CLOSER BY THE HOUR

The Bishop Smoky Mountain Thrillers
Book 3

LAUREN STREET

Chapter One

HE TIED her wrists and ankles to the four posts of the bed, spread-eagle, though he certainly didn't intend any kind of sexual assault. Lord, no, the thought made him slightly nauseous. He wasn't going to rape her, he was going to murder her. But he needed her to hold still while he did it, and the spread-eagle part was the most convenient way to tie her down.

It was a shame that murder victims wouldn't hold still while you killed them.

He almost let out a giggle at that thought, but didn't. He did smile, though, because he was having the time of his life. Rosie Ferguson was also having the time of her life, too, but it was the *worst* time of hers. Her last memories would be her worst memories, and somehow that didn't seem to him to be such a bad way to die, dying at the most extreme moment in your life. That sounded right and good and fair to him.

Besides, this was fun.

He had slapped a piece of duct tape over her mouth to keep her quiet while he hauled her away, but he didn't need the tape now, so he'd ripped it off a few minutes ago, and that's when she'd started screaming. Anticipatory screaming, fear screaming, terror-of-the-unknown scream-ing. She was screaming because she didn't know what was about to happen to her, and if she had known, she'd be screaming much louder.

Should he tell her? Prepare her for—

No, let to be a surprise. It'd be better if it were a surprise, and she certainly wouldn't see a thing like this coming. He almost giggled again, but stifled it.

Preparing the implements of her death didn't take a whole lot of time. Plugging in the iron. Grabbing a bucket and that broken slab of Masonite from the shed. The hardest part had been catching a rat. But hey, Google is your friend, right?

The first thing you needed to know was what species of rat you were trying to catch. Different species ate different types of foods. For instance, black rats were herbivores while brown rats were omnivorous. He would certainly find a target-rich environment for both in the old parts of the building. Probably outside the kitchen, too, around the dumpsters.

He'd been terrified of rats as a boy, but then he'd been terrified of almost everything as a boy. But he got over that. He'd realized later in life that there was a simple solu-tion to constant personal fear. Murder. Kill somebody, just randomly kill another human being, and your own fears are washed away, you're left as white as snow, hallelujah, praise the Lord and pass the offering plate. Once you've taken a human life, once you've seen the light go out of their eyes, why, you're invincible. Nothing can hurt you then. You're Superman. He saw it as a little like taking the spirit of another person, their strength and courage. He supposed there was a Native American legend about that sort of thing, they usually had legends for everything. And even if the person you killed was a weakling, as scrawny and terrified of life as he'd been, their meager portion of strength and courage, when added to your own, was an amount larger than any single person could generate alone.

The more people you killed, the stronger you got.

Google had told him that black rats, which scale trees and enter homes through coin-sized holes in attics, find peanut butter irresistible. Brown rats, the dumpster rats, like just about anything with a strong smell, rotted cheese being a particular favorite.

He had set live-rat traps all over the building, must have been a dozen of them, then went around checking them every evening before he left for home. It took him a week to catch the black rat that now clawed and scratched inside the box in the corner. He'd had it now for four days and hadn't fed it a bite of food. He wanted that rat to be hungry. To be ravenous.

Rosie strained at her bonds, cried and screamed and begged for mercy while he prepared the implements of her death. He'd been planning this for a long time. Maybe for his whole life.

"Won't be long now. Enjoy every breath you take in. Each one you let out too. They're going to be the last breaths you take."

He enjoyed the terror in her eyes.

"Please don't hurt me, don't hurt me, I'm begging you, let me go, I won't tell anybody about what happened, just let me go and I'll… oh dear God, please don't hurt me!"

It all came out in a tear-clotted mewl, accompanied by a slathering of snot out of her nose that dripped down her upper lip and then off the sides of her face. She'd probably shit herself, too, when she died. He didn't like that part, the stinky, body fluids part.

The bucket was an ordinary galvanized steel bucket he'd bought at the hardware store. He turned the box with the rat in it upside down over the bucket, and the rat plopped into the bucket. Then he slid a piece of Masonite between the box and the bucket. Then he removed the box, holding the Masonite in place to keep the rat inside the bucket.

The rat was going crazy in there, clawing at the metal sides of the bucket and scratching at the Masonite.

"Rosie, I want you to meet … Max, I call him Max. You and Max are going to become really well-acquainted."

"What's that in that bucket? What are you going to do with that? Get it away from me, noooo!"

Then she started screaming again.

He carefully flipped the bucket over, keeping the rat inside it by holding firm to the piece of Masonite that was now on the bottom, with the bucket resting on top of it. Then he carried the whole thing to the side of the bed and looked down at Rosie, who lay screaming on the bed.

Though she fought and screamed and tried to cringe away, she couldn't move. And if she could have, she would have, when he placed the piece of Masonite on her fat old belly. He had plugged the iron in and it was hot. He didn't lick his finger and touch it to the surface to test it the way his mother had always done, but it was hot. It'd burn an iron imprint in whatever you tried to iron with it. Not that he was planning on ironing anything.

Holding the bucket down on the piece of Masonite with one hand, he used the other to pick up the hot iron and place it on the bottom of the bucket. It was only seconds before the rat inside the bucket felt the heat and began scrambling to get away from it. He smiled at the screaming, hysterical Rosie as he carefully slid the piece of Masonite out from under the rat.

Now the rat was on Rosie's belly. You could tell she could feel its feet and claws as the horror and terror in her screaming ramped up. The bucket with the iron on it was getting hotter and hotter and the rat had to get away from the heat. It couldn't chew a hole in the side of the bucket to escape. But it could chew a hole in Rosie.

He sat by the side of the bed as Rosie screamed so loud that she must have torn out a vocal cord or something because suddenly she couldn't make any noise but rasping sounds. He saw blood begin to seep out from under the edge of the bucket. Her eyes bugged out of her head like they were about to squirt out of the sockets, and then she began to stop bucking and screaming. She opened her mouth and instead of sound, blood came gushing out as her eyes turned up in her head.

The rat chewed its way through Rosie and all the way through the mattress under her. He heard it plop down on the floor beneath the bed and scurry away, covered in blood and gore, looking for a crack to squeeze through, leaving behind a bloody snail trail of slime.

He turned the iron off and set it on the table beside the bed. Then he picked up the empty bucket, tossed it into a corner, and picked up the machete. Had to chase the rat around and around that room, chopping until he got its tail off, then one hind leg, and finally, sent the blade through the rat's body just behind the head, severing it. Even then, the body kept skittering around, feet working, trying to run.

He went to the bed and lifted the bucket off Rosie's belly, saw the gory hole the rat had chewed through her body. And he smiled.

Chapter Two

It was déja vu all over again.

Rileigh Bishop sat in the early morning sunshine in a parking space down the street from the Rusty Nail Tavern. Again. Waiting to serve a summons on the owner of the establishment, one Walter Thomas Collins, AKA Pinky. Again.

Her boss at the Good GI's private investigations firm in Gatlinburg, Wally Hansford, had given her the assignment yesterday afternoon, and at first, she'd thought he was joking.

"You want me to serve *another* summons on Pinky for DUI? Seriously?"

"If the man keeps getting busted, he's gonna keep getting summoned. That's the way the wheels of justice turn," Wally had intoned, trying to sound pompous and succeeding.

"Why didn't they take his driver's license away from him after the last DUI summons I served on him?"

"You'll have to take that up with the judge. They nail 'em and bail 'em and we…"

"What? Serve 'em and … what rhymes with serve? Curve? Swerve?"

"Whatever. All you have to do is hand the man the summons and collect your two hundred dollars."

"Just find Pinky and stuff a summons in his pocket. *Riiiight.*"

"If it were easy, everybody'd be doing it, and you'd be out of a job."

So now she sat, hoping to catch Pinky as he opened up the bar for the day.

And would you look at that! Rileigh was delighted to see Pinky's big, black Lincoln pull off the street into the parking lot and head toward the back. Customers got the spaces close to the bar. The staff could do the hiking.

She waited, gauged her target, let him get about halfway across the lot before she got out of her car. He spotted her as soon as she moved. He'd have to choose now — the bar or the car — which could he get to quicker? But in taking the time to process the choices, he lost precious time. That was a rookie mistake. He bolted across the lot toward the back door of the bar with Rileigh right behind him. He fumbled with his keys, jammed one in the dead bolt, unlocked it, and lurched inside, turning to slam the door behind him. He missed by a step as Rileigh shoved her foot between the door and the jamb. He grunted, ineffectually pushing his weight against the door.

"Aw, come on, Pinky. Don't make this any harder than it has to be. It's my job to hand you this summons and …"

"It's my *life* and I ain't taking it."

"Yeah, you are. Got you fair and square. Just cry uncle. We can get this over with and both go on about our day."

She shoved on the door, but he had his weight against it and it wouldn't open.

"You got the wrong guy this time. I done took care of

this matter with the courts. Ain't no outstanding warrants against me, I–"

"Save it for the judge, Pinky. *I* know this is a new summons and *you* know this is a new summons, and the only way you're going to take care of this with the court is to stop drinking and driving."

She gave the door a hard shove and he resisted at first, then threw in the towel and stepped back, allowing the door to swing open. She held the paper out toward him, but he refused to take it.

"I ain't signing for nothing," he said.

"Suit yourself." She whipped out her phone and held the summons up to his chest. "Say cheese." She snapped his picture. "So there went trying to pretend you never got the summons. Can we stop fiddle-farting around now and get this done?"

Pinky spewed out a stream of extremely vulgar but colorful obscenities before he snatched the summons out of her hand.

She held out her logbook for him to sign and he sneered at her. "I already told you, I ain't signing for nothing."

"Again, suit yourself. But did it ever occur to you that it might go easier on you in court if you were seen as a cooperative defendant, instead of a defiant asshole."

"I ain't puttin' my name on nothing!" Rileigh inhaled his breath and could tell he was probably well on his way to getting drunk already. It wasn't even nine o'clock yet. This was a man who needed help. He turned to storm off.

"You ever think about going to AA, Pinky?" she asked, switching her tone from confrontational to kind. She saw his back stiffen as he kept walking. Kinda staggering. "You know what the first step is. 'We admitted we were powerless over alcohol. That our lives had become unmanageable.' I'd say you qualify on that score."

"Go to hell," he blustered, a parting shot as he left the bar's storage room and slammed through the door leading to the bar itself.

As Rileigh crossed the parking lot to where she had parked, she tried to evict the sympathy for Pinky that had suddenly staged a full-frontal attack on her psyche. What he got in this life, he chose, she told herself. And if he wanted something different, he would choose it. Nobody was holding a gun to his head and forcing him to drink.

Except, alcoholism was holding a gun to his head, and he was "powerless" to do anything about it. At least, according the the AA brochure.

She shook her head. One of these days he was going to get behind the wheel of his car drunk and end up killing somebody. She hoped the somebody was only himself.

Chapter Three

WHEN RILEIGH DROVE HOME from her encounter with
Pinky at the Rusty Nail, she took the scenic route, as she
called it. There were no routes to her house, or to
anywhere else in the Smoky Mountains, that weren't
scenic. But this way offered some majestic views that
soothed her soul. Particularly now, with the leaves beginning to change. The mountains had that effect on her, they
comforted her. When she'd needed healing, they'd done
that, too. In her darkest moments, fighting an enemy she
couldn't see on the white-hot sand of some god-forsaken
desert in Afghanistan or Iraq, memories of the verdant
green of her mountains kept her sane. And when her own
aunt had crushed her hand with a sledgehammer while
trying to murder her, Rileigh had crawled deep down into
herself in shock and horror and grief. But the mountains
had called her out of her pain and made her whole again.

She loved the smell of the air — so fresh it might have
been scrubbed with lye soap and hung out on the line to
dry in the sunshine. Pine. Spruce. Cedar. And wildflowers.
She rolled down the windows of her car — it was *her* car.

Hers. She ground her teeth, then decided that from this moment forward she would never again think of it as "Aunt Daisy's car." Aunt Daisy had hired one of the Houlihan boys to cut the brake lines on Rileigh's tired old Ford, nearly killing Rileigh when she'd wrecked it. After Aunt Daisy was sent away, Rileigh commandeered the car her aunt had left behind, an old gray Honda Accord, as payment for that car she'd destroyed. Now it was hers.

Yeah, right. She knew better than that. For as long as she drove the car, no matter what promises she might have made in her head to the contrary, this would always be Aunt Daisy's car.

And speaking of Aunt Daisy, Rileigh's mother had gone to visit her today. Correction, Lily Bishop had been "summoned" to the North Tennessee Psychiatric Hospital's criminally insane unit. At least that's the way Rileigh saw it. Aunt Daisy was domineering and manipulative, and even from a mental hospital, she exerted considerable control over her younger sister.

Rileigh pulled into the driveway of her mother's house on Bent Twig Road, executed the maneuver necessary to generate sufficient momentum to make it up the steep driveway and over the rock lump at the top without crashing through the fence around the front lawn. Mama's car wasn't there. She was still at the hospital, also known as the Carrington House because the structure had originally been built as a house on Carrington Ridge. The whole "North Tennessee Psy… etc., etc.," was too big a mouthful to keep repeating over and over.

Rileigh pulled her car around to the back and parked behind the fence, passing the hens clucking outside the chicken house on her way to the back door. When she was a little girl, she'd loved going into the chicken house and feel around under the warm feathers of the birds until she located an egg for breakfast. And oh, how she loved fried chicken.

After she got a glass of cold lemonade out of the refrigerator, she went out onto the front porch and sat down in the silent porch swing — it didn't creak like all the other porch swings of her experience — and settled into the book series she had just started, called Nowhere USA. The books were about a community in the mountains of Kentucky where suddenly nobody could leave. It was like if Stephen King's Under the Dome was mashed-up with Justified, and she was thoroughly enjoying it.

She heard her mother's car engine rev as Mama climbed the steep drive and parked out front. Rileigh knew day was coming when she would have to take her mother's keys away from her, but she just couldn't bring herself to do it just yet. Her mother's dementia manifested itself in quirky behavior and delusions, but didn't seem to impede her ability to perform the daily tasks of life. Even though Mama believed she was dating Rhett Butler and that they were going to run off together as soon as he got better from his neck replacement surgery, she still paid her bills on time, went to the grocery, and cleaned the house, when she wasn't running out to the Carrington House every time Aunt Daisy crooked a finger.

Lily Bishop climbed slowly up the front steps and plopped down with a tired sigh in the rocking chair facing Rileigh on the porch swing.

"Did Aunt Daisy find her legs?" Rileigh asked.

Aunt Daisy had phoned earlier today to complain that someone had stolen her legs. Yesterday's frantic phone call had been to tell Lily that there were rats in the walls of her room, and they came out at night and chewed on her toes. The rats in the wall thing might have a modicum of truth in it. The Carrington House was the kind of place that'd have rats in the walls, if anywhere did.

"They were table legs, Dear," her mother said with a sigh. "That bedside table we bought her… well, it started to sit crooked and she decided somebody had stolen two of the legs off it."

"Did somebody steal the legs off it?"

"Don't be ridiculous, of course not. But by the time I got out there, she'd done forgot that's why she wanted me to come. By that time, she had decided that the nurses were trying to get the patients to drink acid."

"Any particular reason?"

Her mother favored her with a condescending look. "They were trying to poison them, that's why."

"You don't really believe that, do you?"

"No sense in going there, Honey. Aunt Daisy ain't dragging a full string of fish."

Mama got to her feet. "Well, I'd best get busy on supper." There was only the slightest pause. "Rhett can't make it tonight, but I'll make you some chili if you're hungry."

"I'm good, but thanks."

Mama went into the house — through the front screen door that *did* squeak — and left Rileigh sitting on the porch swing, trying to work out in her head how her aunt, who thought the nurses were trying to poison her, was any crazier than her mother, who thought Rhett Butler couldn't make it for supper tonight.

But there was a difference, and when she tried to put a finger on it, she was left with only the vague belief that her mother's dementia was benign. It was a fantasy to color the world rosy and make it a pleasanter place to live.

Aunt Daisy's Alzheimer's was not harmless. She had murdered Tina Montgomery last summer because she believed Tina was Rileigh's older sister, Jillian. And she'd confessed to killing Jillian, too, though they couldn't find a body. She had also come very close to cutting Rileigh's head off with a chainsaw.

Rileigh swung silently back and forth. There was something dark and sinister about Aunt Daisy. Rileigh thought she'd always sensed it even when she was a little girl. And if Mama knew Aunt Daisy had been having an affair with her husband — but she'd never know that, because nobody would ever tell her. What was the point in destroying her fairytale world?

Lily had never gotten lost, never wondered where she was. But Rileigh wanted to be proactive. Like install an app on Mama's phone, so Rileigh could find her if she ever did get lost.

She thought about the look of madness in Aunt Daisy's eyes when she had tried to slice off Rileigh's head — that was pure insanity, not harmless dementia. Rileigh would do anything she could to help her mother continue to function in the world despite her delusions. And she promised herself that she'd have the backbone to take action when her mother eventually lost so much grip on reality that she needed help.

Aunt Daisy was beyond anybody's help. She was locked away for her own safety and the safety of everybody in her life.

If only she'd leave Mama alone.

Chapter Four

On Tuesday morning, Rileigh sat at the breakfast table struggling to focus. She had to clear the fog out of her head because trying to teach her mother anything even mildly techie was something on the order of trying to teach a rhino to crochet. Rileigh certainly wasn't the most tech-savvy person on the block, but she was capable of downloading an app on both of their phones and explaining to her mother how to use it.

At least, she would be if she'd gotten more than about half an hour's sleep last night. She felt so sleepy and groggy now, she could go right back to bed and sleep until noon. But she had things to do, like reporting in to the office in Gatlinburg to file the report on the summons she'd served on Pinky and collect payment for it. Then she'd see what job they might have for her next.

Her wildly spinning thoughts and sleepless night could all be explained with a single name. Jillian. She didn't do it often, but last night Rileigh had dreamed about the older sister who had vanished without a trace when Rileigh was six years old.

In the weeks preceding the last job she'd worked — trying to find the crazy person who was splashing gasoline on tourists and setting them on fire — she had been plagued by mysterious phone calls. The caller ID would identify a number with a Texas area code. She would answer the call, and she'd hear nothing but silence on the other end. Not disconnected silence. Somebody's-there-but-not-talking silence. The last one of those calls came when she left her phone on the kitchen table while she went out to feed the chickens. Her mother had answered it, then had called out to Rileigh, "It's for you. It's Jillian."

Of course it wasn't Jillian, it was nothing but silence. Mama swore she'd talked to Jillian, but then, Mama had talked to Rhett Butler that day too. The number on her caller ID had been the mystery number from a Texas area code. Rileigh had still been a little fragile — from almost being burned at the stake! — and she'd burst into tears, cried out to the not-person on the phone: "Stop it! Leave me alone."

She hadn't gotten a phone call like that since.

But she'd dreamed about Jillian last night, one strange dream after another that melded into a dreamscape of barren desolation, the world after a nuclear holocaust or a zombie apocalypse. Nothing but lifeless land, dead vegetation, a brown sky, an orange sun … and Jillian, walking down the torn up pavement toward Rileigh as if she were on her way out to pick a basket of blackberries. Rileigh had called out to her in the dream, but Jillian hadn't stopped, she'd just kept walking, a small smile creasing her lips as Rileigh begged her to wait, to connect, to interact. Nothing. And when Jillian finally reached where Rileigh, she walked right through her, as if Rileigh were as insubstantial as a shimmering image that only reflected what was real but had no substance of its own.

She had startled awake when that happened. It had been so real, it was as if she could feel the wispy, spiderwebs that were her sister passing through her bones. And her soul. She'd sat there in the midnight dark clutching sweat-soaked sheets, wide awake. It was that hour of the night when all bad things are possible, when the Boogey Man comes out of the closet and brings all his nasty friends. That hour when everyone you love is in imminent danger of plane crashes, brain aneurysms, and drive-by shootings, and death seems as near as the darkness, as cold as the moonlight, and as certain as the coming dawn.

"…asked if you want coffee," her mother's voice made the images disappear like puffs of smoke from a dying campfire. "I can make a fresh pot if this one's too strong."

Mama liked her coffee strong. As in the color and consistency of road tar. She said coffee wasn't fit to drink "less you can trot a mouse 'cross the top of it."

"I don't need any coffee, but what I do need is you."

"Me?"

"Uh huh, you. I need you to listen to what I'm saying. This is important."

"You ain't got no kinda awful disease, do you? 'Cause if you do, don't keep beating around the bush, tell me."

"I'm not sick, Mama." She held up her iPhone. "Go get your phone."

"I don't know where I left the thing, it's around here somewheres."

Rileigh almost reminded her that if she'd gotten that Apple watch like Rileigh had advised, she could touch an icon on it and her phone would ping.

Mama wandered out of the room to search. Rileigh was just getting up to help when she returned triumphantly to the kitchen, holding the phone out in front of her like Darth Vader with a light saber.

"Here it is! what do you want it for?"

"I want to show you an app that I'm going to put on your phone."

"What's an app? No, wait, don't tell me, I know. It's one of them icon thingies that make the phone do stuff."

"More or less, yes."

Then Rileigh proceeded to tell her about the My People app as she loaded it on her mother's phone. She'd already loaded it on her own.

"This app only connects these two phones, yours and mine. If you want to know where I am, touch this icon." She pointed to a cartoon woman with a confused look on her face. "It will immediately drop a pin—"

Mama wouldn't understand that reference.

"It will immediately put this red thing on a map showing you where my phone is. And if I want to find your phone, I touch this icon and it will show me where your phone is located."

"So, this app thingy doesn't hook us up so I can talk to you? It just tells me where to find you? What's the point in that?"

"You can use the phone itself to call me if you want to talk to me, or text me if you just want to send me a message. This app is so I never have to wonder where you are, and you never have to wonder where I am. And if the phone's turned off, it will tell you the location where it was last used."

"Why Sugar, you think I sit around all day wondering where you are? I know you'll come home eventually."

"Sometimes I do wonder where you are, Mama, and with this app—"

Mama's phone rang in Rileigh's hand, so she passed it over. Mama looked at the number and immediately answered and asked, "What is it? What's wrong?"

Aunt Daisy. Had to be Aunt Daisy. Her mother gasped and her hand went to her mouth.

"Oh, Daisy, no!"

"What, Mama? What's wrong?"

Mama put her hand over the phone to silence her sister's hysterics so she could tell Rileigh: "One of her sisters is missing!"

Rileigh didn't have to wonder who Aunt Daisy meant when she talked about her "sisters." Her real sisters were all dead, except for Lily. The girls had formed a bouquet in their parents' home, or so Rileigh had been told, and all of them were named after flowers. Daisy and Lily. Then there was Iris, Rose, Jasmine, Aster, and Della — for delphinium.

But shortly after Aunt Daisy was sent to the Carrington House, she had decided that the women in the dormitory room with her were her sisters, bestowing flower-based names on all of them.

"Missing? What does that mean?"

Her mother gave Rileigh a withering, you-can-be-so-dense-sometimes look. "How many things can *missing* mean? She's gone. Not there. Daisy said she'd been kidnapped."

Who would go to the trouble to break into a psychiatric hospital to kidnap a patient. She could see staging a "jail break" among all the inmates perhaps, to get *out*. But *in?* What for?

"Who is it, Mama," Rileigh said. "Who's missing?"

"Rosie. Daisy saw the whole thing. Says she just vanished."

Chapter Five

WELL, there went trying to have any meaningful conversations with Mama. As soon as Aunt Daisy called, Mama went off the rails. Rileigh was certain that Daisy, the oldest of the six "flower sisters" had always been dominant and domineering, used to giving orders and having her own way. She accomplished the task of keeping her young sisters in line by physical force when she had to. She was a remarkably strong, stout woman who could work alongside the farm hands all day in the field. But mostly, Daisy used psychological intimidation. And Rileigh's mother, Lily, being the youngest, had probably taken the brunt of her older sister's character flaws. Aunt Daisy never married, and there was a reason for that.

Rileigh was powerless to do anything about it when her aunt called and demanded her younger sister do something for her. And she called all the time.

Rileigh paused. Yeah, she called *all the time*. How did she manage that? The patients in the psychiatric hospital where she'd been committed were strictly forbidden to have cell phones, and the three public phones on her wing always seemed to be in use when Rileigh had visited. Yet, her aunt seemed to be able to call whenever she wanted. Rileigh wondered if she could ask the hospital staff to restrict Aunt Daisy's access to the public phones, so she would leave Mama alone. But she wondered if maybe there was more to it than that.

Rileigh made herself some toast and slathered it with the orange marmalade her mother had made last summer. Mama still knew how to cook, could whip up a meal for ten strong men without breaking a sweat, but in recent years — during her "decline" as Rileigh saw it — her cooking skills had remained intact, but they were tied to a memory that was coming unraveled. So she still knew how to make a lemon meringue pie, but she was likely to forget a key ingredient — like the sugar! — or to add something that didn't belong at all. But it wasn't all the time, which made it hard. Sometimes she was still the best cook in eastern Tennessee, and others ... not. It was a crap shoot every time you sat down to eat something Mama had cooked.

As she buttered her toast, Rileigh listened to her mother trying to calm Aunt Daisy, to no avail. Though she couldn't hear much of what her aunt was saying, only the occasional shouted word, it was clear she was genuinely upset over something. The tone of her voice, which was usually assertive and demanding, had changed.

This Aunt Daisy sounded scared.

When her mother got off the phone, she was so dithered and upset, there was no sense in trying to complete the lesson on how to use the My People app. Maybe she'd understood what Rileigh had already explained, maybe not, but her mother wasn't rational enough to listen to techie instructions, so Rileigh gave up and concentrated on trying to calm her mother down.

"Oh, I got to go, I got to go see to Daisy," her mother said, so dithered she was walking around in circles in the kitchen and not going anywhere. "She's powerful upset, seeing that awful thing like she done, ain't no wonder."

"What awful thing?"

"That angel taking Rosie. Daisy seen the whole thing. Took her right out of the room, and with the door closed."

Neat trick. But considering the source, probably a delusion.

"How did the angel convince Rosie to go with him… or her?" Or probably, the correct pronoun was they. "When did this happen, Mama?"

"She said it was last night, after I left to come home and fix supper."

"If it happened last night, why'd she wait to call you about it until this morning?"

"She couldn't get to her phone until the ward was unlocked for breakfast."

"She's not allowed to have a phone."

Mama realized she'd stepped in it and tried to backtrack.

"She couldn't go out into the hall to use one of the wall phones."

"You didn't say a wall phone. You said her phone, she couldn't get to her phone." Mama's shoulders slumped now that she knew she'd been caught. Rileigh didn't let her off the hook. "How'd she get a phone? They're strictly forbidden in the hospital."

"I got it for her." She looked up then at Rileigh and pleaded with her eyes for her daughter to understand. "She felt so lonely out there, so isolated."

"In a room with six other women who she thinks are her sisters."

"Deep down she knows they ain't her sisters. But soon's

I got her the phone, she calmed down and they took her off some of them medications they was giving her for depression and anxiety and such."

That much was probably true. When Aunt Daisy had first been committed to the institution, she was on every chemical compound other than Tidy Bowl, but gradually, over time, she'd been weaned off most of them.

"If you gave her a cell phone, why didn't she call you last night when the angel came into their room and snatched poor Rosie off to … well, to Heaven, I guess?"

"She don't keep the phone in her room. Them other women's too nosey, they woulda seen and called her out about it. She keeps it in a flowerpot in the craft room. It's piped into her hearing aids and—"

"Into her hearing aids. Seriously? How'd she manage that?"

"I don't have no idea. All's I know is it's called 'bluetooth' and it makes her phone ring in her hearing aids, and she can reach up and punch a button and answer it without nobody knowing what she's doing. So she just sits in the craft room making ashtrays and candy dishes and the like, and they think she's talking to herself when I call her. Only time she has to have the phone with her is when she's making a call out. But the craft room is locked at night."

Thank goodness, because if it hadn't been, Mama would've run out there in the middle of the night, maybe driven off the side of the mountain in the dark.

When Aunt Daisy said, jump, Mama always asked, how high, so the phone had become Daisy's chain to her sister. But this was different. Rileigh had never seen her mother so upset by a phone call from her sister.

"Oh, I got to go, I got to go…" She didn't go, though, just walked in tighter and tighter circles in the kitchen.

"No, Mama you're not going anywhere. I'll go see what's going on with Aunt Daisy. You stay here and … make a cake."

"But you ain't seen Daisy since …"

Her mother didn't know exactly what had happened the night Daisy came after Rileigh with a chainsaw, but she'd been on the edge of enough conversations to know it had been something catastrophic, and that Rileigh had ended up with a crushed hand as a result. It hurt that Mama didn't want to know the truth of what her sister had done to her own daughter, but Rileigh didn't want to push it, for fear that the horror of knowing might accelerate Mama's decline.

"You sure you want to?" Mama asked.

Rileigh was sure she absolutely did not want to go see her aunt, but it was better than allowing her mother to go charging off to the aid of her domineering sister when she was this upset. Though if she did go and managed to get lost in the process, Rileigh could at least find her with the My People app on her phone.

"You stay here and … would you make me a… a pineapple upside down cake? I haven't had one of those since—" Actually, it'd been since Georgia had made one trying to "fatten her up" a couple of months ago. But Mama didn't know about that. "Not since I came home from the military. Make me one, please?"

"I'll whip it right up." The task seemed to have pushed all thoughts of her hysterical sister out of Mama's mind.

"I'll be back in time to have a great big piece," Rileigh promised.

Rileigh was relatively certain there was no canned pineapple in the house, so what her mother might use as a substitute — well, it would be an adventure.

Chapter Six

You could spend ten minutes describing the Carrington House in excruciating detail and still not capture the absolute, gut-deep *creepiness* of the place. Rileigh saw the structure for the first time when she was about ten years old, looming at the top of the hill, the windows on the upper floors like dark eye sockets staring sightless at the world. It had filled her with a deep sense of foreboding then, and she'd never been able shake that assessment in the decades since. She was not alone. Most everybody who saw the place was creeped out by it. Its strange blend of Gothic and Tudor architecture creating a singularly ugly edifice with a gray stone facade that had darkened to almost black with age since it had been built in the late 1800's

There were no such things as hospitals in the Smokies until Dr. Isaac Preston set up his practice on Carrington Ridge and brought in a small order of nuns to operate a "recovery center" for the sickest of his patients. From that point onward, the building went through half a dozen different owners, twice as many different uses, and three times as many different renovations. When the nearby cities of Knoxville and Nashville were ravaged by a tuberculosis epidemic in the early 1900s, patients "with means" were cared for at the Carrington House because it was believed the pure mountain air promoted healing. The building was added onto until it could hold one hundred fifty patients, and other wings were added onto the building to care for sick children and the healthy children of sick patients who could not be exposed to their parents' illnesses.

Back then, the death rate from the tuberculosis was about one patient a day, and the sight of the dead bodies being hauled out of the facility so lowered the morale of the patients that a tunnel was dug, running from the building through a hillside to an opening out of sight of the hospital on the other side, where wagons came to cart away the corpses.

It was rumored that tunnels and passageways had been constructed beneath the building as well, used to move bodies out of the facility without upsetting the other patients.

It was also rumored that the building was haunted. Duh. Hundreds of people had died there. What creepy-looking building with that kind of heritage wouldn't gain a haunted house reputation?

The place was closed, opened, then closed again, finally remaining open when Claude Hollister purchased the property right after WWII and turned it into the regional medical center and psychiatric hospital that still served the locals today. Only a portion of the big facility was currently in use as, leaving the remainder boarded up and subject to whatever tall tales the locals cared to create around it.

Rileigh parked her car — it was *her* car — behind the building and went in a side entrance that was close to the "secure" portion of the facility, where patients like her murderous Aunt Daisy were housed.

She checked in at the nurse's station, then went to her aunt's room, which was the last room at the end of a long hallway on the first floor. Rileigh stood at the door and looked at Daisy for a moment before she entered. Her aunt's hair was a color Rileigh thought of as battleship gray, or the color of a ten-penny nail. While Mama's hair had turned a delightful pure white, Daisy's had turned gray and remained there, never completing the transformation into a crown of snow.

Daisy was seated on the edge of her bed, facing the other direction, doing something with her hands, some mindless, rhythmic motion, maybe folding socks together, then unfolding them, then folding them back. Rileigh watched the muscles in her aunt's back move as she worked.

Daisy Gillespie was a big strong woman, had maybe a hundred pounds and five inches on Rileigh. And that had mattered when Rileigh was fighting for her life — and *losing.* She'd have died at Daisy's hands if Mitch hadn't gotten there when he did. The image of her aunt's face, in a great cramp of madness and rage, had been burned so deep into Rileigh's soul, she wondered if she'd ever be able to look at her aunt again without seeing it as a ghostly overlay. That was one of the reasons she'd never come here to visit Daisy.

The other was a lingering rage of her own that she seemed unable to shake. Her aunt had smashed her hand with a sledgehammer! The pain had been staggering. It was a far worse injury than anything she'd sustained during four years of active duty in the Middle East. On that day last summer, Aunt Daisy had slipped the bonds of all restraint. There was literally nothing she wouldn't have done at that time to rid her life of the hated "Jillian" the older sister that she'd mistaken Rileigh for. Daisy had intended to kill Jillian, said she *had* killed Jillian—

Rileigh shook herself to derail that train of thought. It was all so sordid and ugly, her father molesting children, her aunt having an affair with her father — so vile you couldn't even think about it without wanting to wash your mind out with lye soap.

And right in the middle of it had been Daisy. Yeah, she was crazy, genuinely insane, so not accountable for her behavior. But there was a part of Rileigh who secretly believed that Daisy might very well have done the same things if she'd been perfectly sane. If every synapse in her mind had been firing properly, she might *still* have smashed Rileigh's hand with a sledgehammer and tried to cut her head off with a chainsaw.

It was hard to get past that.

Aunt Daisy turned and saw Rileigh standing in the doorway. A flood of emotions washed over her face so quickly that Rileigh couldn't tell for sure what her real response had been. But the response she chose to display — it wasn't involuntary, she got to pick — was a thin veneer of relief painted over fear.

Aunt Daisy was genuinely afraid of something. That made her a little more human, somehow, and Rileigh forged ahead through her own tangle of ambivalent feelings to respond with compassion for that fear.

"Oh, dear Rileigh, thank you for coming!" she cried.

If Daisy had called Rileigh Jillian, Rileigh would have turned on her heel and left, and would likely never have come back. But her aunt wasn't suffering from that particular delusion at the moment. She recognized Rileigh, and that was something.

"I'm so glad you're here," Daisy continued. "You have

to help me or he's going to carry me off into the darkness too, put me wherever he's put poor Rosie."

Rileigh found herself trying to soothe Aunt Daisy in spite of herself. She supposed that was a good thing. Reality was that her aunt was at the very least a sociopath — with liberal doses of dementia and Alzheimer's — and any kind feelings for Daisy that surfaced in Rileigh after all the old woman had done were a tribute to Rileigh's own humanity.

Daisy got up from the bed and made a beeline for Rileigh, like a little kid who's finally spotted Mommy in a crowded store, and almost bowled her over with a bear-hug embrace.

"Everything's going to be okay," Rileigh said. "No need to be upset."

"The angel means to murder Rosie!"

"How do you know he intends to kill her?"

"I just know, that's all. I *know.*" She paused and literally shivered. "And it ain't gonna be no pretty murder, neither!"

That was a bit of a conversation-stopper.

Chapter Seven

NONE of the other women were in the room right now — the not-sisters whose real names Rileigh didn't even know. She and her aunt were alone, so perhaps she could soothe the old lady, ease her slowly out of this delusion, then have a talk with the others out of Daisy's earshot, to see what really might have happened to Rosie.

"Worst thing you can say to somebody who's upset is 'calm down.'" She remembered those words from one of her instructors at the Tennessee State Police Academy. "You want to throw gasoline on a fire, tell a wild-eyed loonie to calm down. Could be a fatal mistake."

So Rileigh did not tell her aunt to calm down. Instead, she took her big hand in her own small one and held on tightly.

"Tell me the story *from the beginning,* don't leave out any details, I want to hear it all."

Aunt Daisy gathered herself, took a deep breath, then began a rambling monologue that was more or less an accounting of everything she had done, seen and heard all day yesterday. By the time, she got to the good part, Rileigh was barely able to concentrate on it.

"So, we was all ready for bed. Me and Rosie was in here, and the others were still in the bathroom."

The six women actually lived in individual enclosures that Mama had dubbed "birdcages." Most of the room was partitioned off, divided into six "enclosures." The partitions were made of wire mesh — chicken wire, Aunt Daisy said, just with smaller holes. The women all shared a bathroom and there was an undivided communal area where they spent most of their time. The room could be locked. Each of the enclosures could be locked, as well, were supposed to be kept locked most of the day, but according to Mama, the women wandered in and out of each other's birdcages at will. From Lily's descriptions of the place, the standard safety protocols for dealing with the criminally insane were sadly lacking. They weren't supposed to be left alone in the common areas. They weren't suppose to leave their room without an aide, or go to the craft room or the game room or out into the grounds unattended. They did, though, and apparently, always had.

"So, Rosie and I were in here and Rosie was singing that song she always sings, you know the one about, 'I've been cheated, been mistreated, when will I find love?'"

"The old Vince Gill song."

"Rosie gets songs on the brain and they kinda go around in there in a continuous loop, and it's the same song for at least a week. And when she ain't singing, she's humming. I wasn't paying no attention to her. I was working on my puzzle." On a table beside Aunt Daisy's bed was an intricate puzzle, the kind that advertised five hundred pieces, or maybe a thousand. Rileigh couldn't see the box for this one, but the partially-completed puzzle occupied half of the table, and a pile of unused pieces rested beside it.

"Then she just stopped singing. Just stopped. I didn't look up right away because I'd found that piece of the flower I'd been looking for all evening. Then she made a kinda funny sound, and that's when I looked up and I seen the angel."

"What makes you think whoever you saw was an angel?"

"He looked like an angel, that's what. He was dressed in white robes. He didn't have no wings, though, or a harp, but I think them things is just what people have decided angels ought to have, not what they really do. Well, except the wings part. There's places in the good book that talks about angels having wings, but this one didn't."

"Describe him to me."

"I done described him."

"But what did he look like? Was he a white man or a black man? Tall or short, skinny, or fat? What color was his hair?"

Aunt Daisy seemed flummoxed.

"I didn't notice none of them things about him, don't even know for sure it was a him and not a her. All I seen was he was dressed in white. And he just appeared out of nowhere, like poof, there he was. That's how I knew he was an angel, because he could just appear out of thin air like that."

"Did he say anything?"

"Nary a word. He just took Rosie by the hand and started leading her away."

"Was the door to the hallway open?"

"The door was locked from the other side. He didn't come in no door. He just appeared out of nowhere. Ain't you listening to what I'm telling you?"

"So this being dressed in white, who was neither male nor female, black nor white, tall nor short, skinny nor tall, took Rosie's hand and led her away... through a locked door? How?"

"I don't know."

"You said he kidnapped her, but from what you're describing, she went with him willingly. "

"If an angel appeared out of nowhere in front of you and took your hand, wouldn't you just kinda go where they told you?"

"So, she did what he told her."

"He didn't tell her nothing. You need to listen to what I'm telling you. He just took her hand and started leading her... well, into nowhere. Into where he came from. After a few steps Rosie decided she didn't want to go, and she tried to pull away. That's when he done that thing. I don't know what it's called, where you kinda pinch somebody's neck and they just pass out. He did that. He reached up and pinched her neck and she just folded up like a dead accordion. Then he picked her up—"

"Picked her up?" Rosie was a good-sized woman.

"Yup, lifted her off the floor like she didn't weigh nothing at all, and then he walked away."

"You keep saying that — *away*. Where did he go?"

"See, there's the thing. I don't know where he went, I just know he was here and then he wasn't here anymore, and when he wasn't here no more neither was Rosie. And I didn't even think until then to do nothing. But by then it was too late. He was already gone."

"You're telling me that a man dressed in white came into your room, but not through the door, he literally picked Rosie up and carried her out of a locked room, but he didn't go through the door."

Aunt Daisy nodded her head frantically up and down.

"Yeah, that's what happened. And I woulda called Lily right then to tell her about it but—" She caught herself then. "I mean, I woulda got one of the nurses to—"

"Mama told me she gave you a cell phone. Where is it?"

"I ain't got no idea what you're talking about. Cell phones ain't allowed. Rosie didn't have no phone either, or might be she'd have called, like maybe dialed 911 or something."

"I'm not sure if the 911 dispatcher can direct an ambulance to heaven."

"You think that's where he took her?"

"You're the one who said he was an angel."

"He didn't take Rosie to Heaven. He took her to Hell, where the demons is gonna rip her apart."

Daisy squeezed Rileigh's hand so tight that it hurt.

"You got to find her. She didn't want to go with that angel. He kidnapped her." Daisy let out a sad sigh. "Ain't gonna do no good now, though. Whatever awful thing he was planning to do to her, he's had plenty of time to kill her."

Chapter Eight

NOW WHAT? Rileigh stood outside the door of Daisy's room, knowing little more about the disappearance of sister Rosie than she'd known when she got here. She supposed she could talk to the other "sisters," find out if they saw or heard anything.

Right now, she didn't even know for sure if Rosie was indeed missing. Aunt Daisy had pointed to her made-up bed as evidence that she hadn't slept in it last night. Was possible she'd gotten up early and made her bed before Daisy woke up?

The only possible course of action Rileigh could see was to report her aunt's bizarre allegations to whoever was in charge and let them handle it.

She went to the nurse's station on that floor to speak to Nurse Miller, the charge nurse who'd let her into Daisy's room. Nurse Miller was a sour woman who clearly did not want to be here, and when Rileigh had explained why she'd come, the woman brushed her off with, "Shoot, you can't b'lieve anything any of them says. They're all batty as loons."

Rileigh asked the nurse to direct her to the head administrator or whoever was in charge.

"We got a new sheriff in town," Nurse Miller told her, and it was clear she wasn't thrilled about the revelation. "Mr. Pettigrew got fired is what I heard, and this new young fella has taken over. He's a Hollister, the son of the man who owns the place."

The nurse gave Rileigh directions to the bank of administrative offices on the first floor in the front of the building, but within minutes, she was hopelessly lost in the cavernous hallways of the institution. She noticed several things in her unintended self-directed tour of the institution. For one thing, it was in far better shape inside than it was outside, but that wasn't saying much — both needed a lot of work. A lot. Somebody needed to throw a whole shit ton of money at this place to get it up to anything that didn't register a ten on the creepiness scale.

She was sure the structure would pass code inspections. Otherwise, they would've shut it down years ago. But there were several whole wings of the building that were closed off. She'd gone to the end of one corridor and looked through the window on the door. On the other side was a deserted hallway in a state of total disrepair. Ceiling tiles hung down in places where there had been water damage. The hallway floor between the sets of doors was littered with debris, maybe construction debris, or maybe just the walls and the ceiling crumbling.

She finally pushed through a set of double doors, determined to find somebody she could ask directions, and found herself in a newly renovated lobby with upholstered chairs, a winding staircase that led up to the floor above, a bank of elevators and a hubbub of activity.

She went to the information desk and asked to see Hollister.

"Do you have an appointment?"

"No, do I need one?"

"Well, Mr. Hollister's a busy man and–"

"Just tell him my aunt is a patient in the ... and she believes her roommate has been kidnapped."

That lit a fire under the young woman. Within minutes, Rileigh was ushered into an outer office that was all new, modern, shiny, minimalist right angles — glass and chrome — a glaring departure from the architecture of the rest of the building. It was jarring, like finding folding-chair seating in the Sistine Chapel. A sleek, long-legged secretary invited her to have a seat, saying that she'd tell Mr. Hollister she was here. Rileigh expected the secretary to show her into the man's office, but a dark oak door on the other side of the reception area opened and out strode a man who managed to exude confidence without seeming cocky.

He extended his hand to Rileigh. "I'm Brandon Hollister," he said. "Do I understand correctly that you want to talk to me about a missing patient?"

He was neither condescending nor dismissive, which was also a plus, because surely to goodness he got crackpot relatives constantly wanting some of his time. He was a strikingly handsome man — not a pretty-boy — good looking in a camping-gear commercial sort of way. His blond hair was in stylish disarray, wide-set blue eyes under contrasting dark eyebrows, and he had the square jaw of a 1960's western hero. He wore a sport coat over jeans and a white tee shirt. When he smiled, his whole face lit up, and Rileigh found herself surprisingly flustered.

"Well, my aunt ... she's crazy, of course, or she wouldn't be here ... and she believes her sister — well, her roommate, her name's Rosie. My aunt says she's missing."

Saying it out loud like that — and stumbling and

bumbling to get it out — highlighted how truly ridiculous it was. But he kept smiling, like what she'd said was perfectly normal and he heard things like that all the time.

"And you are …?"

She hadn't introduced herself when she shook hands, bad manners.

"I'm Rileigh Bishop. My aunt is Daisy Gillespie. She's in room 105 in the North Wing." She saw a slight tightening around his mouth, indicating that he was processing the source of the complaint.

"Please, come into my office and let's talk about it," he said, and his was such an easy friendliness that Rileigh found her embarrassment fading away. "Would you like some coffee? A soft drink? Popcorn?"

"No thank you … excuse me, did you just say popcorn?"

He chuckled, a warm sound that for some reason reminded Rileigh of caramel syrup dripping down off an ice cream cone.

"I had a little office get-together last week, to introduce myself to the staff, and somebody — okay, it was me — had the brilliant idea to bring in a carnival popcorn machine. I thought it'd kind of lighten the grim spirit, since I fired the man I'm replacing."

"And did it?"

"Not so's you'd notice. I guess it was asking too much. I've made it clear that everybody's job is on the line, so they were a little too uptight to be won over by a bag of popcorn. Consequently, we've got a lot of left-over popcorn to get rid of." He gestured to a comfortable looking chair— with soft upholstery, no right angles and chrome, that sat across a coffee table from a small settee and another chair. "Please have a seat."

Rileigh settled herself on the settee and Mr. Hollister

sat down in the chair across from her, rather than behind the large desk in the back of the room, which sat in front of floor-to-ceiling bookcases.

"So, tell me about your aunt, the patient who thinks her sister—"

"It's not really her sister. But Aunt Daisy thinks all her roommates are her sisters. And it's not just that she thinks Rosie's missing. She thinks...." Oh, go ahead, spit it out. "She thinks Rosie was kidnapped."

"Somebody kidnapped her? From this facility?"

"That's what Aunt Daisy says." He hadn't made fun of anything she'd said to him, so she decided just to get the whole thing out, plop the absurdity out there hot and stinking between them. "She says she saw the kidnapping, that Rosie was abducted by an angel."

"An angel."

It wasn't a question, and there was no derision in the way he said it, but it just suddenly struck Rileigh as funny, and she had to choke back a giggle. "I didn't get the impression that it was any *particular* angel. You, know like the Angel Gabriel or Michael or anybody like that. Just an ordinary, run of the mill, garden-variety angel."

"Are you serious?"

"I'm trying to be, but it's getting harder and harder the deeper I get into my aunt's mental illness. It's hard to say shit like this with a straight face."

He burst out laughing at that, a full merry, inclusive, come-laugh-with-me kind of laugh that washed away the last of the moorings that bound the two of them to the dock of I-just-met-you awkwardness and carried them out into the sea.

"As a matter of fact," he said when he got his laughter under control, "we were already looking into a patient missing from Room 105 before you arrived."

"You were?"

"She wasn't in the room for breakfast this morning and the charge nurse reported it." He held up his hand to curtail her response before she could speak. "That's not terribly unusual. Everybody in that wing is in some stage of dementia, so it's absurd to expect normal behavior from any of them. Maybe she got up, decided she wanted to bake a cobbler and went out to pick blackberries." He made an all-encompassing gesture. "This is a big place. She could be anywhere."

"So, you're looking for her?"

"Not a formal search, if that's what you mean. We have to go through all the usual suspects before we get to that point. I believe she's no longer on the grounds."

"Where'd she go?"

"I think she went somewhere with her son."

Rileigh could tell that assumption didn't please him.

"And that's not good news because?"

"Because her son is ... well, I will keep my personal opinion about his character to myself. What I know as fact is that he has been coming around a lot lately. Left his mother here for twenty years and never bothered to visit, and now he's suddenly omnipresent, with some paper he wants her to sign."

"What kind of paper?"

He shrugged. "It isn't any of my business what kind of paper it is. I just know that I heard him in the courtyard a couple of days ago, badgering her. I told him to back off, and he didn't take my interference well."

"So you think he took—"

"I *suspect* he *might* have taken her off the property, which is a violation of our rules of occupancy. Perhaps he believed if he could get her off by herself, he could convince her to do whatever it is he wants her to do."

He smiled a little smile. "But I wouldn't bet the rent on that if I were him. It has been my experience with people who have dementia that once they have an idea in their heads, you couldn't pry it out of them with a jackhammer. If she's decided she's not going to sign his precious paper, there isn't anything he can say or do to change her mind."

"Well then …" Rileigh rose to her feet. "I've accomplished what I came here for." She held out her hand. "Thank you for your time, Mr. Hollister–"

"*Mister* Hollister? It's Brandon."

"Brandon." She smiled. "Let me know when you find her. I'm Rileigh, by the way… and my aunt really is Daisy, but I don't know the real names of the rest of the flowers in her little garden, so it's hard to say who it is my aunt thinks got carried away by an angel."

"Her name's Thelma Ferguson. If you'll leave your number with the receptionist, I'll give you a call when we locate her."

She left her phone number. So he could get in touch with her about … Thelma. He'd said *he* would give her a call, not that he would have his receptionist get in touch with her.

Rileigh flat out wouldn't let herself look forward to the call.

Chapter Nine

AFTER RILEIGH LEFT the Carrington House, she headed to Gatlinburg to file her report with the Good GI's. She had slapped a summons on Pinky's chest and she had the picture to prove it, which meant she'd completed her assignment and should get paid for it. As a freelancer, they'd cut her a check for contract work on a job-by-job basis. Which sucked. She wished the agency had more work to give her. She didn't really want to join the firm, become a full-time employee or anything like that. She wasn't ready yet to have to become a part of that culture — co-workers, and office parties and depending on each other. Always having each other's backs. She wasn't up to that kind of responsibility yet, couldn't handle it.

Besides, she didn't really see herself spending the rest of her life delivering summons and sitting on boring stake-outs trying to catch cheating spouses. She did not aspire to climb the corporate ladder and become a... what? Lead investigator? Something like that.

She let that go, concentrated on enjoying the scenery. Full-on autumn had not yet arrived. The mental image of its coming was butter melting on top of a stack of pancakes, then dripping slowly down the sides. It was only the eleventh of October, not yet the peak season for fall colors, but give it two weeks, maybe three, and it would be breathtaking. Looking out over the Smoky Mountains from Clingman's Dome during the peak season was truly a staggering sight, almost holy. The mountainsides would be splashed with every hue of red and yellow — butter and daffodil yellow, claret-wine red and the rusty red of a roan foal or an auburn-haired toddler.

Now, she drove down winding mountain roads where the trees had just decided in the past couple of days that they needed to be about the job of becoming too beautiful for words. The birch trees were usually the first, white trunks and yellow leaves, looking like birthday candles among the greens of the fir, pine, and cedar trees.

She rolled down her windows to let in air that just had a bit of a chill in it. By midday, it'd warm up into the mid-seventies, but right now there was the sense that maybe somewhere out there deep in the woods, frost was decorating a spider web with diamonds.

She breathed deeply, let out a long sigh, and thought about Brandon Hollister. He had been an unexpectedly nice man and that had thrown her. She'd been expecting some uptight, suit-and-tie dude as animated as a clothing store mannequin. This guy had been real. Standing there in his fancy office in a sport coat over a white tee shirt and jeans... he had been refreshing.

That was all. Just refreshing.

She stomped into the dust the tiny flicker of a flame, something that'd been ignited by the spark she'd felt when she was in his office. No, she didn't need sparks right now. Resolutely shoving those thoughts and any attendant emotions aside, she turned her mind toward the anticipation of another job from the Good GI's.

Just please, not surveillance. She had run completely out of audio books.

When she stepped into the Good GI's offices a few minutes later, a couple of things were readily apparent. One, the air conditioning wasn't working. They usually had it cranked up to a point just short of an Arctic winter, necessitating a few minutes of thawing out after she left, until her fingers warmed up enough to curl around the steering wheel. Ok, exaggeration, but close. But today, it wasn't cold in the building. It wasn't even cool. Thankfully, it wasn't hot outside or the place would have been cooking, sitting as it did on a hillside in the direct morning sun. Rileigh actually enjoyed the normal temperature, but those who'd worked all summer in the freezer were probably sweating buckets.

The second thing she noticed was something else that wasn't there: the ever-cheerful Stephanie Papadopoulos, their receptionist. Hers was among the most annoying voices Rileigh had ever heard, reminded her of a sour note on a violin. But today neither her smiling face nor her annoying voice were in evidence.

Instead of Stephanie, there was a young man in a coat and tie at the reception desk. Emphasis on the "young." He likely hadn't shaved more than half a dozen times in his life. His voice was normal when he picked up the phone and recited the cheery little speech: "Hi, we're the Good GI's. If there are bad guys in your life, we're on it."

When he was through with the caller, he turned his attention to Rileigh.

"What can I do for you, ma'am?"

Was she a "ma'am" now? Yeah, to someone his age,

she probably was. Maybe she should rush out and purchase long-term care insurance.

"I'm looking for Wally. Is he here?"

"Yes, ma'am, he—"

Before he could complete the sentence Wally appeared in the hallway talking to another man. They both looked like they were trying not to sweat. Wally spotted Rileigh and excused himself, then approached her. She could tell by the look on his face that he didn't have any work for her.

"Sorry, Rileigh, but business is kinda slow right now."

"You mean, school has started, so all the cheating wives are home checking homework and giving out spelling words?"

"You did a good job wrangling Pinky for that summons," he said, and the compliment felt genuine, not of the say-something-nice-to-the-loser variety. "One of these days, that guy's gonna…" He let it go. "I'll get Philip to cut you a check."

Rileigh gestured with her chin toward the young man at the desk. "Is that Philip?"

"No, *that* is Trevor Hargraves. The second, I think. Maybe the third. He's replacing Steph while she's out on maternity leave."

"I didn't know Stephanie was pregnant."

"She isn't. But she wants to be. So, she's taking some time off to … well, you don't need a biology lesson. She and her husband are going to the beach."

He showed the first indication that the heat was bothering him then, moving his head in the universal way of those whose collars are sticking their necks.

"Probably not any warmer there than it is in here," he muttered, then turned his attention back to Rileigh.

"Give me a call the first part of next week and I might have something for you."

Rileigh didn't let her disappointment show. "I'll be around," she said cheerily, then turned and left the building.

She got it. The Good GI's employed a staff of private investigators and she was just picking up the slack, helping out when there was a surge in cases or somebody was on vacation. This wasn't regular employment. She tried to make herself be as glad about that as she had in the beginning, glad for the freedom to refuse a case, glad she didn't have to fool with all the accouterments of "a job." And she was still glad about all those things... but it sure would have been nice to know where her next paycheck was coming from.

Chapter Ten

RILEIGH SPENT the rest of the afternoon in Gatlinburg —
shopping, picking up the laundry, returning a book her
mother had ordered from Amazon. Since Mama had
begun her "romance" with Rhett Butler, she'd developed
all manner of new tastes. She'd never cared much for
music one way or the other, hummed whatever tune was
current on the radio and that was about it, but apparently
her new love had introduced her to classic rock 'n' roll.
Two days ago, Rileigh had heard her mother jamming to
"Peggy Sue" by Buddy Holly, for crying out loud. You
couldn't get any more classic than that. She also decided to
cut down on the salt in her diet. Why? She was a stick, just
like Rileigh. And she'd taken to reading poetry. She'd
started with the sonnets of Shakespeare and made her way
through Keats and Yeats all the way to Dylan Thomas,
commenting in somber tones last week that she did not
intend to go gentle into that good night.

Mama … quoting Dylan Thomas. Right.

Her mother had also ordered another book that
Rileigh intercepted at the last minute and censored. Mama

had no idea what the letters BDSM stood for, but she liked the black leather boots on the scantily clad girl on the cover image on Amazon so she'd ordered a book that featured "hard kink/edge play."

Where in the world had Mama heard about bondage? Was Rhett into kinky sex? Even thinking about sex in the same paragraph as her mother gave Rileigh hives, so she'd merely snatched the book out of the box before her mother found it and would return it for a refund.

There was some grocery shopping to do, too. She needed to pick up the dry cleaning—

Her phone rang and Rileigh's heart kicked into a gallop. She had custom rings for the people who called her often — her mother, Georgia, the Good GI's, even Mitch — so she knew by the sound who was on the other end of the line. And could therefore weed out the rest of unknown numbers as SPAM.

But that's not why she did it. She wasn't trying to avoid SPAM calls; she was trying to avoid calls from an unknown number with a Texas area code where the caller merely sat on the other end of the line and breathed.

She hadn't gotten a call from that number since she'd screamed at the caller to leave her alone.

Was it starting again?

Keeping her eyes on the road, she looked at the number on the screen. It was an unknown number, but it had a local area code.

She answered tentatively, and let out a sigh of relief when she heard Brandon Hollister's voice. Then instantly sucked the sigh back in as a gasp of surprise that *it was Brandon Hollister!* The back-and-forth movement of air was too confusing for her diaphragm to process. She choked on the whole breathing thing and went into a coughing fit on the phone.

"Rileigh," he said. "Are you all right? This is Rileigh, right?"

She managed a fairly normal-sounding, "Sorry, got choked on my coffee." Her face turned red as she fought the reflexive heaving of her diaphragm.

"If this isn't a good time ... I didn't mean to interrupt anything. I just promised you I would call you if I had any news about Thelma Ferguson." When Rileigh didn't reply right away he continued. "Thelma, you know, the woman your Aunt Daisy believes is her sister, Rosie."

"Yes, Rosie." Her voice was hoarse and she sounded breathless, like she had a python wound around her neck, but otherwise she had mostly regained voluntary control of her breathing.

"Turns out she really is missing."

"Really?" One-word answers were suitable for now, while she cleared her throat, swallowed, and tried to get her composure back along with her voice.

"I checked with her son and he hasn't seen her at all today." He paused, then said conspiratorially, "That's his story and he's sticking to it. Right now, I don't have any reason to believe he's not telling the truth. Just about everybody who might have been inclined to aid and abet some clandestine meeting with Rosie 'off-site,' or to witness it happening, was busy at the time."

"Busy?" Her voice was a little strained, but otherwise normal.

"Rosie was at dinner last night. Sometime between dinner and lights out, she disappeared. I was conducting one-on-one staff meetings for the three-to-eleven and the eleven-to-seven shift personnel from right after dinner until almost midnight. Which is a reason — not an excuse but an explanation — for why she wasn't reported missing right away. The people who should have been doing head

counts were discussing employee evaluations, policy violations and benefits packages with me. And they dropped the
ball." He paused. "*We* dropped the ball. It happened on
my watch." He let out a breath. "I was about to notify the
authorities, but thought I'd give you the news first."

"Thanks." His little *mea culpa* speech had given her time
to get her breathing squared away, so she launched a whole
sentence out into the air, hoping it wouldn't send her off
into another coughing fit. "The authorities would be the
Yarmouth County sheriff. His name is Mitchell Webster."

"A friend of yours?"

Was Mitch a friend? Oh my, oh my, oh my, was *that*
ever a loaded question. Her best friend Georgia would
have answered with a resounding — "That man's way
more than just a friend." But Brandon hadn't asked Georgia, he'd asked her, and Rileigh didn't believe there was
anything between her and the sheriff but a shared dedica-
tion to police work and a mutual respect and admiration.

Even after he had saved her life. Twice.

"We've worked on several cases together."

That wasn't an answer to the question he'd asked,
more like politician-speak where you talk after somebody
asks a question, so it seems like you answered it when you
really didn't.

"Cases?"

"Yes. I work as a freelance PI for Gatlinburg Investigations — the Good GI's — so Mitch and I have crossed
paths a lot."

"Well, since you're a private investigator, maybe you'd
like to pitch in here, given that it involves your aunt and
all."

"I'd be glad to help any way I can."

"Right now, we need bodies." He sounded like he
might have chuckled, but she couldn't be sure. "I mean, we

need people to search the buildings and the grounds. If you're up for that, I'd appreciate the help."

"Glad to do it. I can be there in half an hour."

Rileigh punched the red icon on her phone to disconnect the call, grabbed her emotions in a choke hold and pinned them to the floor. She was glad he'd called. Okay, but that was *all*. She was *not* thrilled to hear from him and she did *not* like the sound of his voice and she did *not*—

Oh, put a sock in it.

Chapter Eleven

When Rileigh had volunteered to help search for the missing Rosie on the grounds of the Carrington House, she hadn't factored the location into the equation. But when she pulled up to park behind the building, the whole *presence* of the huge edifice was nothing less than intimidating.

She found Brandon in the well-lit lobby, coordinating search teams. The Carrington House sat on three hundred and fifty acres of wooded land that backed up on the Great Smoky Mountains National Forest, which meant that if Rosie had wandered off, she had hundreds of square miles of woods to get lost in. Given that nobody had laid eyes on Rosie since last night, she could have wandered a considerable distance from the hospital.

Or not.

She might also be curled up in a corner in the huge laundry room, sucking her thumb and crying for her Mommy.

Or somewhere in the cavernous basement, which was

nothing short of a doppelgänger for the catacombs under Rome.

Or in one of the empty rooms off one of the empty hallways, in one of the empty wings of the building.

"Why don't you come with me? We can check off some of the obvious places." Brandon picked up a powerful flashlight and headed toward the back door.

Rileigh hurried to catch up with him.

"Didn't you just get here? Like a couple of weeks ago? How do you know the hidden holes in the property if—"

"I took charge a little over two weeks ago, and fired Norman Pettigrew the next day." Brandon opened the door for Rileigh and she stepped through it, mildly marveling that here was a man who still did such things. "My grandfather bought the property sometime before WWII, I think, and when he died, my father inherited it. My father was not a particularly hands-on kind of businessman. He was more the corporate boardroom kind, and he left the actually daily operations of all of his holdings to managers."

The darkness settled around them like a blanket as soon as they were out of the spill of lights from the windows on the first floor.

"I've made a grid in my head of this whole back side of the building," Brandon said. "We'll search it one quadrant at a time. Sound like a plan?"

"Works for me."

The two of them headed out into the darkness, following the bright tail of the flashlight sabering out into the black. The building was surrounded by shrubbery. Old shrubbery that had been growing untended for decades. What had once been a dignified hedge following the edge of the property had become a fifteen-foot, impenetrable wall.

Rileigh gestured toward the hedge as they approached it.

"Somebody is in serious need of a gardener."

"I think they allowed this hedge to grow out of control so it would be a barrier between the property and everything else around. Both to keep patients in and to keep snoopers out. It wasn't as intimidating as a wall."

"Or razor wire."

He looked at her with a surprised grin.

"Or razor wire. But it accomplished the same purpose." He stopped and surveyed the towering greenery. "We're going to have to make some adjustments here. We need ways to get through it, so you don't have to go all the way to one end or the other to get on and off the property."

He made an imaginary mark in the air.

"Added to the to-do list."

They traveled along the length of the hedge, pointing the flashlight into the undergrowth, which was so dense it was impossible for anybody to bulldoze their way through.

"You still haven't answered my question," Rileigh said. "You just got here. How do you know so much about the property?"

"I've been studying it my whole life. Seems like my whole life, anyway. Of all my father's properties, this was the most fascinating to me. Even as a kid, I begged him to take me with him on those rare occasions when he actually physically showed up here."

"You were asking your father to take you here. I was begging my mother to take a different way home so we didn't have to drive past it."

He stopped in his tracks.

"Seriously?"

"Seriously. I was scared shitless of this place when I

was a little girl. Believed all the haunted house tales people told about it."

"Like what?"

"There was one that said a patient had hanged himself from a chandelier in the main entryway."

"There is no a chandelier in the main entryway."

"Don't let the facts get in the way of a good story. The patient in question had murdered his whole family, had cut them into little pieces and fed them to the pigs."

"People actually believed that story?"

"Oh, I don't know if *people* did, but I did."

"Why was that?"

This time, she was the one who stopped.

"I'm not completely sure." She looked up at the shadow of unlighted building laid out on the black velvet sky with stars as big as chunks of bright ice. "The way it's built, like whoever did it was crazier than the patients. Or at the very least couldn't decide what style to use, so they just hodgepodged them all. That pointed arch over main entrance and the ribbed vault in the ceiling of the reception areas, that's pure Gothic. But the steep pitched roof, the iron railings and all the fireplaces — who puts fireplaces in a hospital?"

"This structure had been many things during its lifetime, besides being a hospital."

"The parts of it don't seem to fit with each other, or with the surroundings. It seemed like some kind of zombie building that wasn't meant for this world, and I didn't want to get anywhere near it."

"You were really that scared of the place."

"Yup. But clearly you weren't."

"Just the opposite. On the rare occasions when I could get my father to bring me here with him, I would always sneak away and go exploring. When I was only about five or six, the place had completely shut down and was deserted. My grandfather was losing money hand over fist, so my father came down to put in his two cents. We spent three or four days here, trying to gauge how much money it was going to take to renovate it. During that time, I went exploring."

He pointed up at the black shape of the building, toward one of the upper floors on the south end. "I found what looked like a torture chamber up there, in a room with padlocks on the door."

Rileigh shuddered. "Seriously?"

"I said it *looked like* a torture chamber. To a six-year-old. Turns out it was a physical therapy room, which by modern definition amounts to the same thing."

They had come to the end of the hedge behind the building. Rileigh pointed to a small stone structure nestled in a corner, where the north and south wings met. it was snuggled up there, with bushes in front and a small rock wall in disrepair around it, almost completely hidden from view.

Brandon shone the flashlight on the building.

"I've been wondering where that was," Rileigh said. "The house where the witch lived who captured Hansel and Gretel and planned to fatten them up before she ate them."

Brandon cocked his head to the side. "Does look a bit medieval, doesn't it."

"What is it?"

"There was a caretaker resident on the grounds of the place during several of its various renovations. That's the caretaker's cottage."

They approached the old stone building and Rileigh looked around her in the darkness and shivered. It felt like cold water was dripping down her spine, from one vertebra to the next.

"Could you have made this any more sinister looking? It's right off a movie set. Stone cottage, thick walls—"

"The better to muffle the screams, my dear." He feigned an evil laugh. "Heh, heh, heh."

"Stop it!"

"It's not nearly as creepy in the daylight, I promise you."

"Said the man who pleaded to come here as a child when he should have been running away in the other direction screaming."

They approached the cottage and Brandon swiped the bright flashlight beam over the sides, the walls, the windows, and the door. The windows were boarded up, the door locked with a hasp and a padlock sealing it. More important was the layer of dust and tangle of spiderwebs around the door and windows. Clearly, they hadn't been opened in ages.

Rileigh and Brandon turned away from the cottage and headed back along the hedge behind the building, following it until it ended at the wall of some kind of outbuilding. A garage or a storage facility. That, too, was locked up tight.

"Well, we've searched our quadrant and come up snake eyes. Rosie may be somewhere on the property, but she certainly wasn't in here."

They both looked toward the driveway as a white police cruiser with bright red and blue flashing lights pulled slowly across the parking lot. A handheld searchlight beam sliced into the darkness, illuminating everything it touched with a light so bright Rileigh though it might peel back her corneas. The cruiser continued its slow circuit around the back parking lot, then turned and went back down the road that ran along the side of the building.

"Guess that means your sheriff friend is on the job."

They went back into the building, into the bright lights of the reception area. Brandon excused himself and started going from one group of searchers to another, gathering information, then dispatching them to some unsearched portion of the grid.

When he came back to stand beside her a few minutes later, he told her what she expected to hear. None of the search teams had turned up anything yet. If Daisy was to be believed, which she probably wasn't, Rosie had "left" their room wearing a white cotton nightgown. That would surely have shown up in the glow of all those flashlights. But there was nothing.

It was like Aunt Daisy said — Rosie had vanished.

Chapter Twelve

Yarmuth County Sheriff Mitchell Webster decided that he would wait until morning to call out all the troops. There were various organizations that operated as rescue teams in the mountains. It wasn't like tourists went bopping off into the woods never to be seen again every week, but it was surprising how many people who had absolutely no experience with the woods — city dwellers who only knew asphalt and concrete and electric lights — would take off for a stroll among the trees with no concern for how they'd find their way back.

One tree looks pretty much like another in the woods. Combine that with a total lack of understanding about the nature of … well, nature, and most discovered that "retracing" your steps to return to the cabin or campsite was much harder in practice than you'd think it'd be. Footprints in wet leaves will vanish in an hour or so, and the outlines of rock faces and vegetation is a *mirror image* of what you saw when you left the cabin, it doesn't look the same. If a novice made it more than half a mile away from the cabin they'd rented for the week, it was just about guaranteed he wouldn't be able to get back to it.

So finding lost people, though not a common occurrence, was certainly not a rarity either. The worst times were when children wandered away from a campsite. When an alert went out over the network that volunteers were needed to do a grid search of some portion of the mountains, the mention that a child was lost brought out herds of people.

An old lady who wandered away from a mental health facility would be cause for alarm, but she wouldn't have the stamina to wander far, and he was sure there would be a plethora of hands on deck to search for her. So he'd made a decision not to call out the troops at night. They could start fresh in the morning, if the Carrington House staff didn't find her tonight.

It'd been his experience that even people who should know better were likely to ignore the single best plan of action for anyone who finds themself lost in the woods: hugging a big oak tree.

"Hug a Tree" was taught in most of the elementary schools in the mountains, though kids who grew up in the woods were less likely to get lost than other kids and more likely to know what to do if they did get lost.

The goal of Hug a Tree was to make the search for a lost person easier and more efficient. But staying in one place, though it made perfect sense from a searcher's point of view, was hard advice to follow when you were out in the woods alone. Your knee-jerk response to being lost was to try to find your own way back. And because of that, searchers were faced with trying to find a moving target, frustrated when they found signs that the lost person had been in one spot but had moved on to somewhere else.

For the rest of the night, Mitch would concentrate his

efforts on checking all the possible sites on the several rural roads that connected with the main lane leading to the hospital, assuming that if the old lady had been lost in the woods and came across a road, she'd follow it. So, he had squad cars out patrolling those. He also made sure to notify the media. If it happened to be a slow news day, a tourist lost in the trees could end up being a big story. And the bigger the story, the more volunteers would show up to help search.

If nobody found "Rosie" by dawn, Mitch would pull out all the stops. He'd establish a command center at the hospital, her last known whereabouts, and deploy specialized search teams from there — there was a K-9 unit in Gatlinburg, but Mitch would start by calling on the aid of Jim Baumgardner, an old farmer on Coon Track Hollow who had the best bloodhounds for five hundred miles in every direction. Or so was the word of mouth.

Mitch had already plotted out a grid search for the area, too — ten miles from the hospital in every direction. Once there was enough light, teams would be deployed within that area. The businesses that served campers, fishermen and others who might venture out into the trees told every customer the "lesson of the whistle" — that the sound of a whistle carried better and farther than the sound of a human voice, and whistles didn't get hoarse from overuse.

But Rosie probably hadn't thought to take a whistle with her. She was last seen in her room, barefoot, in a white nightgown.

Mitch found himself getting wound tighter as the hours ticked by and there were no clues. A woman with dementia wouldn't need a reason to wander off and likely had no destination in mind. Which meant there was nothing he could do to find her faster.

It would be dawn soon "out there on the flat", but it wouldn't get light in the woods for hours after that. Sunrise in Gatlinburg would be a little after 7:30 a.m., but it would be nine o'clock before he could mobilize search teams here.

He'd already spoken to the hospital administrator, so he knew that Rileigh was out there looking. He called her twice to find out how things were going on that end.

"You sound worn out," he told her when he called the second time.

"That's probably because I'm worn out. I was just about to call it on this one, I need to get home to Mama, who is worried sick about Rosie. Well, she's worried about Daisy, who's upset about Rosie. I'm really surprised she hasn't turned up yet."

"I'm sure she's fine. We'll find her tomorrow."

Mitch wasn't completely lying. He did believe they'd find Rosie tomorrow. But the "she's fine" part... not so much. It had gotten down below fifty degrees after sunset yesterday, and the woman was wearing nothing but a cotton nightgown. He was concerned about what condition she'd be in when they did find her.

And he had every right to be.

Chapter Thirteen

THE OWNER of the Blarney Stone Realty Company checked out his appearance in the rear-view mirror of his car before he got out and he didn't like what he saw. Absolutely did not.

Charlie Hayden would definitely have to do something about the lines around his eyes. They looked deeper with his perpetual spray-on tan, so he'd backed off. He usually went in about every three weeks for touchups, but he'd waited an extra week this time. That had been a mistake.

It was all coming unglued and he didn't seem to be able to grab hold of it anywhere long enough to change the course of his life.

He was thirty-eight years old, but looked twenty-five. Okay, thirty. Yeah, he looked at least thirty now. He was good-looking, fit and healthy. Except the fit part wasn't as easy now as it'd been when he was younger. Three days a week in the gym wasn't getting the job done anymore: he could see the beginning of a little pooch above his belt line, and he went on a binge of 100 sit-ups a day to get rid of it. All that got him was sore abs under the flab.

He had never had a washboard abs, wasn't ripped, didn't want to be. That kind of thing was for pretty boy bodybuilders, not for Charlie. But he did want to appear fit and healthy. The tan helped, but letting one extra week go by before it was reapplied had been a mistake. He could see that now. He turned his head to the side and examined his ear. That was the tell-tale place with spray-on tans. It was easy to get the rest of the body right and totally screw that part up, and now his ears were noticeably much lighter than the rest of his face.

He'd make another appointment for Friday.

Then he glanced again at the mirror image and wouldn't let himself look away. You could slice and dice it any way you wanted to, but the truth in long johns with the butt flap down was that Charlie Hayden was losing his hair. He couldn't even call it a receding hairline anymore, it had gone beyond that. He'd tried that Rogaine stuff for six months and couldn't tell that it had made a lick of difference. He couldn't very well wear a rug — God no! But hair transplants? The only ones he'd ever seen looked like somebody'd planted corn on the man's head in straight rows. You could have driven a tractor down the spaces in between those tufts of hair.

He shook his head, tried to shake it all off.

Right now, he couldn't do anything about the hair, and he already had a plan to do something about the tan. That left only the fit and healthy thing, and that's what he was doing up here at the Maple Stump trail at such an ungodly hour. He'd been up late last night, catching the results of the horse races he'd bet on in California. Getting up at seven after staying up until two… that used to be a piece of cake. Now his eyes looked puffy from lack of sleep. He couldn't keep doing that kind of thing. Being a good-looking young man was all Charlie knew how to do, and he damned well didn't intend to learn how to be a middle-aged man with a receding hairline, too-white ears, and a paunch.

He got out of the car and shivered in the early morning chill. He ran on a treadmill at the gym, or sometimes at the track at the high school. He used to run often up and down the streets of Gatlinburg. It was an image he liked to foster, the strong young man glistening with sweat, muscles taut on his calves, flat belly. He liked to show it off.

But he hadn't been doing a lot of showing off lately because ... he looked down and grabbed the "belly" in both hands. That it was even grab-able was horrifying, and he had to put a stop to it right now.

He did a couple of stretching exercises, mostly for show, then set his running watch and headed out into the woods. He did not run on trails ordinarily. But the trails were more strenuous, more ups and downs, and he knew he wouldn't run into anybody on the trail that he had to impress. If he got a stitch in his side, he'd stop. Nobody to see. And eventually he'd get into the kind of shape where he could run the whole three-mile length of the Maple Stump Trail at a sprint. That was his goal. Sprinting the whole length of the trail.

Somewhere inside Charlie, a little voice of reason told him matter-of-factly that he was blowing smoke up his own ass. He wouldn't be able to get into that kind of shape in the few months of good weather left this year before it turned too cold or too snowy to keep running. And that little part of his brain was glad that there wasn't time, because it would give him an excuse not to do it. What that little part of Charlie's brain kept from the rest of his mind was the clear and certain understanding that Charles Edward Hayden wasn't as strong as he once was, and he would never get that strength back — or that hair, or that unwrinkled skin.

He was getting old.

If he let himself listen to that little voice, he would sit down on a stump and cry. He did not want to get old. He had too much living left to do. Too many beautiful women out there. Too many bets left to win.

He took off at a slow jog across the small parking area, then into the trees. He felt tired and sluggish, but his body would respond when he demanded it do so. He'd done it before.

About a quarter of a mile in, his muscles staged their customary revolt, demanding that he stop this running foolishness at once. They'd get over it in another quarter of a mile, and by the half-mile mark he would be hitting his stride. He would struggle to keep up his pace on the uphill portion of the trail up ahead, but he'd gut it out.

He had come around a bend in the trail and there was something lying right in the middle of it, about fifty yards ahead. A lump of some kind.

Allowing his long stride to carry him forward, he was almost up to the lump before he realized what it was. It was a person. It was a body.

A dead body.

Charlie stumbled from the shock of the realization, caught his toe on a rock and then he was falling, putting his hands out in front of him to break the impact.

His knee struck the ground and screamed at him in pain. The skin on his palms was scraped, and then his belly hit the ground, knocking the breath out of him.

He lay for a moment where he was, then lifted his head. He had fallen to the ground only a few feet away from the body.

Oh, dear God, it was a woman. She was wearing some

kind of white dress — no, a nightgown — but she was barefoot, and some part of his analytical mind took note of the fact that the bottoms of her feet were clean. She had not walked here barefoot. She had been … carried.

And then he saw why.

As if in a nightmare, Charlie rose up onto his elbows, then onto his hands and knees, his eyes racing across the horror in front of him, attempting to see every detail, while his mind struggled to block the whole horror out of his mind and see absolutely nothing at all.

The elderly woman was lying on her left side in the dirt, and the whole front of her nightgown was a shredded mess of blood, guts, and gore. He pushed himself back away from the body, didn't want to get that good a look at it. But what he saw, he couldn't un-see. She had died some kind of horrible death — if he were to guess, he'd say she'd been shot in the belly at close range with a shotgun. Her whole torso was torn up. Pieces of her guts were lying on the trail.

He threw himself backwards, scrabbling away from the horror before vomiting in the grass. He heaved and heaved, then dry-heaved when there wasn't anything left in his stomach to throw up.

As soon as he could stop, he crawled, then got to his feet and staggered away. He pulled his phone out of his pocket, but his trembling hands couldn't hold onto it and he dropped it on the ground. It hit a rock. Dammit, cracked the screen.

He picked it up carefully with both hands, holding tight as they shook. But there were no bars, he had no reception. He'd have to go back to his car to call the police.

That was absolutely fine with Charlie Hayden. He turned and bolted back down the trail in the direction from which he'd come, going faster and faster, trying to outrun the images he carried along with him in his mind. He came barreling down the trail out of the woods toward his car, and he literally crashed into it, hit it hard and bounced off.

There was another car in the pull-off and a young couple, all decked out for hiking, were standing beside their car, staring at him.

"There's a body..." he began, and found that as soon as he tried to talk about it, the heaving sensation returned to his stomach. "Just call 911. I can't get coverage. Call 911 and report a–"

A what?

Well, somebody had carried that body down the trail and dumped it in plain sight. And the old lady sure as shit didn't die of natural causes.

"Tell them you want to report a murder."

Chapter Fourteen

MITCH HAD BEEN afraid for hours that he'd find Rosie and she'd be dead. Well, he did, and she was.

He'd feared she'd died of exposure. But clearly that wasn't what happened. Unfortunately, the only thing that *was* clear was what hadn't happened. She hadn't succumbed to hypothermia.

She'd been murdered.

The crime scene was pretty much secured by the time he got there. The dispatcher had received a strange 911 call that reported a dead body on one of the labyrinthine hiking trails that crisscrossed the mountains both inside and outside the national park. The Maple Stump trail was one of the older trails. It wasn't level, but it didn't offer the inclines some of the more expert trails did, so it wasn't a trail for beginners, but because of its short length — just three miles — it was a favorite for families and people intimidated by the prospect of hiking in the woods.

Thankfully, this crime scene had only a handful of looky-loos and rubberneckers, unlike the last couple of murder investigations Mitch had conducted. It was good to be able to stand and stare at the scene, just stare at it, see what you could figure out about what had happened, without an audience videoing your concentrating face, posting still shot close-ups online with captions like, The Sheriff is Clueless. Mitch thought he knew what a toad in a shoebox must feel like as it looked up at an eyeball pressed against the hole in the lid.

Charlie Hayden had gotten restless, unhappy that he'd had to hang around until Mitch arrived so he could tell Mitch what he'd seen. Which was nothing much.

"Look, I was running, I came around a corner on the trail and there she was... and then I... I threw up, okay?" He made a gagging noise, as if to demonstrate. "Jeez, what happened to her? Did somebody shoot her in the belly with a shotgun.?"

The gory wound in her belly did look like it must have been caused by some weapon that inflicted maximum damage on the victim. But Mitch wasn't ready yet to declare that it'd been a shotgun. For starters, even a cursory examination revealed there was no buckshot in the wound. And for another, a shotgun would have blown the internal organs out through the exit wound in the back of the body. But the exit wound on Rosie's back was actually much smaller than the entrance wound in the front, just a small hole about the size of a fist.

Mitch was glad to put the whole conundrum in the hands of the coroner when he arrived. His name was Gus Hazelton, a tall, thin black man from Kentucky who moved with the grace of a former athlete, though he claimed not to have participated in the basketball madness of Tennessee's neighbor to the north. His full name was Dr. Augustus Lafayette Hazelton. And besides the M.D.

after Gus' name, he had an alphabet soup of other initials that apparently indicated associated degrees as well.

Mitch had taken a liking to the man the first time they met.

That had been at the scene of a fatal traffic accident, when the coroner showed up on the scene in combat fatigues, carrying his rifle. He'd been hunting, he said.

Then he'd stood with Mitch looking at the mangled car, where a young mother had died. The two teenagers in the car that had plowed through a red-light and t-boned the young woman's car were only slightly injured. The driver maintained that she didn't know where the other car had come from. She'd been watching the road the whole time and it was just … suddenly there and she crashed into it. There had been an aggrieved quality to her voice that indicated she was quite put out with her day being inter-rupted by something as insignificant as a dead woman when she had important things to do. She let it be known she had to leave the wreck site when her mother came to pick her up because she was trying on prom dresses this afternoon.

"Kid was texting," Gus had said to Mitch under his breath. "You know it and I know it, and that's as far as it'll ever go, because there's no way to prove a thing like that."

"I'm trying to get the traffic camera feeds from beyond the next red-light."

"Which are so far away, you'll be lucky to see the car at all, let alone the kid in it."

"Likely, but I'm going to try."

Gus had looked at Mitch then, actually looked at him as if he'd just been introduced and had not been at the scene of two previous accidents with Mitch

"What do you expect to find?"

"Oh, I'm not looking for a view into the car. All I want is the timestamp on the video. If I can establish where this car was at a specific time, I can compare it to the kid's cell phone."

"Which she surely has sense enough to—"

"Took it away from her the moment I got here. She was not happy about that."

"You know who her father is, right?"

"Nope, and no point in telling me, because I don't know enough about Yarmouth County to be properly impressed or intimidated."

Gus had grinned, showing the space between his two upper front teeth. Mitch found out later that Gus referred to it as his "Madonna Gap."

Reaching into his pocket, he drew out a cigar and offered it to Mitch.

"You can smoke it if you like. I just keep one handy to light when I'm examining a floater. Ever examined a floater?"

Mitch offered that he had not had the pleasure of examining a drowning victim whose body hadn't been found right away.

"Other people use Vicks in their noses, but that always opens up my sinuses so wide you could drive a Humvee through them. A cigar, though. Just the right amount of stink to mask the smell."

As if summoned by Mitch's thoughts, Gus came trudging up the trail to where the body lay under a blanket.

"Mornin', Sheriff. I hear you've got a corpse with a hole in it, and you'd be interested in finding out what implement of destruction was used to create the opening."

"Something like that. Take a look for yourself."

Gus went to the body, knelt on the ground beside it,

and lifted the blanket away. He pulled something from the breast pocket of his shirt that looked like a six-inch-long end of an ice pick, but pointed at both ends. He used the points to carefully move around pieces of the victim's clothing — and pieces of her internal organs — to get a better view.

He studied the body, then got up and went around to the other side of it and knelt there, looking at the back side. He poked at it with his examining stick, then got to his feet and walked back to where Mitch was standing.

"I'll have to get the woman back to the lab to take a look," he said, "but it wasn't a shotgun that made that wound."

"What did?"

"I'm not prepared to say right now." That was surprising. Gus was usually very upfront with conclusions he'd come to without a whole lot of information — which were usually right.

"Being mysterious, are you?"

Gus gave him a serious look. He shook his head. "If this is what I think it is …"

He wouldn't say any more, just nodded at the ambulance attendants who'd been waiting for the coroner to arrive so they could haul away the body.

RILEIGH WAS sound asleep Thursday morning when Mitch called. Still she tapped the little green "yes" icon and tried to sound like she'd been wide awake.

"Oh, hi, how are you?" Her voice sounded clotted, and that was a totally inane remark.

"I'm sorry to wake you up."

He didn't buy that she'd been awake, and she almost tried to bluff her way through, but she'd been up all night, why wouldn't she have been sleeping? Still, she had a neurotic need to be so on top of things that she could go a night without sleep and not miss a beat. Which begged the question — why did she always need to convince Mitch she was superwoman?

That was definitely something to ponder. Just not right now. The slow turning of the cogs in her brain finally got around to wondering why he'd called. Then a thought occurred to her and she was instantly awake for real.

"Did you find Rosie?"

"Yes, we found Rosie." She only had the brief moment between that statement and the next to feel relief that the woman had been found. Then the other shoe dropped. "I'm sorry, but she's dead."

She had absolutely not been expecting that. She sucked in a breath in surprise.

"But how? Why? Where—?"

"Which do you want answered first. How, why, or where?" Before she could answer the question, he forged ahead. "I can't answer the first two questions. I don't know how she died and I don't know why it happened. But the where is on Maple Stump Trail."

"How'd Rosie get all the way from the hospital to that walking trail?"

"I couldn't tell you how she did it, but I can tell you how she *didn't* do it. She didn't do it under her own steam."

"What does that mean?"

"It means she didn't die on Maple Stump Trail. She died somewhere else and her body was dumped on the trail."

"Somebody killed her."

"It appears that way."

"How?"

"Don't know?"

"You don't know how? There are a finite number of ways to kill somebody. What method was used on her?"

"I don't know the answer to that question."

"Then what do you know?"

"I know that she's been dead for a while, probably since the night she went missing."

"And somebody just kept the body until now?" There wasn't really a question in what she said, and he didn't answer. "If the body was left, whoever killed her wasn't trying to hide the crime." She paused, trying to process it all. "Who found her?"

"Charlie Hayden."

"He's a gym lizard, hangs around there so he can sweat and swap lies with the other lizards. I never pegged him for a guy who really does for-real working out."

"Well, he was for-real working out this morning." Mitch paused. "And he looks god-awful, by the way. Pale under a spray-on tan is not a good look."

"Have you notified anybody? Brandon or Aunt Daisy?"

"Not yet. I was wondering if you'd be willing to go along for that. The telling Aunt Daisy part."

She could understand why he wouldn't want to deliver bad news to her crazy aunt. She could leap on him in hysterics and try to gouge out his eyes.

"Aunt Daisy's not going to take the news well."

"That's why I want you to come along."

"All right. I will meet you there in, say, half an hour."

"Make it an hour. I want to swing by the coroner's first. After we talk to Daisy, I want to talk to the other sisters in Daisy's room, and the staff who were working last night."

Rileigh almost told him what Brandon had said about his one-on-one interviews occupying the time of the care-givers who might have seen something. But she didn't. Let Brandon explain it himself.

Instead, she pointed out what Mitch already knew, which was how futile it was going to be to try to get information from five dementia patients. "I bet every one of them will have a different explanation for what happened to Rosie."

"I suspect Aunt Daisy's still going to come out in first place in the *can you top this?* competition."

Rileigh couldn't argue with that. She ended the call, gathered herself, and went looking for her mother. Mama was in the kitchen, cooking up a whole package of bacon and at least a dozen scrambled eggs.

Were they expecting company for dinner tonight? The Mormon Tabernacle Choir, maybe?

"Mama, I have bad news for you."

Mama had her back to Rileigh and Rileigh watched her stand up straight.

"It's about Daisy ain't it. She's dead."

"No Mama, Daisy's not dead. Why would you think—?"

"She's been telling me for ages that somebody's trying to kill her, says she knows too much and eventually they're gonna have to shut her up. I just figured they'd finally succeeded."

"It's not Aunt Daisy who's dead. It's Rosie, the woman Aunt Daisy said was kidnapped by an angel."

He mother turned around slowly.

"*This time* it ain't Daisy. But how about the next time? She's living on borrowed time."

Rileigh hadn't expected that answer. "Aunt Daisy's fine, at least as far as I know. But Rosie, they found her body this morning on a walking trail."

"And she was murdered?"

Again, Rileigh was surprised.

"How could you possibly know a thing like that?"

"I know a whole lotta things you don't think I know."

Then Mama turned back around to attend to the bacon that was sizzling and popping in the black iron skillet. She didn't cry out loud, but Rileigh could see her shoulders shaking.

Chapter Fifteen

The coroner's "lab" was a tidy brick building beside a stream, set back from the road that led to Dollywood. It was expertly landscaped, blending into the woods so well it was almost invisible. There was no signage to indicate the purpose of the building, nothing but a dignified, Dr. Augustus Hazleton, M.D. on a post beside the mailbox.

If the outside of the building was impressive, the inside was jaw-dropping, especially for a coroner's office. Mitch had no idea what kind of equipment a fully-stocked coroner's lab should have, but it was clear that this lab lacked for nothing. There was no receptionist at the desk in the small waiting room just inside the front door, but the decor of the room was elegantly understated. Gus' office off the lab in the back of the building, on the other hand, was anything but elegant. No degrees on the wall, just hunting and fishing pictures, and the stuffed remains of the fish, fowl and land animals Gus had bagged — so many that Mitch figured if Gus shot anything else bigger than a muskrat, he'd have to open up a whole new room for the trophy. The office also appeared to be home to all the fishing and hunting gear Gus used, including a locked gun cabinet that had enough firepower to start a revolution in a third world country. Mitch's thought the first time he saw it was *Man Cave*.

Mitch knew that a county coroner's salary wouldn't have purchased enough ammo to load the rifles.

"I won the lottery," Gus told him the first time he'd come to Gus' office, answering Mitch's question before he could ask it.

"Seriously?"

"Don't you read the signs, man? Says right there in big letters above the scratch-offs in every convenience store from Louisville to the Tennessee border: 'Somebody's got to win. Might as well be you.'"

"You won on a scratch-off?" Mitch thought those tickets never returned prizes bigger than a few thousand dollars.

"More amazing than that. I won on a ticket — not a handful of tickets but a single one, that I bought because I needed change from a hundred-dollar bill and the clerk wouldn't give it to me out of the register. I told him, 'Fine, then sell me a lottery ticket.'"

Gus grinned when he said it, revealing the Madonna Gap in his front teeth.

It had been a big win, a Power Ball, and Gus had walked away with his pockets full of cash and a guaranteed annual income for the rest of his life. That was why Mitch always felt lucky when he was with Gus, like maybe he could draw a straight flush in a poker game, or land on one of the big money slots on a roulette wheel. Like maybe Gus' luck would somehow rub off on him.

"I spent the cash money pretty fast. Win the lottery and suddenly everybody in your life is destitute and needs money to pay for Mama's brain surgery. It was the annual income that set me up. I discovered then that operating the medical practice I'd planned to set up, with the degree I'd sweated blood for, was not the way I wanted to spend the rest of my life."

"You thought it'd be more fun to perform autopsies on floaters than to treat some poor schmuck's case of the clap?"

"I went back for the additional degrees because I loved medicine or I'd never have become a doctor in the first place, but with live patients, it can turn into a time suck. I'd rather go fishing."

Gus didn't care that he came off sounding shallow and self-serving, both because he didn't give a fig what anybody thought of him and because he was anything but. He'd written a book on criminal pathology that made him famous — in doctors-of-the-dead circles — and he traveled all over the country doing consulting work in his private Leer jet, which he flew himself. Turns out, Gus Hazelton was not only one of the most imminently qualified pathologists in the country, but he was also single-mindedly determined to hang an accurate cause of death on every "patient" that crossed his autopsy table. He was as dedicated to his dead patients as any good doctor was to his live ones.

But there was none of Gus' typical cheery good humor about him when Mitch went to his office to find out how Thelma Ferguson — Rosie— had died. He was all business.

"Yes, I'm *sure*," he began. "So don't bother chasing after some alternative scenario because you don't like the one I give you."

Mitch merely nodded.

"Thelma Ferguson died from massive injuries to her internal organs — lungs, heart, liver, spleen, intestines."

When Gus didn't go further, Mitch prodded, "Caused by…?"

"There's not a firearm on the planet that would inflict that kind of damage. She wasn't shot, or stabbed or impaled."

"What did cause the injuries?"

"An animal of some kind. A rodent. You can see the teeth marks in the flesh. Simplest answer is a rat. I've collected a couple of hair samples, still need to analyze them."

Mitch was utterly confused.

"Are you saying … what *are* you saying?"

"I'm saying that a rat chewed through Thelma Ferguson's body, through her torso and out her back."

Mitch was too stunned to react.

"*Chewed* through?"

"Yup."

"But how… ?" Mitch didn't even know how to phrase the question.

"I've done my part, the how is your job." Gus' words were clipped, his tone curt. Both of those behaviors were out of character. Something was wrong.

"There's more to it, isn't there?"

"I can't tell you how it happened, if that's what you are asking." He paused. "But I can tell you this: Thelma Ferguson was alive when it happened."

"You mean—?"

"I mean, I'm not talking about a rat chewing through a body that died from some other cause. I'm saying the rat was the cause of death. A rat chewed through her internal organs. She might have survived until it got her heart."

"I've never heard of anything like that. Have you ever had a case—"

"Of an animal killing a human? Sure. You don't want

to see what a pissed off Kodiak bear can do to the human body."

"I'm not talking about a bear. A rat! If she was alive, why didn't she—?"

"There are ligature marks on her wrists and ankles."

Mitch felt like the earth beneath him had opened up and he was tumbling down into darkness.

"Ligature marks." He almost didn't have the air to push the words out into the world. "You're saying somebody tied her up and then … what?"

"I've checked under her fingernails, thought maybe she clawed at somebody, but there was nothing. Based on the angle of the marks, her hands weren't tied together, neither were her feet. They were each were tied individually to something."

"She was spread-eagled."

It wasn't a question.

"The marks are consistent with that kind of restraint, but there's no way to know for sure."

"But why would the rat try to chew through her?"

"Like I said, I've done my part. The rest is up to you to figure out." Gus paused, then ground his teeth. "If I can help in any way, any way at all, you let me know."

Then he drew another breath and said what Mitch was already thinking. "I can't imagine a worse way to die."

Chapter Sixteen

RILEIGH MET Mitch outside the front doors of the Carrington House, and the moment she saw his face, she knew something was wrong.

"Okay, spill it," she said. "What do you know that I don't?"

"Can we talk about this later?"

"Yeah, we can, but I'd rather we didn't. Whatever it is has something to do with Rosie, doesn't it?"

"Okay, you're going to hear this eventually. I guess you need to hear it from me." Mitch's face looked grave, as grave as she'd ever seen it. "I just talked to Gus. He gave me the official cause of death for Rosie."

Mitch stopped there, didn't say anything else.

"Well, what is it? How did she die?"

"According to Gus, she died from internal injuries caused by some kind of rodent, probably a rat, chewing through her torso."

Rileigh couldn't have heard that right. He couldn't possibly have said what she thought she heard.

"A rat?" she sputtered.

He nodded.

"Chewed through?"

"Yeah, that's pretty much the response I had. But Gus is sure." Mitch stopped again.

Was she going to have to drag every single word out of him, one by one?

"What? Tell me!"

"He also said that she had been tied down" Mitch rushed on, as if he didn't say it all at one time, he wouldn't be able to say it at all. "And she was alive when it happened."

Rileigh gasped.

"Let's go inside and have a talk with your Aunt Daisy." He shook his head as he turned toward the doors. "See if we can make some sense out of what she said happened to Rosie."

They went to the nurses' station on Daisy's floor, and the charge nurse showed them to Daisy's room. Thankfully, her roomies were somewhere else at the time. The instant Daisy saw her, she leapt up and raced into Rileigh's arms, grabbing her in a bear hug that stole her breath. "Oh, Rileigh, I'm so glad you're here."

Daisy turned her head toward Mitch.

"And you, Sheriff, You need to hear this. You need to know there's a kidnapper out there on the loose, snatching people out of their rooms. Taking them off to do who knows what to them."

"How about we sit down and talk about it?" Mitch suggested. "I'd like to start out by talking about Rosie. I never met her, and you knew her well. I'd like to hear what she was like."

"What does that have to do with that angel taking her?"

"The more I know about Rosie, the better I will be able

to figure out what happened to her." When Daisy was still unconvinced, he pushed. "You don't have to understand why I want to know. Just trust that I'm asking because I want to do my job and tell me about her."

Aunt Daisy let out a sigh of submission and walked to the edge of her bed, plopping down on it. She looked a little more bedraggled today than usual. Her hair was a tangle of bedhead that was all on the right side, suggesting she had slept on her left side. She wore an old pair of faded jeans with holes in them, but they weren't fashion statement holes. They'd been worn there. Rileigh thought Aunt Daisy might very well have been wearing that same pair of jeans for the last 20 years. Above the jeans, she wore a wrinkled t-shirt with some kind of design on the front that Rileigh couldn't make out. Either it was intentionally blurry, or it had so faded with age that you couldn't tell what had been there to begin with.

Aunt Daisy looked at Mitch. "Rosie was the best of them, of all my sisters."

Rileigh thought about her real sister, Rileigh's mother Lily, who did Aunt Daisy's bidding no matter what, who came running every time her older sister crooked her finger, who—

Rileigh let it go. Daisy Gillespie was a narcissist with dementia. At the very least, she was literally incapable of caring about anybody but herself.

"Well, let me see. We called her Nosey Rosie because she was always sticking her nose in somewhere it didn't belong."

"How?"

"Any way she could, like she was always digging into something. You'd best not leave your purse unattended around Rosie or she'll go through it, just to see what's in it, not stealing nothing. She liked to get up near the closed doors when the shrinks come to do consults, listening to the crazy things some of these people say. She wanted to hear every conversation, particularly the ones she wasn't a part of. Why, as a matter of fact, she broke into the administrator's office about a month ago. I don't know how she got in there, but when they found her the next morning, she had files spread out all over the floor and she was reading everyone's private information that she didn't have no right to know. Probably took them three days to get it all straightened back out again."

"So how did she get out of here? I thought the doors were locked."

Daisy made a snorting sound.

"The staff in this place is so careless, they might just as easy lock you out of your room as lock you in it. Bunch of incompetent assholes. But even when they did lock us in, Rosie could always get out. She knew how to pick the lock."

Daisy got up and went to a dresser, opened the top drawer, and dug around in what looked like pairs of socks and underwear until she came out with what looked like a bent bobby pin. She went to the door and pointed to the locking mechanism.

"I can't do it. I've tried but I can't. Rosie was the only one of us who could. She could stick this thing in that little hole and wiggle it around and listen to the clicks and clacks, and the next thing you know, the door would pop open. I figure she must have picked the lock on the door to the administration room."

Mitch got up from where he was seated on the side of somebody's bed and went to the framed pictures set up on a table by the window. They were family pictures, all jammed together, so many that you couldn't see any particular one without picking it up.

"Is there a picture of Rosie in here? Or her family?"

Daisy got up and went to the table where the pictures were sitting. She fumbled around through them for a few moments, then picked up one and handed it to Mitch.

"That's Rosie."

It had probably been taken in the past year or two, and she was standing outside under a tree with a young man who had his arm around her, either protectively, or possessively, depending on how you interpreted the body language. Rileigh wondered if that was the son that Brandon had suspected of taking Rosie off the grounds. He seemed too young. A grandson, maybe.

"Pictures reach out and grab a moment from the past and yank it into the present," Daisy said. "This, here, was Rosie before she come to the Carriage House. She was happy as she could be living on a farm, taking care of her chickens and her goats. She had a cow and she milked it twice a day, every day. She had to get up at four o'clock in the morning, because if she waited any later than that, the cow would start to baying in the barn, making so much noise it would wake up the whole family. She liked to can vegetables out of her garden and make jelly and preserves out of the blackberries that grew wild in the bushes. She'd been a widow for so long when this picture was made, she'd gotten over missing Harold by then."

Daisy looked up at Rileigh and Mitch. "What I'm saying is she was happy. She was getting along fine, living her life the way she wanted to, doing what pleased her. And the next thing you know, she's in here, stuck in a locked room, with nobody ever coming to visit her. They said she was crazy, but all of us is crazy, and she wasn't any crazier than anybody else. In fact, it seemed to all of us that Rosie was the most sane person on the floor, and that includes the nurses, the doctors, and the orderlies. But here she was, locked up in the loony bin. I think she learned how to pick the lock because she was bored and lonely. She wanted more out of life than looking at four walls and the ugly faces of five women who wasn't really her sisters at all."

Daisy turned her gaze full on Mitch then, glared at him with eyes that could be as cold as stone one minute and empty the next, like looking into some barren wasteland where nothing lived. "Then that angel come in here out of nowhere and carried her off. She didn't deserve to be yanked away like that."

"Did she fight back?" Mitch asked.

"Nah, she didn't do nothing. She just looked him in the face and told him she wasn't ready yet. She said she hadn't done everything she wanted to do and wasn't ready to go over to the other side yet, but it didn't matter what she said. He grabbed her by the arm, yanked her across the room, and…"

She didn't finish the sentence. So Mitch asked, "And what?"

"And then the two of them vanished," Daisy said. "Just went poof like a puff of smoke and wasn't there anymore."

Chapter Seventeen

MITCH AND RILEIGH left Daisy's room and checked out at the nurse's station, then headed out into what Rileigh thought of as a rabbit warren of hallways in the rest of the building to the administrative offices to find Brandon Hollister. As they walked, Rileigh told Mitch what she'd learned about the man who had just recently taken over hands-on management of the hospital.

"He seemed competent enough to me." She kept her words devoid of any emotional subtext. "He owns the place, inherited it from his father when the old man died. His first act as the new owner was to fire the administrator of the facility. He also put the rest of the staff on notice that they did not have job security here, that he would gauge the competence of the staff, keep the ones doing the best jobs, and replace all the others."

"He actually told them that."

"Yeah, I think he did. But even if he didn't say it that way, he told me that the administrator his father had hired to operate the facility was at best a moron and at worst a crook, and that during his tenure at the Carrington House, there had been many questionable hires. He said he would have to weed out the good ones and cut bait on all the others."

They only got lost twice in the twisting hallways, before finding the renovated wing where Brandon and the rest of the administrators had offices.

"I'm sorry, but Mr. Hollister isn't in right now," said his secretary. "He's down at the morgue with Mr. Mackay."

Rileigh asked for, got, and promptly confused directions to the morgue, at the bottom of a wide, dark stairway that led to the basement.

The basement was the facility at its worst. The ceiling was too low in places, making even short Rileigh duck her head. The walls were rock, like the outsides of the original building. Water stains abounded. It was damp and musty, with that odor common to closed-up places and thrift store clothing.

The morgue itself could have been right out of a Dr. Frankenstein movie. Old equipment, a rough concrete floor, and drawers in the wall where the "occupants" were kept. When they entered, they found Brandon standing beside a body on a metal table covered with a sheet. The right foot was exposed and there was a tag on the big toe.

"Brandon," Rileigh said as she approached him, "I'd like you to meet 'the authorities' you called to look into Rosie's disappearance. This is Sheriff Mitchell Webster."

The two men shook hands, and in spite of herself, she thought of two male dogs meeting, squaring off against each other, their ears laid back, hackles raised. Sniffing each other's butts.

Mitch wasted no time getting to the point.

"The dispatcher advised that we found the body of the missing woman, Thelma Ferguson?"

"Rosie," Brandon said.

"Yes," Rosie.

"You know that this is now an active murder investigation, right?" Mitch said.

"I do now. All we were told was that she died under questionable circumstances."

"Thelma Ferguson was murdered somewhere, probably shortly after she disappeared out of her room, and then her body was taken to Maple Stump Trail and dumped there. A jogger found it this morning."

"Murdered," Brandon said, seeming to test the texture of the word in his mouth. "How was she killed?"

Mitch didn't exactly squirm, but it was clear he really didn't want to talk about that point.

"Coroner's completing his autopsy and you'll have a copy of the full report as soon as he submits it."

Brandon blinked. "Okay. So, you're not saying she was stabbed or strangled or shot or … whatever… until the coroner signs off on it?"

Somehow that must have felt like a criticism to Mitch, because he bristled.

"Like I said, she died under 'questionable circumstances,' but it was definitely not an accidental or natural death." He paused. "What I'm interested in now is finding out how she got out of her room. Do you have any information about that?"

"Not yet, but I'm looking into it. What I can tell you is that I was meeting with the 3 to 11 shift staff as well as the 11-to-7 shifts from noon until about midnight, which includes the period of time when Rosie went missing. The people who should have been in charge of securing her whereabouts, and the people who might have witnessed something out of the ordinary, were not on the floor at the time."

"You often leave whole wards of the hospital without staff for long periods of time?"

Now it was Brandon's turn to bristle. They were acting like a couple of mail dogs, sniffing each other's butts.

"I have been in charge of the overall operation of this facility for less than two weeks and what I discovered when I arrived was that a large portion of the staff is incompetent. I haven't found but a handful of them who don't need to be fired on the spot." He paused, lowered his hackles. "But I have a hospital to run and I can't do it by myself. All I can do is systematically weed out the employees who shouldn't be here. That's what I was doing at the time that Rosie went missing."

Mitch might have picked up the ball and continued toward the goal line with it, but instead he said, "Did you know that Rosie could pick the lock on her room, and did so often? I'm told that she was discovered in one of the administrative offices some time ago, where she'd picked that lock to access confidential information?"

"I did know the offices were broken into. I did not know that Rosie was the culprit. I will see to it that a new lock is installed on the door of that room immediately."

"Kind of locking the barn door after the horses are already out," Mitch said, then surprisingly, held up his hand. "Sorry, that was a cheap shot. This is a disturbing case, and close to home, since she was Aunt Daisy's roommate."

Rileigh saw Brandon pick up on the reference to "Aunt" Daisy — and what that might imply — before Mitch continued.

"Is there anything that I don't know right now that I ought to as I investigate Rosie's death?"

"As a matter of fact, there is." Brandon cleared his throat. "Rosie's son has been hanging around the hospital a lot in the past couple of weeks, noteworthy because he hadn't been to see her a single time before that in almost two years. I overheard the two of them talking in the courtyard. Carl Ferguson, I think his name is, but my staff can give you all his contact details. He was insisting, in a vehement and almost threatening way, that his mother sign some kind of paper. I had to make him leave the premises. As soon as we figured out that she really was missing, I called him, and he said he hadn't seen her in several days."

Mitch nodded. "Anything else?"

"If I think of anything, I'll let you know. Meanwhile, I will get you copies of all the personnel files of anybody who might have had any reason to be on her floor that night. I figure that's at least two dozen people, perhaps more."

Mitch nodded curtly.

"So, are we done here?" Brandon asked. "I'd like to finish paying my respects to Fred." He glanced toward the metal table holding the dead body with a toe tag. "He died today. He'd been living here for more than forty years. Had a traumatic brain injury and the family didn't know how to take care of him, so they brought him here."

Brandon looked at Rileigh. "You know how I told you I used to beg my father to take him with me when he came here?"

She nodded.

"Fred was one of the reasons. He was a little boy in a man's body. A delightful child who loved to laugh and play jokes on the nurses, and hang out with a shy kid twice his mental age and half his size who had ... what shall I call it ... limited people skills."

He patted Fred's hand under the sheet. "I'd been looking forward to spending time with him."

"We'll be going then," Mitch said, without consulting Rileigh on whether or not she was ready to go.

As they walked out of the building, Rileigh said, "You're going to dig into the past of two dozen people by yourself?"

Mitch shrugged. "You got a better idea?"

"How about we split the list down the middle? You poke and prod half of them and I'll go after the other half."

"Deal." He smiled at her, but it was a distracted smile, either because he was thinking about the case he was working on or because he was fuming over his dislike for Brandon Hollister, which couldn't have been more obvious if he'd written it in the sky.

Chapter Eighteen

PINKY COLLINS WAS BEING CAREFUL, very careful, doing everything slowly, deliberately, determined to appear sober, stone cold sober.

He wasn't. He absolutely was not sober. He was drunk on his butt, barely able to stand up, but he had to get Smitty's car back to him tonight 'cause he'd need it in the morning to take his kids to school.

Pinky had to borrow Smitty's car because after his last DUI, they'd put that thing on his car. Shoot, he didn't even know how to operate the device, wouldn't have been able to if he had been as sober as they all wanted him to be. The upshot of the thing-a-ma-jig was that the car wouldn't start unless Pinky blew in that little tube and the machine indicated his blood alcohol level was less than .5 mg. He probably couldn't have passed that test the first thing in the morning before he even had a beer.

But he couldn't live life without a car. And the reality that didn't none of them want to acknowledge was that Walter Thomas Collins could hold his liquor so well he could drive better three sheets to the wind than somebody who'd never had a drink in their lives. When you drank as much as Pinky did, you learned to handle it, learned to function just fine even when you tied one on. You—

Pinky stumbled, caught his toe on a bump in the asphalt and fell flat on his face in the parking lot. The pain of his cheek hitting the asphalt informed his sluggish brain that he was likely to have a shiner tomorrow.

Dammit.

He got to his feet, swayed, might have gone down again if he hadn't reached out to hold on to the hood of the car he'd fallen in front of. That steadied him.

He shook his head to clear it and that was a colossal mistake, because it sent the whole world off in a spinning whirlwind around him. He had to hold on tight to the hood of that car to keep from face planting a second time.

Smitty was the best bartender Pinky had ever had, was a loyal guy who minded his own business. He'd been reluctant to let Pinky have the car. But Pinky had sworn on a stack of Bibles he wouldn't have so much as a beer, that he'd go straight to Gatlinburg, pick up the order, and come right back. Wouldn't be gone more than a couple of hours. Swear to God.

Pinky squinted down at the watch on his left arm. Took him a few tries to focus.

Shit. He'd promised to return the car by five o'clock and it was damn near ten. Where had the time gone? He'd just stopped off at Tucker's to have a beer ... he'd shot some pool ... the rest was a blank. He didn't know where he'd been, but he was damned sure where he was going. He was going to Smitty's house on Lenwood Drive and hand him the keys. He'd apologize for being late. Smitty would understand. He didn't really need the car until in the morning anyway. Pinky would get an Uber to take him home.

As soon as he got behind the wheel, he felt better, more in control. Shoot, Pinky could drive from Gatlinburg to the Forge with one eye tied behind his back. He opened a window, let some fresh air blow in his face and he felt even better. He turned on the radio, or tried to, but he couldn't figure out how. Which one of these damn knobs was for the radio? The middle one sent air shooting up onto the windshield, so it must be—

The car Pinky was driving crossed the center line all the way into the other lane. When he looked up and saw headlights coming at him, he yanked the steering wheel to the right to get out of the way and sent the car flying off the road and into the woods. The other driver swerved left, crashed through a guard rail, and plummeted five hundred feet before hitting the rocky slope below, then bounced off the rocks, turning over and over as they pinballed down the mountainside, coming to rest as an unrecognizable hunk of twisted metal smashed against the side of a boulder in a small creek.

MITCH HAD to drag himself out of bed after the call from the Tennessee Highway Patrol woke him at 3 a.m. He'd been up all night Wednesday searching for Rosie, and had been so tired when he finally fell into bed around midnight last night that he'd fallen asleep almost before his head hit the pillow. He'd been jarred from that blissful sleep three hours later when his phone rang.

There'd been a fatal wreck — a vehicle went off Putnam's Overlook — and the Tennessee Highway Patrol trooper working the traffic accident had called the sheriff's department to report that he'd made a discovery that shoved this wreck out of the ordinary category and into you're-gonna-want-to-see-this-land.

Mitch drove down Turner Pike to get to the site of the wreck in Piddly Creek below Putnam's Overlook. Crews from the rescue squad, the fire department, and the ambulance service had forged a trail through the woods there, back about seventy-five yards, to get to the vehicle that had gone over the embankment above. The other vehicle was in the woods at the top of the ridge, and apparently the driver had not been seriously injured.

Mitch made his way by flashlight through the woods to the creek. On the other side, the rescue squad had set up big lights that lit everything in fifty yards with a harsh, glaring light that cast dark back shadows with sharp edges. Mitch didn't know the trooper working the accident, so he introduced himself to the young man, who couldn't be more than a year or so out of the academy. He led Mitch to the mangled piece of metal that had once been a vehicle.

"It's a hearse," the officer said. "Well, was a hearse. The driver was killed, but at least the only passenger was already dead."

The rescue squad was packing away the jaws of life they'd had to use to get the body of the driver out of the front seat. The back part of the vehicle had been torn open in the fall, and the gurney with the corpse attached had gone catapulting out and tumbled down the rocks, somehow managing to end up under what remained of the hearse.

"There wasn't much left of the corpse," the young trooper said, keeping his voice level. But Mitch could tell that he hadn't quite gotten the "detachment" part of his job down right because he was visibly upset by the sight of the mangled corpse — so torn apart it was only apparent it was a human by the presence of an arm, and a leg with the bottom portion missing, still attached to the torso.

The trooper got out his notebook, grateful to have something to focus on besides the body, and read off what he'd learned about the vehicle and its occupant. *This is a hearse from Dargenio's Funeral Home in Gatlinburg, it was transporting a mister* ... he studied the notes, like maybe his handwriting had been a little shaky when he wrote down the information. *...Mr. Fred Mackay, from the North Tennessee State Hospital to the funeral home.*

Fred Mackay. That was the body in the morgue of the Carrington House when Mitch and Rileigh had been there this afternoon. The new director, Brandon Hollingsworth, had been there "paying his respects" when they arrived.

The trooper continued speaking, but Mitch missed the name of the deceased driver of the vehicle. He tuned back in in time to hear that the driver of the other vehicle involved in the accident, the one that had crashed into the trees at the top of the overlook was one Collins, Pinky.

"Let me guess," Mitch said. "Mr. Collins ran the hearse off the road — right?"

"Good guess."

"Wasn't a guess. Pinky's a drunk, an accident looking for a place to happen. I guess he found it tonight."

"He's not badly hurt," the trooper said. "I talked to him but apparently he was in a blackout and didn't remember a thing. We took him into custody."

Mitch almost commented that the people who ought to have been arrested were the county prosecutors, who kept amending Pinky's DUI charges down to reckless driving, "improper equipment," or some other lesser offense, and the judge who should have taken the man's driver's license away from him and left him in jail long enough to dry out.

Mitch let that go. The trooper was looking up from his

notes and pointing to something laying in the rocks beside the stream.

"That's the body, the corpse that was in the back of the hearse. What's left of it." The young man paused. "I left it where I found it as soon as I noticed. It's why I had the dispatcher call you."

The young man walked resolutely over to the mangled body. There was no blood, at least, which somehow made it even more horrifying. The internal organs had been ripped out of the body and were spread around on the creek rocks and in the creek.

The trooper pointed his flashlight on what was apparently part of the corpse's torso, though what he was highlighting was clearly visible in the bright lights all around.

"There," the trooper said. "As soon as I saw that, I figured you'd want a call."

The "that" he was describing was a sandwich bag full of some kind of white powder, stuck in among the various unidentifiable organs. Somebody had apparently used the dead body as a mule to transport drugs.

Yup, that definitely put a different shine on the apple.

The body of Fred Mackay had been transported directly from the wreck site to Coroner Gus Hazleton's office. It would have been standard procedure to take a dead body to the coroner to rule on the cause of death, but Mitch didn't need a ruling on what'd killed the man. He needed Gus to examine the corpse and tell him anything he could figure out about the drugs that had been jammed into the man's insides.

Gus was leaned over a microscope when Mitch came into his office. He always felt a little intrusive, just walking in the unlocked front door of the building and right into the lab. But Gus didn't even employ a receptionist — "that desk is just for show" — so Mitch settled for hollering something inane, like.

"Yahoo, Domino's Pizza, we deliver."

Or: "Hello, Betty's Brassiere Shop, we fix flats."

Today he settled for: "Buddy the Elf here, what's your favorite color?"

Gus didn't look up from the microscope, just said over his shoulder, "You're not cute enough to be an elf. There's coffee in the break room. It probably won't kill you. Bring me a cup when you get yours."

Said break room featured a refrigerator, a microwave, and a coffee pot, for Gus and all the non-existent employees who wouldn't be gathering there to eat lunch.

When Mitch returned, Gus still leaned over the microscope, but he stood up when Mitch entered the room.

Thankfully, the remains of Fred Mackay were not stretched out across the exam table but lay demurely under a lumpy white sheet there.

Gesturing toward a stool on the other side of the exam table, Gus said, "Sit."

"Roll over," Mitch replied. "Fetch."

"Play dead," Gus joined in. "Definitely a command for a pathologist to teach his dog."

Mitch tasted the cup of coffee he'd just poured for himself and grimaced.

Gus took a big swallow, and said, "Aaaah, nectar of the gods." He let out a sigh. "I hear our friend Pinky finally fulfilled the prophesy we made about him the first time he was in a wreck."

Mitch nodded. "And he's fine. Oh, his arm is broken, and he won't be winning any beauty pageants — face was pretty bunged up and all his front teeth were knocked out. But he's still breathing. That's more than you can say for the guy who was driving the hearse. Had to use the jaws of life to get his body out of the wreck and they won't be having an open casket at his funeral."

Mitch paused. "How come the drunks always come out of these wrecks without a scratch?"

"That's a myth. People say, 'oh the drunks are relaxed and that's why they're not hurt.' Horse shit. I've worked hundreds of wrecks over the years and I'm here to testify that it doesn't matter whether you're drunk or sober, if your vehicle comes into contact with one going in the opposite direction at sixty miles an hour, you're not going to walk away from it. It's just the blame factor that high-lights DUI wrecks. You tend to notice some drunk stag-gering away from a wreck he caused where some little kid got killed. You don't notice all the times the drunks are just as dead as the people in the other car."

He set the coffee cup down and indicated the micro-scope he'd been peering through.

"Black rat, genus Rattus, in the subfamily Murinae, had a bite range of … well, you don't care about that. The point is the rat that chewed a hole in Thelma Ferguson's body was a basic, garden variety creature, the kind you'd find in any barn or dumpster anywhere."

"So, somebody just went out and caught a rat and then …" Mitch couldn't finish that sentence, because he had no idea how the killer had persuaded the rat to kill Thelma.

"Apparently." Gus turned back toward the exam table. "There's not much I can tell you about Mr. Mackay, other than the fact that the plastic baggie of drugs nestled in his innards is not endemic to the species." He pointed to a side table. "I kept the baggie for you, put it in an evidence bag. Not that you're going to find out anything with it. Standard kitchen sandwich bag, too gooed up with fluids to have retained any prints."

"The thing I need to know from you is how did the baggie get into the body."

"Well, duh, somebody cut him open."

"Was it a surgical incision, like maybe a doctor did it? He'd been in the hospital. I didn't ask what the cause of death was, but perhaps he'd had recent surgery."

"Wish I could help you, but I got no clue, the remains were so torn up. Fred Mackay's gut could have been cut open by a surgeon with a scalpel or sliced open by the janitor with a letter opener. No way to tell."

Gus reached to remove the sheet from the body, but Mitch shook his head.

"I've seen. I don't need to see again. I'll take your word for it."

Mitchell called Rileigh as he drove from Gus' office to his own, to give her an update on Rosie's murder case. Which was no update at all, because he didn't know anything more about the case than he did when the body was found. Well, other than the species of rat, but he doubted that'd be a very useful factoid to possess.

"I heard there were drugs in the corpse in the hearse that went off Putnam's Overlook."

Mitch shouldn't have been surprised. The "grapevine" in Yarmouth County probably wasn't any more effective than the rumor mills in any of the surrounding small towns. But it sure seemed like word about every tragedy was out on the street here, faster than anywhere he'd ever seen. Hundredth monkey, he supposed. Thankfully, the cause of death of Thelma Ferguson still wasn't common knowledge. Just the buzz about it — the hole in the body that was probably a shotgun blast but maybe not. He sure would like to keep the lid on the details of that one for as long as he could.

"What'd you hear?"

"I just told you. That there were drugs in the corpse. It was on its way to Dargenio's Funeral Home, wasn't it?"

"Yes."

"I know the owner. His name's Whit Nash. He's older than I am, was a senior in high school when I was in the eighth grade. He came to Memphis for an emergency responders' convention a few years and I was there with the Memphis PD. We ran into each other in the convention center lobby, did the whole homie dance, and had dinner together. He started Nash Ambulance Service."

"Good guy?"

"If you're asking if I think he's the kind of man who'd be involved in an illegal drug ring, I'd say not, but we only spent those few hours together. I will say that I admire him. He has cerebral palsy. He's high functioning, but it affects his speech and his walk. I've always respected that he hadn't let a disability get in the way of what he wanted to do in life." She paused. "While you find out who was supposed to dig those drugs out of the corpse, would you like me to talk to Whit?"

"You talk to him, and I'll talk to Brandon Hollister about how the drugs got into the corpse in the first place."

Mitch didn't like that he was glad to put Rileigh on some assignment that didn't involve her speaking to Brandon Hollister, but there it was.

Whether or not she'd picked up on how he felt about her spending time with Brandon, Rileigh didn't seem to miss a beat.

"Clearly somebody at the Carrington House was in the wholesale drug business. Maybe that's what got Rosie killed."

"How do you figure?"

"Well, Aunt Daisy called her Nosy Rosie, remember? Maybe she was wandering around when she shouldn't have been, *where* she shouldn't have been, and she saw something she shouldn't have seen. Maybe she stumbled upon the drug operation and they had to kill her to keep her quiet."

"That's a reasonable motive for murder. But that kind of murder? Seems like a whole lot of trouble to go to when they could have put a bullet in the back of her head or slit her throat."

Mitch paused, didn't like the images that filled his brain when he did. "She was awake when it happened. Gus said she was. Why would you do something like that to somebody unless you really hated them?"

"Or unless you were batshit crazy."

Chapter Nineteen

By lunchtime, Mitch was pulling his cruiser into a parking space at the Carrington House.

He didn't exactly demand to see Brandon Hollister, but he did what he didn't ordinarily do, which is intimidate with his badge. He was as willing as anybody else to wait in the reception area, but he indicated by his unwillingness to "have a seat, he will be with you shortly" that he had better things to do with his time and he was here on official business.

He looked around the office while he waited for Hollister to grant him an audience.

He stopped himself right there. He had no logical reason not to like Hollister — but he had an emotional one that he didn't want to acknowledge because it would require him to open up all kinds of doors he would much rather keep shut and locked right now. So he did his best to set aside his feelings for Rileigh and tried to figure out what it was about the man that raised his hackles. Something definitely did.

Too good looking? Too poised? Too relaxed? Relaxed

like a man who's very comfortable in his own skin. It wasn't that Mitch was uncomfortable being himself, but Mitch hadn't grown up in money. He had grown up in horror. You didn't come out of a childhood like Mitch's unscathed. He should be grateful that he wasn't more poorly adjusted than he was. His brother had fared worse. He'd gone to shrinks and psychologists, and knew all the phrases for what was necessary, how he had to process what had happened to them, experience it and embrace it or some other kind of horseshit. None of it made any sense to Mitch, but he'd encouraged his brother because he could tell that Hank was hanging on by his fingernails.

Mitch should have been there for him, he should have—

No, he was not going to *should* on himself. Not today, bigger fish to fry. What had happened to his brother was as predictable as sunrise on Easter Sunday morning. The only thing about the whole scenario that wasn't predictable was that Mitch hadn't gone down the same drain. For a while, he'd been circling it.

"... see you now," said a pleasant voice, and Mitch realized the secretary was talking to him. She showed him to the wide oak door, rapped her knuckles on it softly and opened it a crack, then said, "The sheriff is here to see you, sir."

Hollister said something to her from the other side of the room. She opened the door wide and ushered Mitch inside with a gesture.

Brandon stood by the window, looking out, and Mitch could only envy his view of the forested mountains. Mitch's view out of the courthouse windows of his own office offered a picturesque, eight-by-ten, glossy, suitable-for-framing view of the dumpsters behind the building.

"Sheriff Webster, I'm surprised to see you today. Is there any news on Rosie Ferguson's case?"

"I'm not here to talk about Rosie. I'm here to talk about Fred Mackay."

"Where was his body taken after the accident? His family is planning a service for him."

Well, the grapevine apparently didn't extend all the way into Hollister's office, because he had not heard about the drugs in the dead body.

"So, you didn't know there were drugs found in the body."

"Yes, Fred was on medications of some kind but—"

"I was called to the scene of the accident early this morning, where the state police trooper showed me Fred's body. It had been ripped open by the accident, and the trooper pointed out to me that there was a baggie containing a white powder that had been *inserted* into the body."

Brandon looked genuinely surprised. "What are you saying?"

"The coroner has not yet determined the nature of the white powder in the bag. But I doubt somebody would go to the trouble of hiding a bag of confectioner's sugar inside a corpse."

Hollister's realization knocked him off his game, and Mitch liked watching that. He also liked driving the point home before Hollister could try to deny it. "That somebody works here."

Hollister sat down abruptly in the big chair behind his desk. He didn't offer Mitch a seat, but he was fine standing. The better to loom over the suspect as he was figuring out that he was a suspect.

"I'm here to find out what you know about this. How did those drugs get into Mackay's corpse."

"Well, I certainly have no idea." Hollister shrugged, not a dismissive shrug, but a confused, uncertain one. As if he genuinely had no idea. Mitch was a little bit ashamed of the part of him that was disappointed by that.

"I need to know the names of everybody who had access to the body—"

"That'll be easy, I'll just give you an employee roster." Hollister spread his hands out in front of him. "You were in that morgue. There's not even a lock on the door. It was accessible to anybody who wanted to go in there."

He ran his hands through his hair before continuing. "I can get you a list of the people who were responsible for the body. The charge nurse, the orderly who wheeled …" His voice trailed off. "But they certainly weren't the only people who had access to the body."

Hollister remembered his manners then. "I'm sorry, Sheriff. Please have a seat."

"I'm good."

The man at the desk looked up at him with a discernment Mitch wouldn't have credited him with. "If you think standing there above me is going to make me so nervous I'll spill the beans and tell you everything I know, you don't know me at all. I already have told you: everything I know is nothing."

Mitch could see Hollister begin to process all the information he'd just given the man, saw him respond to the conclusions he was reaching in his head, conclusions he was not sharing with Mitch.

"You know something more about this than you're telling me. Care to share it?"

To Mitch's surprise, the man stood up abruptly and paced over to the window.

"Fine, you want to know what I know that you don't. I know I have a staff of incompetents. I told you before that my father wasn't a hands-on manager, but it was way worse than that. He didn't really care about people, didn't care if they were managed properly, didn't care about their work environments. He just looked at the bottom line and if it was a number he liked, he didn't rock the boat. Now it's my job to clean up his mess."

He grabbed hold of his irritation, but it was still apparent.

"I just got here, and I fired the guy who'd been running the place on the spot. I'm the new kid on the block, and in case you haven't noticed, you locals aren't particularly welcoming of strangers — unless they're tourists. I have to interview and hire a competent staff, when the people I talk to as references won't say anything bad about a neighbor to a–"

"The proper word isn't stranger. It's 'Away from here.' If you're not from here, that's what they call you."

"They?"

"I've had this job for less than a year, and I discovered quick that the locals wouldn't tell me diddly squat about one of their own."

What he didn't tell Hollister was that the way around that dilemma he had found was getting a local, Rileigh, to help him bridge the gap to the public.

Hollister sighed. "Then you get it." He sat back down. "I will give you a list of those responsible for the body, which we both know doesn't mean much in terms of this investigation." Then he looked directly into Mitch's eyes, appearing to be asking for approval, or at the very least trying to make a connection with a fellow outsider. "I promise I will tell you anything I find out, as soon as I find it out."

Then he sat back with what appeared to be a dejected sigh in his big chair.

"Looks like some members of my staff aren't just incompetent. They're criminals running some kind of drug operation." He paused, then said softly, "Goody."

Mitch left the Carrington House with a slightly different read on the man running the place than he'd had when he arrived. He'd caught glimpses of real humanity in Brandon Hollister, and had been pleasantly surprised that the man's first response was not CYA. He didn't try to avoid the issue or hand off responsibility to somebody else.

At the very least, Mitch had to respect that.

Chapter Twenty

RILEIGH WAS grateful to have something to do to get her out of the house. Ever since Rosie's body was discovered on the walking trail yesterday, Mama had been in a dither. Rileigh was sure she'd fielded at least a dozen frantic phone calls from Daisy, but she'd gotten close-mouthed after she'd let it slip that she'd given her sister a cell phone.

Though Mama wouldn't admit to the calls, it was clear Daisy had worked her up into a snit about the Carrington House being dangerous, that she wanted her sister to bring her home. Like that was going to happen. Or maybe Daisy was pushing to be transferred to some other location. If they put Aunt Daisy in some hospital on the other side of the state, Mama couldn't go running out there every time Aunt Daisy crooked her finger. Which didn't sound to Rileigh like a bad outcome at all — except that if she couldn't go "see to" Daisy, Mama would just stew about it. That'd be worse.

Rileigh had promised Mama that she would see about getting Aunt Daisy moved to another facility, find out what the steps were, how to initiate the transfer. She'd said it just to ease her mother's mind, but realized she really ought to look into it.

As she drove to Gatlinburg to talk to the director of the funeral home, she knew Mitch was on his way to talk to Brandon, and she would not let herself dwell on the possibility that Mitch had orchestrated the separate interviews just to keep her away from the other man. That was nonsense. In fact, she actually did need to talk to Brandon — about moving Aunt Daisy.

On an impulse she picked up her phone and dialed the cell number he'd given to her. He picked up after the first ring. "Hello, Rileigh, what can I do for you today?"

"How about you go out to dinner with me tonight?"

She hadn't meant to launch the invitation out there so abruptly, but she'd only reached the decision to invite him to dinner for the moving-Aunt-Daisy conversation a few seconds before she hit the button on her phone to call him.

"Well, I—"

"Mama has been after me to consider moving her sister to some other facility besides the Carrington House. I told her I'd look into it. I don't think moving Daisy is necessary or even a viable option, but ye have not because ye ask not, so I'm asking. Could we perhaps talk about it over dinner?"

"Sure we can. I'd like that."

"Do you like Mexican food?"

"Is the Pope Catholic?"

"How about Cuban?"

"Does a bear shit in the woods?"

"Great. I know a little mom and pop I, not a touristy place at all, that caters to the Hispanic population around here, mostly families with kids, so it's a little noisy. But the food is great."

"Give me the address and I'll meet you there at … how about seven o'clock?"

After she hung up, she did a frantic time calculation — could she make it home in time to wash her hair and blow it dry and get cleaned up and then back to Gatlinburg? The math worked and she relaxed. Though it was overcast, threatening rain, Rileigh enjoyed the drive. She wondered if Brandon had ever been in the mountains in the fall, but pushed that thought and all attendant thoughts out of her head so she could concentrate on the task at hand.

She had never been to Dargenio's Funeral Home, and was surprised that it was such a … going concern. The building was large — tasteful, but large — and the parking lot was full. She went up the wide front steps and found a sign directing her to one of four viewing rooms. Thomas Thurgood was in VR1, Emily Atchison was in VR2. There was currently nobody in VR3, but the family and friends of Emilio Flores were informed that visitation would begin there at 5 p.m.

The hallways were crowded with people, and the soft sound of crying came from the room where the Thurgood family was morning the loss of their father/brother/husband/son Thomas.

It wasn't difficult to find somebody on the funeral home staff. They all wore dark gray suits with black name tags bearing their names and positions in gold calligraphy that was hard to read. She thought the outfits made the whole lot of them look like flight attendants. She got one of them to direct her to Whit Nash's office, where he sat behind a desk so neat and tidy, she couldn't imagine he was ever able to get anything done there.

"Hello, Rileigh," he said, straining on the words to pronounce them properly. He stood up and extended his hand in a jerky motion to shake hers. "It's good to see you."

He spoke slowly, but in the years since she'd seen him

last, he had gotten better control over his speech. "Please have a seat and tell me what I can do for you."

She sat, and when she did, she saw a family photograph on his desk, showing him with a small, plump wife and two small children.

"I'm not here to arrange a funeral. I'm here to talk about the body of Fred Mackay."

He knew instantly what she was talking about.

"Yes, he was in one of our hearses when it was in an accident last night. There is only one daughter and a niece surviving. We notified them that the viewing set for this afternoon would have to be postponed."

She noticed that he clasped his hands on the desk in front of him, perhaps in an effort to keep them still.

"Do you know the rest of the story?"

"You sound like Paul Harvey." She was surprised at the injection of humor and chuckled with him.

"Well, the rest of the story is that there were drugs in the corpse."

"Drugs?"

"Officers on the scene discovered a baggie containing white powder in the abdominal cavity of the body."

"Oh." It was like the word had been punched out of his belly. She watched him make the connections.

"So somebody was using the dead body to transport drugs. Is that what you're saying?"

She nodded.

"Why are *you*—"

"The Yarmouth County sheriff has asked me to help in the investigation. Somebody put the drugs into the body at the Carrington House. There must have been somebody on this end waiting to take them out."

"Someone on our staff?"

"How many people would have access to a corpse before the service?"

He thought about the question, then shook his head. "We have a staff of sixteen, full- and part-time. There are three people on the administrative staff, so make that nineteen."

Then he spread his hands out in front of him in a jerky motion. "But they're not the only people who'd have access." He gestured to the door of his office, outside which was a growing crowd of people. "It's not like we keep the bodies locked up somewhere. They're downstairs in the preparation room until we bring them up for the viewing. There are 'employees only' signs on the doors, but they're not locked. anybody in the building could go in the room."

Great. There were at least two dozen people who'd have had both access and opportunity to retrieve the drug shipment. And an unlimited number of people who were merely in the building and could conceivably have gotten the job done.

It had seemed from the beginning to Rileigh that using a corpse for a drug mule was a singularly unusual mode of transport. She couldn't imagine why anybody would go to that much trouble. Oh, sure, to smuggle a kilo of fentanyl across the border into the US from Mexico—yeah, a plan as elaborate as this might make sense. But to carry a sandwich bag full of whatever from the Forge to Gatlinburg? That was some major overkill.

"If you wouldn't mind, could you compile a list of all your employees, both full- and part-time? And anybody else who might have a key to the building."

Whit said he would be glad to give her a list.

As she got up to leave, he asked her the question that had been bounding around in her own mind.

"Why would somebody go to the trouble to conceal drugs in a dead body? You'd think there are more convenient ways to transport them?"

Rileigh shrugged. "You got me. But I think figuring out the why will go a long way toward answering the who."

Chapter Twenty-One

RILEIGH DIDN'T TELL Georgia about her date. Not *date*, it wasn't a date. She was just having dinner with the man, for crying out loud. Everybody has to eat. The vehemence with which she slapped down her own response should have been a clue to the sea of emotional depth charges she was about to go swimming through, but she chose to ignore the whole thing. And that was why she hadn't told Georgia about it. She would make it into some kind of big deal, and it wasn't. It really wasn't.

La Familia Restaurant was on a little side street, away from all the touristy bright lights. It was possible the Ortega family, who ran the establishment, had actually made the sign small on purpose, to keep away the crowds. The front of the building was nondescript, none of the garishness of the businesses in downtown Gatlinburg. Those souvenir shops were in a perpetual game of *Can You Top This?* with each other. Oh, you built a storefront that looks like a haunted house? Well, I'll build a bigger store front down the block that looks like a haunted *pirate ship*! A haunted ship, you say? Lame! I'll go farther down the block and build a store front shaped like a flying saucer, and put little green men out front, *dead* ones, zombie aliens. Anything to draw in the customers.

What La Familia lacked in charm out front, it more than made up for inside, and out on the back deck that extended up the hillside into the trees. There it was all bright colors and palm trees. Red tablecloths and yellow napkins. A mural on the back wall portrayed a stunning view of the ocean across a sandy beach. It was the most beautiful mural Rileigh had ever seen —or she would have said that until she saw the mural of the Smoky Mountains Sara Park had painted inside her house to serve as a map for placing the incendiary devices she intended to use to burn the Great Smoky Mountains National Park to the ground. But that was yet another thing in Rileigh's life she wouldn't allow herself to think about.

Brandon arrived just as she was pulling into a space in the parking lot, so they walked in together. As they waited for a table, Rileigh told him that La Familia sold Mexican dishes and Cuban dishes — in entirely different parts of the divided restaurant. Each side was decorated authentically.

"It would have been easier just to put Mexican dishes on one side of the menu and Cuban on the other," Brandon said.

"Easier, but not as much fun. It's like they're two different restaurants. There'll probably be a singer on the Cuban side and a Mariachi band on the other. The last time I was here, Mama and I did Cuban and a woman sang Celia Cruz's song, La Vida es un Carnaval. She was so good the crowd gave her a standing ovation, and when I sat down, I spilled my flan all over the front of my dress."

"Which side do you prefer?"

"You pick."

They stepped inside the building, where a big sign proclaimed that Friday night at La Familia Restaurant was karaoke night in the whole restaurant.

Brandon must have seen her reaction. "What? You don't like karaoke?"

"Oh, it's fine. With a little tequila to fortify my soul, I sometimes end up bellowing out something."

"I can't wait!"

They were seated on the Cuban side of the restaurant and ordered tostones con pollo as an appetizer. Brandon got ropa vieja as an entree and Rileigh got vaca frita. They both ordered tres leches for dessert. Rileigh ordered a strawberry daiquiri. Brandon bourbon and water — Maker's Mark bourbon.

"Not Jim Beam?" she asked.

"Maker's Mark is smoother."

"You do know that it's brewed exclusively in a historic little distillery in Kentucky, a few hours' drive from here, don't you?"

"I did not know that."

Rileigh told him the distillery provided tours for visitors, but stopped short of saying the two of them ought to go see it sometime. She was trying to keep the brakes on. But she had to admit, he looked particularly handsome tonight in a sport coat over a button-down shirt and khaki pants.

There weren't a lot of small children in the restaurant, so the noise level was considerably lower than it sometimes was, which made it possible for the two of them to have a conversation without shouting.

They'd come here to talk about getting Daisy transferred out of the Carrington House and into another facility. Except, no, they hadn't. They both knew that.

"So, tell me the life story of Rileigh Bishop in a few

succinct sentences. You can leave out the whole *I was born a small child* part."

"But that's my best line. I was born a small child in a family that was too poor to have any more children. So, a neighbor had me."

Brandon groaned.

"I'd have gotten at least a few points for that if Georgia were here. She's my BFF since kindergarten, and when we're together, lame humor happens. We're powerless to control it."

"I have no friends like that. I bounced around a lot because my father was career Navy. I was always the new kid in class. What's it like to have a BFF you've known since childhood?"

"Mildly schizophrenic. We finish each other's sentences. But we took very different paths in life. She stayed here, settled down, had a yard full of kids. I went into the military."

That led the conversation to Rileigh's deployments, two in Afghanistan, two in Iraq, and Brandon's years in college studying psychology.

"The diplomas aren't on the wall yet, and I may decide not to hang them at all, but I'm a certified clinical psychologist, had always planned to start my own practice, but life happened. My father's death was unexpected, I didn't build my life plans around owning and operating a psychiatric hospital. It's jarring."

"Do you like it, running the hospital?"

"I can give you a firm sometimes on that. I don't like the administrative headaches and I loathe the HR stuff. I'm scrambling to get to know these people while I'm planning to fire half of them."

"You're not a paper pusher."

"I got interested in the psychology of the criminally

insane when I lived in Virginia. I worked for a long time with the FBI's Behavioral Analysis Unit at Quantico. That was fascinating."

They'd already devoured the appetizer, but their entrees came just in time.

"So, you'd rather be doing the psychology part of the business you inherited?"

"I like working with the patients — like your Aunt Daisy."

"Who believes women she hardly knows are her long-lost sisters, which is the least of her delusions. But the others appear to have signed on to the delusion themselves. The one Aunt Daisy calls Iris thinks I'm her daughter. And that'd be fine, if she weren't convinced that her daughter tried to poison her."

"Daisy doesn't cause problems, not the usual kind anyway. There are other patients who are constantly in conflict with the staff. I don't know right now if the staff members or the patients are to blame." he paused. "This ropa vieja is delicious. Want a bite?"

Rileigh gave him a bite of her vaca frita and the conversation took up where it had left off. When Rileigh finished her entree, she ordered another strawberry daiquiri. She didn't often drink, but she could hold her liquor.

"You do know what landed Aunt Daisy in the Carrington House, don't you?"

"She tried to kill somebody, right?"

"I was the somebody."

"She tried to kill you?"

"With a chain saw."

Brandon's face paled and he put down his fork.

"Your aunt tried to kill you with a chainsaw, and you

still keep looking after her, trying to fix whatever imaginary thing's broke in her life. That's admirable."

If he only knew all the other horrible things her aunt had done in her life, how she'd had an affair with Rileigh's father, and when her older sister, Jillian, caught him molesting Georgia, Aunt Daisy killed Jillian and cut out her tongue. At least, she'd said she did.

"Not so much. What I'm really doing is looking after my mother. If Mama ain't happy, ain't nobody happy, right? Substitute 'Aunt Daisy' for 'Mama,' add water and stir. As long as my Aunt Daisy is doing well, I only have to worry about Mama's mental issues. She has dementia too, and right now she thinks she's dating Rhett Butler."

"*The* Rhett Butler, of 'frankly my dear, I don't give a damn' fame?"

"The same."

The karaoke had begun while they were eating. Somebody took the microphone and began to belt out Sweet Caroline, and the rest of the crowd joined in. When the song was finished Brandon asked, "Are you going to try?"

"Only if you will." A response that had always worked before to get out of having to sing.

"Sure, I'll try. But you first."

Rileigh squirmed. "You know I'd rather get stuck in an elevator with Kim Kardashian than do this, right?"

He merely grinned and gestured for her to go for it. Rileigh waited through woman struggling to sing a song by Adele and failing miserably. Then came a girl who was way too drunk to sing Wonder by Natalie Merchant, but she tried. A kid who didn't look like he was sixteen sang Places I've been. When he finished, a middle-aged man did a pretty good job singing I Want It That Way by the Backstreet Boys. Rileigh was up next. She decided on the fly to sing the kind of song people would join in singing, so she'd have backup.

She spoke to the sound guy for a moment, who nodded and gave her a microphone. When he nodded again, she tilted her head back and belted out, "Sooooomewhere over the rainbow" and the crowd joined in on the parts everybody knew. The crowd dropped out and let her finish alone. "If happy little bluebirds fly beyond the rainbow, why, oh why, can't I?"

She had good voice and she'd stayed on key. The crowd's applause seemed genuine.

When she returned to the table, Brandon didn't move.

"Your turn," she said.

"I was just calling your bluff."

"I'm not going to let you wiggle out of it."

"Please don't make me make a spectacle of myself," he begged.

She pulled him to his feet and pushed him toward the small stage. "Go ye therefore and spectacle yourself."

"I can only sing one song and it's not–"

"Go!"

He went when it was his turn, took the stage graciously, but refused to take the microphone from the previous karaoke-er. He looked out over the crowd and announced, "I'm being forced into this," gesturing toward Rileigh. "And I only know one song. This is it."

He paused for a beat, and then began, "Oh say can you see, by the dawn's early light–"

Laughter began in the audience but quickly died as the sound of his voice filled up the room. Surely he was one of those people called upon to sing before sporting events, because his rumbling baritone voice filled up the whole restaurant. All conversation died. A few people sang along quietly. Then an old fellow down front stood up. Someone else did. Parents with young children stood and urged their children to their feet. Rileigh could see the open door to the kitchen and the staff there had paused as well. By the time, the song was over, most everyone in the restaurant was standing. When he hit the final high note on "free" the crowd burst into a roar of applause.

Brandon gave a little smile and quickly vacated the stage.

"Why didn't you tell me you could do *that?*"

"You didn't ask. My father got promoted because they'd trot me out to do that in front of the admirals when I was just a kid."

"You have to admit, it's a bit of a conversation stopper."

"Well, if we're not going to talk, let's at least order some more dessert." He hailed the server and ordered a second tres leches.

Chapter Twenty-Two

STELLA ROUNDTREE WAS TIRED. Her feet hurt, she was afraid she was getting a toothache again, and she'd heard that funny rattling sound in her car on the way to work this morning that meant yet another repair bill on the pile of junk. But it was her own fault. She'd said in the divorce settlement that she wanted the car, pitched a green fit to be awarded the car. She should have known by the fact that Doug didn't put up much of a fight over it that the car was a piece of shit. He had certainly put up a fight over every other damned thing they owned.

But not the dog!

She had by god nailed his ass on the dog.

She'd seen it on some dumb television show years ago, about this couple who were fighting in front of Judge Judy or somebody about custody of their dog, and the judge said she would let the dog decide. So she put the dog on the floor and let the two people call it, then awarded custody to the one the dog went to. Turns out later, that the husband had found out what the judge was going to do and rigged the whole thing: rubbed ground meat all over his hands and the dog came running to him so fast it knocked him over.

Stella hadn't done anything quite that elaborate, but she had spent three days with the dog before their court date, had taken Critter with her everywhere, gave him treats, taught him to beg and stay. Well, he didn't get the stay down part down, but he was all over beg. When the final court date came, her attorney managed to get the judge to agree to the call the dog method — and Critter had come right to her.

She pulled into her driveway and the dog bounded out to the car. Where was Casey? She was supposed to keep Critter pinned up in the yard so he wouldn't run out into traffic.

Stella stalked into the house, hollering for her oldest daughter.

"Casey, where are you? Didn't I tell you to keep Critter in the back—"

Then she heard the music from upstairs. Some awful song — or rap, which in her humble opinion wasn't music at all but chanting— playing so loud the kid wouldn't have heard a nuclear explosion.

"Casey Marie, you get down here right now and put Critter in the backyard where he's supposed to be."

The sullen fourteen-year-old did as she was told, grunted something like *sorry* as she passed Stella on her way outside. Stella had surprised her by coming home early. She had left the Carrington House before her three-to-eleven shift was over, because her new Sugar Daddy had told her she could have the rest of the evening off. Big surprise there. The man was tee-totally pissed at her, but she had him over a barrel and he knew it. He either paid her to keep her mouth shut or she would start singing like a birdie, and there were all kinds of people in uniforms with badges and guns who would absolutely love to hear the song she'd be singing.

She had gone into the break room, where her take-home thermos of coffee was waiting for her. She'd expected to see him there, but the room was empty. Yeah, the guy was definitely falling into line. They hadn't discussed her demands yet, so she would make a point to take him aside tomorrow and arrange to meet him somewhere private to seal the deal.

The deadbeat ex-husband of hers wouldn't pay his child support, was five months behind, and she had already called her lawyer about it. Trouble was, she hadn't paid the lawyer's bill either, so he wasn't eager to take Doug back to court.

But now, her financial troubles were over. She would have a guaranteed income that wasn't dependent on whether Doug was able to stay sober long enough not to get fired from his job. And the guaranteed income would increase. She'd asked for what she believed to be a reasonable amount, but this was just the beginning. She knew he was making money hand over fist with his little operation, so there was no reason she shouldn't be able to get rich, too.

But that was all for later. Right now, there was the roast in the oven, if Casey had done as she was told and left it there to keep it warm. Stella got up from where she'd plopped down into the recliner ponderously — her back had been giving her trouble. She couldn't keep doing what she was doing forever. Working with those crazy people was hard work, and she didn't get paid nearly enough to compensate her if she messed up her back permanently.

She had considered going on disability. But no, she had to stick around, be there every day where she could keep her eye on things so her new business arrangement wouldn't go south on her.

Casey stalked through the kitchen on her way back to her room from putting Critter in the back yard.

"Don't you turn that music up so loud. I got a headache."

Her daughter mumbled some kind of monosyllabic grunt and went back to her room.

Stella leaned over to get the big roast out of the oven and her back screamed at her. She'd have to see a chiropractor. Setting the roast on the table, she got a plate and silverware, and sat down to eat her delayed dinner.

But first, *coffee!*

All the nurses on her wing had gotten together last Christmas and gave themselves a present, a coffee maker that actually made good coffee. Outstanding coffee. It was so good, that Stella took a thermos to work with her every day so she could bring coffee home with her after her shift was over.

She lifted the steaming coffee to her lips, inhaled the aroma rising up out of the cup and smiled. She took a big gulp and it warmed her all the way down. She drank the whole cup before starting on the roast. Then she left the kitchen for Casey to clean up, going into the living room and plopping back down in the recliner to watch Family Feud.

When it was over, she went into the kitchen for more roast, had barely gotten seated when the room suddenly tilted, and she felt her chair sliding across the room toward the far wall.

What the …

The room continued to tilt and she cried out, tried to keep from sliding with the furniture to the other side of the room, but the floor on the door side kept rising and rising and rising.

The doors to the cabinets on that side of the room opened and al the contents fell out into the floor. Dishes broke, plates shattered, canned goods hit the floor and rolled down it toward where Stella now lay on the floor on her belly, gawking up at the rising wall on the other side of the room.

She watched the pot roast slide off the table and crash to the floor, spilling the meat and vegetables out in a steaming heap. The juice became a little river that carried the contents of the pot down to the lower side of the room where Stella stared in slack-jawed terror.

When the piece of meat slid right into her face, Stella knew she had to do something. She had to get out of here. Out. Yes.

She couldn't run, all she could do was crawl, and the floor was still moving steadily up on the far side. She clawed her way across the un-level floor to the doorway, and through it. She crawled into the bathroom on the other side of the hallway.

And the bathroom was fine. The floor there was flat. She lay panting on the bathmat in front of the tub. Then she slowly got to her feet and looked out the door, across the hall into the kitchen. The kitchen floor was almost vertical by now. Everything that'd been on the walls or in the cabinets or on the counter now lay in a tumbled heap on the wall on the other side of the room.

How? Her mind was spinning around in circles so fast it made her dizzy. The colors in the room were all wrong. The white toilet and tub were a bright purple color, like they were made of eggplant. And there was something dangling down from the ceiling. It was blue and looked like the Spanish moss on those trees she'd seen when her family went to Louisiana on vacation when she was a kid.

She looked back into the kitchen. Though the sides weren't rounded, it was revolving like that drum they put bingo numbers in, and she watched in horrified amazement as everything in the kitchen slid down the wall, which was now the floor, except it wasn't. The ceiling was revolving around to be the floor and the contents of the room shifted with the geography.

Where was Casey? Her bedroom was on the second floor above the kitchen. Was the same thing happening up there that was happening down here? Stella couldn't stand watching it. She reached over and slammed the bathroom door shut. Flicked the lock shut, then sat down on the floor with her back braced against the door and her legs extended so her feet were on the bathtub. That door wasn't opening with her sitting like that.

"Mama, Mama, what's wrong? Why were you screaming?"

It was Casey's voice, right outside the door.

"Run," she screamed at her daughter. "Get out of here before the rest of the house rolls."

"What are you talking about? Mama?"

Stella stuck her fingers in her ears so she couldn't hear her daughter's voice and it faded away. She looked across the yellow bathroom floor at the eggplant-colored tub and toilet. Sitting on top of the toilet was a bottle of wine. Not wine, champagne. That's what she needed. She needed *a drink.*

She got up from the floor and crossed the small room, snatched up the bottle and was relieved to see there was no cork, just a screw on lid. She unscrewed the lid, didn't even bother to pour the champagne in the bathroom glass. She just turned the bottle up and chugged.

It tasted so fine. She took two big gulps, then lifted her face and turned the bottle up and poured the contents over her face and head.

And it felt so fine.

Then it didn't. Suddenly, it burned. Stella was on fire, but she couldn't breathe or scream or see.

She screamed silently then, fell to the floor and screamed silently then, writhing there in silent pain on the yellow floor while her house tumbled over and over around her.

Chapter Twenty-Three

Mitch normally would have let one of his deputies take the call, but he was only a half a mile away when the dispatcher informed him that there was some kind of domestic disturbance at Hummingbird Lane. When he got to the residence, he could hear someone inside yelling,

He knocked on the door and a teenager opened it immediately.

"You have to help me. Something's wrong with Mama. She's in the bathroom, the door's locked, and she won't come out."

Mitch followed the teenager through the house. Whatever had happened had interrupted dinner. There was what smelled like a delicious pot roast sitting in the middle of the table and one plate with a little food on it.

The girl stopped at a bathroom door and began to bang on it with her fist.

"Mama, can you hear me? Come out now. The sheriff's here."

Mitch could hear nothing from the other side of the door.

"What's your name and what's your mother's name?"

"I'm Casey Roundtree. My mother is Stella."

Mitch knocked on the door. "Mrs. Roundtree, this is Sheriff Mitchell Webster. I need you to open the door now. Your daughter's worried about you."

There was no response from inside the room.

He tried again with no response. Casey was getting visibly more upset by the moment.

"Something's wrong, something's bad wrong. I heard her scream before."

"Tell me what happened."

"Nothing happened. Nothing that I know of. She came home from work early and … "

Her voice trailed off.

Mitch put his hand on her shoulder. "You're not in any trouble, but I need to know what *really* happened."

"Okay, she came home early, and I was up in my bedroom… smoking weed. She wasn't supposed to be here, but suddenly there she was, pulling up in the driveway. So I turned my music up really loud and opened the window. I don't have a fan, so I used a pillow, swishing it around in the air, trying to get the smell out of the room."

He said nothing so she continued.

"But she didn't come up to my room — thank god! — just yelled at me as soon as she got in the door because Critter wasn't in the back yard. I don't know how he got out. He does that sometimes, I think maybe he'd learned how to use his nose to lift up that lever on his kennel. Anyway, he was out in the front yard, and she was furious. She told me to come down and put him back where he belonged."

"And did you?"

"Uh-huh, and then I went back up to my room. Then I

heard her screaming. She sounded really scary, screaming for me to get out of the house and run away. I went downstairs and she was in the bathroom with the door locked. I asked her if everything was all right and she didn't answer me. But she was making, I don't know … strange sounds."

"Describe them."

"It almost sounded like she was choking or maybe throwing up, and I heard a clunk, so I think she fell down. But she never answered me, and she wouldn't open the door. I didn't know what else to do but dial 911."

Casey was holding onto her composure by her fingernails. He turned and knocked on the door again. Still no response. The fact that she heard her mother fall down mattered.

Mitch picked up the mic on his shoulder and spoke into it. This is Unit 1. I have a 10-59 on Hummingbird Lane. Request backup."

The number he gave to the dispatcher told her to send an ambulance as well. Clearly there was something wrong with Mrs. Roundtree.

Mitch needed to break down the bathroom door, but this was an old house. Not some subdivision with weak hinges and hollow-core doors. This door was a standard size and made of solid wood. He would need help to break into the room.

"Is there a window into the bathroom, or any other way to get in?"

"No. There's no window. What's wrong with her?"

The girl turned back to the door and began to bang on it again, calling out, "Mama! Mama!" And crying.

Mitch needed to distract her.

"Tell me about your mother, Casey. You said she came home from work. Where does she work?"

"She's a nurse at the Carrington House. I was surprised that she came home early because she's been working late almost every night since … well, for a long time. My parents just got divorced and everything's been different since Daddy left. I had to drop out of band because we couldn't afford to pay for the saxophone rental. But then about a week ago, she said everything was going to be better, that soon we'd have all the money we needed, so I should talk to the band director and see if I could have my old place back."

"Did she tell you why your finances would be looking up?"

"It wasn't because of Daddy, that's for sure." The venom in her voice was heartbreaking. "He doesn't give a rat's ass what happens to us. He's supposed to pay child support. Well, he doesn't. He's way behind. Which is why mama was working such long hours. He's supposed to have visitation rights with me. He showed up once. Then the next weekend, I just sat there and waited all afternoon and he never came."

The sound of the siren had started while the girl was talking, getting older and louder. It cut off abruptly and Deputy Mullins came to the front door. "In here," Mitch called out. "We need to break this door down."

On TV cop shows, there were handy devices, like sledgehammers or battering rams, that the SWAT team used to break down a door. The sherif''s department in Yarmouth County, Tennessee didn't own one of those. Movies often portrayed officers ramming their shoulders into a door, but that was a good way to dislocate a shoulder. Instead, Mitch told the girl to stand back, then he and Deputy Mullins coordinated their efforts. "On three. One. Two. Three" The two men leaned back and both of them kicked the door in the middle near the knob, hoping to break the piece of wood in the jamb where the knob closed.

The door remained solid.

Again.

The two men kicked again and this time the door gave with the blow.

The third kick loosened it even more, and on the fourth kick, the wood splintered and the door was knocked into the room. Or it would have been, but there was something on the floor, blocking it, so it could only open a foot or so.

Mitch cocked his chin at the teenage girl, and Mullins told her to step away so she would't get in the way. Mitch shoved on the door, trying to open it, but it was jammed tightly shut. Mitch put his eye to the opening and could see that what was blocking the door was a body on the floor.

The ambulance and rescue squad trucks pulled up in the yard then, and Mitch instructed Mullins to get the rescue squad team in ASAP. When Mitch showed them the door, they returned with an instrument like a sledge-hammer that they used to get into wrecked cars. With three or four blows the whole knob unit was just dangling. The Rescue squad then attacked the other side of the door, aiming at the hinges. The top one gave easily. The bottom one held fast for longer, but finally it gave too — the door came off in the ma's hands and he pulled it through the opening.

When Mitch saw what was on the floor in the bath-room, he was glad he'd called the ambulance. And glad Deputy Mullins had moved Casey away from the door so she could't see. She pulled away once, tried to get to the door, but he grabbed her and held her firm.

The body on the bathroom floor was clearly beyond help. The woman's head, face and hands had been eaten away. The flesh was blistered and dissolved. She had no face anymore. Her eyes, nose and mouth were mounds of unrecognizable flesh, eaten away by some kind of acid.

A bottle of Drano lay on the floor beside her. She must have poured it over her head. Probably drank it, too.

What could have prompted Stella Roundtree to drink Drano?

Chapter Twenty-Four

"You're not going to tell me about it are you?" Georgia said.

"What's to tell? We had dinner and …"

"And…? Hello, Earth to Rileigh. This is Georgia here. The same Georgia who put gum in your hair when we were in kindergarten and threw up all over your shoes after we stole that bottle of bourbon and tried to chug it. You can't bullshit me."

"It's not bullshit. It was just a dinner." Georgia gave her an evil eye. "We were talking about the case I'm working on, so it was a business dinner."

"I'm not the IRS. You don't have to convince me you talked about business so you can take the price of the dinner off your taxes. But what *else* did you talk about?"

"We really did talk about the case."

Georgia sat down abruptly on a plastic crate where the Christmas tree stand, most of the lights, and the tree skirts were stored. Rileigh had volunteered to help Georgia clean the junk out of her mother's attic for a yard sale, because it was dusty in that attic and Rileigh didn't want Georgia up there any longer than she had to be. Georgia still had some breathing issues from inhaling smoke from the fire that had almost killed her.

Georgia didn't keep badgering Rileigh. That got Rileigh's attention. She turned and saw what Georgia was holding in her hand. It was a roll of duct tape. *Red* duct tape. Georgia said nothing, just sat with the tape in her hand, looking through Rileigh with that a thousand-yard stare in her eyes.

Rileigh put down the clot of coat hangers she was trying to untangle, went to Georgia, and took the tape out of her hand.

"Didn't do a bit of good," Georgia said, her eyes on the tape.

"It was a clever idea, though, don't you think? I get points for that much."

"Duct-taping me to a chair on my birthday is more on the order of a symptom of major mental illness than it is a clever idea."

"Seemed like the right thing to do at the time" — Rileigh looked down at Georgia and their eyes locked — "to an eighteen-year-old who didn't know any better."

Rileigh and Georgia were silent then, after the roll of red duct tape had grabbed a frozen moment from the past and dragged it into the present. It was the kind of companionable silence that happens between people who know each other so well that words would just mess up the communication. Finally, Georgia spoke.

"Well, is it funny yet?"

Rileigh grinned. "I thought it was funny all along."

But Georgia got even more serious.

"You gave me my life back. I'd still be in prison right now if you hadn't stolen those drugs. And if you'd gotten caught, you've have been right there with me."

"I'm always with you, Georgia." Rileigh's eyes started to get wet and her throat started to tighten. She had to clear it to continue. "You think I'm going to let the girl who put bubble gum in my hair and barfed bourbon all over my feet take the fall for a scumbag like Bradley?"

Georgia finally cracked a smile. "You never did say I told you so."

Rileigh smiled back. "You never did say you forgave me for duct taping you to the chair, but I figure we're even."

She picked at the tape until she got the end free, pulled up a piece with that distinctive sticky-tape sound, bit a tear in the edge of it and ripped it away.

"Don't point that thing at me," Georgia said. "It might go off."

"That's good," Rileigh said as she closed the ends of a cardboard box and used the tape to seal it. "Not great but good. You get points, a few."

"Don't think you can distract me with a roll of duct tape and a stroll down memory lane. I want to know about dinner last night."

Rileigh sighed. "I told you. We were talking about a case."

"What case?"

"I'm trying to catch a murderer."

"What does the new head honcho at the Carrington House know about Rosie's death? Is he a suspect?"

"Brandon?" Rileigh burped out a little laugh. "God, no!"

"I caught that, the way you said his name. There *is* something going on, isn't there?"

Rileigh threw in the towel.

"Okay, fine. I had a really good time, better than I expected. He was witty and fun and... I liked him."

Georgia fairly glowed. "I knew it! Spill it, the whole thing. I'll know if you leave something out."

So Rileigh told Georgia about the evening, where they'd eaten, what they ordered. She said that she'd told him that Daisy tried to kill her, but she hadn't told him about the whole is-Jillian-alive-or-dead? saga.

"And last night was a Friday night, so it was karaoke night at La Familia."

Georgia actually rubbed her hands together.

"You sang, didn't you? Tell me you sang."

Georgia had decided when they were in choir together in high school that Rileigh could sing — not just the school choir kind of singing but real, professional singing. She loved Rileigh's voice, which was reasonably good but certainly not professional-level. Georgia was always pushing Rileigh to sing somewhere, made sure that it was Rileigh they called when her girlfriends started getting married and needed a soloist for the ceremony. Rileigh had hated that part. After she left the Forge for the military, she'd decided that she'd rather face a mortar attack than sing The First Time Ever I Saw Your Face ever again. Can't Help Falling in Love With You was right up there, too.

"Yes, I sang."

"What?"

"Somewhere Over the Rainbow."

"Seriously. You should have picked something sexy, like—"

"I had no desire to sing something sexy on a first—" She caught herself before she uttered the dreaded "date" word. She quickly covered by blurting out, "You should have heard Brandon."

"He sang?"

"Indeed."

"What?"

"The Star-Spangled Banner."

"He sang the national anthem in a karaoke bar?"

"It was one of those, 'you had to be there' moments. He brought the house down."

Georgia said nothing else, just sat grinning up at Rileigh.

"Okay. What?"

"Just listening to your voice, watching your face when you talk about it." When Rileigh tried to brush her off, Georgia hung on. "Seriously, Riles, you haven't looked or sounded like that about a man in a long, long time." Georgia paused. "Shoot, maybe never."

Chapter Twenty-Five

WHEN MITCH PULLED up at the coroner's office on Saturday morning, he found Gus' Lexus RX SUV parked beside the back door. Gus was hauling supplies out of his office and loading them into the SUV.

"Going on a trip?"

"Man, I'm glad you came by. I have lots to tell you about. And the answer's yes, I'm going on a trip."

"Where?"

"Deep sea fishing, somewhere off the coast of Florida. A travel agent booked the whole thing. All I have to do is suit up and show up, then they take me out on a boat and I catch the biggest marlin anybody's ever seen, and–"

"Put it where? In case you haven't noticed, pal, you're plumb out of wall space in there. Unless you take some of it down."

"Bite thy tongue, heretic. The trophies in that room are sacred. Each one of them represents an adventure. I can look at that mountain goat and remember how I was sighting in on him from the other side of a huge crevasse. I wasn't looking for game on that side, but then he was just there. And as I'm sighting in, I'm thinking: 'How in the hell am I going to get that thing out of here? It probably weighs six, maybe seven hundred pounds.' But it was too good a shot to pass up."

"If you're going on a boat, what's all this for?" He gestured to the camping gear.

"After I catch that big marlin, I'm going wild boar hunting in Texas."

"There are wild boar *on the hoof* in Texas?"

"Hell, yeah!"

Mitch waited patiently as Gus described the last time he went boar hunting in Texas before interjecting politely, "You said you have information for me."

"Oh, indeed, I do, my friend. Indeed I do."

The two men went into the building, edged past sleeping bags and camp stoves stacked in the hallway.

"Had to dig out the fishing gear," Mitch said, pointing to the flotsam and jetsam they were stepping over.

They went into Gus' lab and a switch flipped somewhere inside the man. He changed from the red-neck hunter to consummate scientist. He just didn't look like a scientist, or a coroner either, in his fishing cap.

"I got this information in from the laboratory that tested the white powder you found stuffed in the corpse of Fred Mackay."

"Fentanyl, right?"

"Hell if I know. The lab sure didn't."

"Didn't know—"

"The report made it clear that the lab had never seen a compound like that white powder. It was very similar to fentanyl, but it had been chemically altered in some way."

"In what way? What for?"

"Don't know and don't know. The lab was stumped."

"You're not just going to accept that are you?"

"Hell, no, I'm not going to just give you back the baggie and put question marks in all the applicable places and be done with it."

"That's the Gus we all know and love."

"I was planning to do some testing myself, but then the fishing/hunting trip came up, so I'm paying an associate to do the work."

"What's he going to test?"

"Simple stuff. I just want to know what that white powder does. I figure I'll know in a few days, or at least know more than I know right now."

Mitch shifted gears. "What about the toxicology report on the woman who drank Drano last night. Any information on that?"

"Yup. And I can tell you, I wouldn't have been surprised if you'd told me she was standing naked on a street corner whistling the Ave Maria out her left nostril. She had enough LSD in her to trip out all the blond men in the Norwegian Army." Gus grinned. "Did I ever tell you about my misspent youth?"

"Not the good parts, I'm sure."

"I was quite a wild child. Did some pretty substantial mind expansion."

"That stuff was around when I was in college," Mitch said, "and I considered experimenting, but then I decided I was pretty happy with the size of my mind the way it was."

"I went on some wild trips." Gus sat down on the edge of his desk and got a far-away look in his eyes. "I don't remember anymore where we were. It was somewhere hot and dry, but at that moment it could have been the sunward-facing side of the moon or a tanning bed in the Bronx. And I also don't know exactly what I was tripping on. It might have been one of those occasions when there was a gathering with a big bowl on the table filled up with pills and you just scooped up a handful and swallowed them down."

"Did any of your friends survive the experience?"

"Surely they did. I mean, I'd remember it if somebody died, wouldn't I?" He shook off the thoughts. "Anyway, I was lying on the floor on my back under a coffee table. The table had a glass top, and I looked out through it and decided that I was a snake in a terrarium."

"A snake in a terrarium."

"Uh, huh. And one other time I thought I was a golf ball."

Mitch reserved comment.

"Anyway, the point I'm making is that the woman whose blood I examined could have thought she was absolutely anything in the world. If she drank Drano, there's no telling what she thought it was. Maybe she thought it was champagne."

Chapter Twenty-Six

When Rileigh got home from Georgia's mother's house, she immediately took a shower and washed her hair to get all the dust out that had finally triggered an allergy attack. Her eyes were red and swollen, and she sneezed, like, a thousand times.

As she was blowing her hair dry, she looked out the window and saw her mother in the chicken yard, talking on the phone. She was probably fielding a call from Daisy and didn't want Rileigh to hear the conversation.

By the time Rileigh dressed and went downstairs, she found her mother gone and a scrawled note on the kitchen table.

"I got to go out. There's tuna salad in the frig if you want lunch. I'll be back by dinner."

She'd gone to the Carrington House to see her sister. What was wrong this time? Had there been an invasion of Tooth Fairies? The residents were all gone, but there was money under all their pillows and their dentures were missing, too.

She was instantly sorry for making fun of the situation.

Aunt Daisy might be as crazy as a nuclear waste dump rat, but what had happened to Rosie, no, Thelma Ferguson, was absolutely real. Brutal murder. That was nothing to joke about.

Which brought Rileigh back to her mother, who'd probably dropped her life and gone barreling out to participate in whatever delusion Daisy had cooked up today. She'd be out there for the rest of the afternoon, and come home more upset than she'd been when she left because she hadn't been able to solve whatever Daisy's imaginary problem was.

Not today.

Rileigh grabbed the keys to her car — she didn't even have to remind herself that it was her car, except she just did. As she pulled into the Carrington House parking lot, she saw her mother's car, so she'd been right, it was Mama to the rescue!

When she went into Daisy's room Mama was indeed trying to calm an upset Daisy, who got even more upset when she saw Rileigh.

"She's gone, she's gone, just like Rosie, can't find her nowhere, won't nobody find her ever because he come for her just like he done Rosie, he come and whisked her away and ain't nobody ever gonna see—"

"Stop!" Rileigh commanded, and it had the effect of slapping somebody who's hysterical. Daisy froze on the spot, shut her mouth, then sank down on the edge of her bed and put her head in her hands. She didn't cry, just sat there like that, silent.

"Rileigh Joseph Bishop, you hadn't ought to talk to your Aunt Daisy like that," Mama said, turning on her. "You didn't listen to a word she said, just shut her down. You ought to be ashamed of yourself."

And Rileigh was ashamed of herself. Ashamed she'd

blown up like that with her mother present. If only her mother knew all the things Aunt Daisy had done over the years … she let it go.

"I'm sorry, Mama." She turned to Daisy. "Tell me what happened, slowly, without undue hysterics."

"He come for her, just like he come for Rosie, took her away to do terrible things to her."

"You saw the angel take her?"

Daisy paused. "Well, no. I didn't see it this time. But it had to be him, because she's gone and the door's locked, so what else coulda happened to her?"

Actually, the door had been unlocked when Rileigh had arrived. Now maybe it'd been left that way when her mother came in, or maybe it was yet another occasion of staff incompetence.

"Don't you worry about nothing, Daisy. Rileigh told me she's gonna get you moved out of this awful place and into somewhere you'll be safe. And comfortable."

Rileigh had never told her mother any such thing, but Mama never was one to let reality stand in the way of how she wanted things to be.

"What was Della wearing when you saw her last?" Rileigh asked.

"She had on that yellow dress that has the little flowers on it. The one with that coffee stain on the front where she spilled a whole cup in her lap."

"Yellow dress, right," Rileigh said, "I'll be right back."

Rileigh went to the charge nurse and wanted to know if Daisy's room had been left unlocked — again. The woman adamantly maintained that it'd been locked up snug as a bug in a rug. Rileigh didn't believe her. This was a big place and searching for one little old lady here all by yourself was a lesson in futility. But she could do what

Brandon said he did as the first line of offense. He checked the usual suspects.

Rileigh set out to the dining room, where residents were seated together, talking or silently staring into space even though it wasn't mealtime. She searched their faces. Nothing. She went from the dining room to the crafts room. Then to physical therapy. Then to the room where a group of residents were playing some kind of game that appeared to involve dominoes instead of cards. She paused for a moment to watch them, amazed that their minds could be so damaged they did strange — sometimes horrible — things, and yet there was still a place in their twisted circuitry sound enough to understand the rules of a game.

She went to the other activity rooms. There was chair aerobics going on in one room, and some kind of instruction going on in another. No Della.

Then she turned a corner and literally bumped into Brandon.

She was gratified that he seemed to be as glad to see her as she was to see him.

"Long time no see," she said.

"How's your stomach?"

"It's fine, how — oh, please tell me all those spices last night didn't make you sick."

"Okay, I won't tell you. but I will say next time let's just stick to the basics, maybe Cracker Barrel."

She smiled. Next time.

"What are you doing here?"

"Looking for a lost roommate."

"Oh, no. Not again. Who this time?"

"Della of the yellow dress, who was whisked away by an angel this morning. Aunt Daisy knows that because, well, that's how her sisters roll."

"She didn't witness the kidnapping, you mean."

"No, she didn't see it, but she's just as convinced as she was about Rosie. And the instant she missed her, she called Mama and Mama hauled ass out here—"

"I've been wondering about that. You say your aunt is constantly bothering your mother about something, but I don't know how she could have that much access to a phone. The phones on the wards are—"

"Mama gave Aunt Daisy a cell phone."

"Really?"

"Yup."

"Well—"

"There she is!" Rileigh said, pointing out the window to a woman in a yellow flowered dress emerging from the trail that led to the fountain in the woods. "That's Della. I'm sure of it."

Rileigh and Brandon went to the door at the end of the hallway that led to one of the patios on the side of the building. No Della.

"Where'd she go? Was I hallucinating?"

"I saw her, too."

Then they both saw her crossing the grass, heading toward the impenetrable hedge around the back of the facility. They caught up to the woman in the yellow dress when she stopped, seemed to be assessing the hedge.

"Della?" Rileigh said. The woman looked at her uncomprehendingly. Then Rileigh remembered that only her Aunt Daisy thought she was the long-dead sister Della — short for Delphinium. "I mean—"

Rileigh didn't know her real name, but surprisingly Brandon did.

"Mrs. Cramer. Lucille. What are you doing out here by yourself."

"Don't be a twit. You think I'd come near the trolls

without an escort?" She gestured around at thin air. "Does it look like I'm alone?"

"You need to come back into the building now. We've been worried about you. You didn't tell anybody you were going out and we were afraid you'd gotten lost."

Another withering look.

"I have forgotten more about the grounds of my estate than you will ever know."

"Fine, then," Brandon said. "Why don't you lead us back into the building? I'm not sure I could find my way by myself."

"Come this way," Della said condescendingly. "They should issue you young ones a compass with your swords, or we could lose the whole army."

Rileigh and Brandon formed the end of Della's parade as she marched back into the building at the head of her troops.

When Rileigh showed Della into her room, Mama and Aunt Daisy were deep in discussion and all Rileigh heard was "Rhett" and "meatloaf".

"Della wasn't lost after all," Rileigh announced triumphantly. Daisy looked up at her confused. "Why would Della be lost? You've got it all wrong. It's Rosie who's lost. We ain't seen Rosie in days."

Outside in the hallway, Brandon told Rileigh that Daisy would have to surrender her telephone.

"It's not just us. It'd against state regs for patients to have cell phones."

"Can't you make an exception for Daisy? I get furious at her for bothering Mama all the time, but it will make her feel really isolated not being able to connect."

"Sorry, no can do. State inspections next week, and if we pass muster at all, it will be a miracle comparable to the parting of the Red Sea."

Rileigh couldn't help being disappointed. Daisy abused the phone, but when Rileigh thought about how she'd feel in her aunt's place, stuck in a home like this, she understood why she kept calling Mama.

"I tell you what," Brandon said. "After the state inspectors leave next week — if we're still open — I'll give it back. But she has to keep it a secret."

"She's had it for months and nobody's noticed yet. But are you serious? Is it possible the state will shut this place down?"

"The place was on life support when I took over, and the longer I'm here, the more I find out about just how bad it really is." He spread his palms out in front of him. "We'll just have to wait and see. At least, if we close, Aunt Daisy will be granted her request to move."

Rileigh didn't like the thought of the facility closing. Where would they put Aunt Daisy? How far would she and Mama have to travel to see her?

And would Brandon leave if they shut the place down?

Chapter Twenty-Seven

MITCH STEPPED through the door of the Ferguson Nursery and Lawn Care Service on the road between Gatlinburg and Dollywood and a little bell rang above him.

"I'm coming, I'm coming, keep your pants on!" came a voice from the back of the building, as if it were Mitch who'd summoned him and not the bell. "If you're here cause your lawn ain't been mowed, I'm working on it. Crew didn't show up—"

An enormously large man lumbered through the door at the back of the shop and stopped talking when he saw Mitch and the uniform. Malcolm Cranston Ferguson — Crank to his friends and he didn't have many — was the son of "Rosie" Ferguson, the woman who'd been murdered. He was the man Brandon had said pressuring Rosie to sign some kind of paper.

"About damn time you showed up," he said as he made his way toward Mitch. The man was so large he had to turn sideways to get down the rows of merchandise he had for sale. He almost tipped over the display of yard art gnomes and elves. "Have you caught him yet? The man who killed Mama?"

"No, sir, we haven't made any arrests in the case yet."

"Why in the hell not? How hard can it be to catch somebody who kidnapped an old lady out of a nursing home? Surely somebody seen it happen."

"There was one witness, yes, but she'd not a very reliable witness."

"Yeah, you mean she was nuts. Ain't nobody in that place dragging a full string of fish, and that goes for the staff, too." He grunted. "I'm gonna sue their pants off."

"You're planning to file a lawsuit against the facility?"

"Damn straight I am. They couldn't keep up with one little old lady. It's their fault she's dead and they're going to pay for it." He made the motion of rubbing money between his fingers. "As in *pay.*"

"I'm here to ask you some questions about your mother."

"What are you bothering me for? You need to be out trying to catch the guy who done this."

"When was the last time you saw your mother?"

"I went to see her two days before they lost her."

"And before that? Did you see your mother often?"

"I'm a busy man, Sheriff–" he read the last name off Mitch's name tag. "—Webster. I got things to do, places to go, people to see. I ain't got time to be running over to that nursing home every time my mommy crooks her little finger."

"Did she do that often? Ask you to come see her?"

"In the beginning, yeah. When me and Becky put her in that place she howled to high heaven about it, called five or six times a day, liked to drove my sister crazy. I told her, 'just block her calls.' But she wouldn't. I did, but she wouldn't."

"When was the last time your sister—?"

"The last time my sister done anything was this spring and what she done was die. She had all kinda things wrong with her, surprised she lasted as long as she did." He spit on the floor. "Didn't neither one of us inherit Mama's constitution. That old lady was strong as an ox. I got emphysema, diabetes, chronic pancreatitis and heart problems, and I need both my knees replaced, but Mama, she just kept on going like that little pink energizer Bunny."

His mother was also two hundred pounds lighter than he was, maybe more. Not that that had anything to do with the man's physical problems.

"When Pa died three years ago, me and Becky got together to see what we'd ought to do about Mama. She was already half nuts, done stupid things like freezing her hearing aids in an ice tray, shit like that. We tried to get power of attorney then, but nooooo." He grunted in derision. "Mama had more on the ball than the moron judge who would only grant us 'medical power of attorney.' What the hell good did that do? All we could do was make decisions about her medical care, but we couldn't even touch the estate."

"Your mother had a big estate, did she?"

"Hell yeah, she had a big estate. My daddy was a, what do you call it, an entrepreneur. He started and ran all kinda businesses, mostly for tourists. He rented out rafts and inner tubes and kayaks for the flatlanders to play in the river. Sold camping equipment — tents and sleeping bags and camp stoves. And he had cabins he rented out all over the mountains."

The little bell over the door where Mitch had entered rang, and he stepped aside to allow a young couple into the building.

"What can I do for you?" Crank asked. "Looking for anything special?"

"What you can do is mow our lawn," the young man said, and his wife nodded agreement like a bobble head doll. "You were supposed to come—"

"I ain't got no say over them yard crews." Crank had his reply ready, and had, most likely, delivered the speech before. "Them crews is independent contractors. There's four of them, and right now one's out of commission with mower problems and another one hasn't shown up for work in more than a week. With only two crews doing it all, they're behind."

"They don't work for you?"

"No, ma'am, they do not."

"Then why is it that we write the payment checks to Ferguson Lawn Care Service?"

"It's just a business arrangement. They have to work out of a local—"

"They're illegals, aren't they? Have to be. I couldn't find a one of them who could speak English."

Crank looked at Mitch, and instantly became conciliatory. "I can't speak to their immigration status — like I say they're independent contractors. But I tell you what. You give me your name and address and I'll see to it that one of the crews that's working gets to your yard next."

That satisfied the couple, who gave Crank their address and left.

"Like I told them, Sheriff. The immigration status of them guys running lawn mowers ain't none of my concern. If they come over the border illegal—"

"I'm not here to talk about immigration issues. I'm here to talk about your mother's death."

Crank relaxed and shrugged. "What's to talk about? Them dumb shits couldn't keep up with their patients, didn't take proper care of her, and that's why she's dead. And they're going to pay for that."

"I understand that the last time you spoke with your mother, you were trying to get her to sign some kind of paper, is that right?"

Crank became cagey. "Maybe I was, but it don't matter one way or the other now. The whole damned thing is tied up in probate court and I ain't gonna see a dime out of it for months. Shit, I'm going to have to pay for her damned funeral out of my own pocket. She's sitting on a fortune and I'm the one gets saddled with the bill for planting her. At least the court ought to be willing to let go of enough money put her in the ground."

"Where were you the night your mother was killed?"

Crank looked uncomfortable.

"What difference does it make where I was? What … you think I killed her? I blew a hole in my own mama's belly with a shotgun?"

Apparently there was still a lid on the actual cause of death. At least for the time being.

"Where were you that night?"

"Ain't none of your business where I was." He puffed himself up into something he must have hoped resembled indignation. "You want to know a thing like that, talk to my attorney."

"I'll do that. You'll be able to call him when we get down to the station."

"The station? What the—?"

"If you won't answer my questions here, I will take you down to my office and ask the same questions there. You'd save us both a lot of trouble if you'd just—"

"I's with a hooker. Name's Cheyenne. She works out of a place on the south side of Pigeon Forge. I's there all night." Crank paused. "I get 'em for a whole night so's I…

you know, don't have to get in no hurry." He gestured down at his body. "Ain't about manhood or nothing like that. It's just about blood flow. And my plumbing don't work the way it used to when I's out cattin' around as a young buck."

Crank Ferguson was unable to supply the legal name of the prostitute he'd spent the night with that night. But he provided a phone number and the address of a massage parlor where she could be found.

Mitch walked out into the sunshine and realized how fresh the air smelled. Crank's personal hygiene wasn't up to a standard Mitch would find acceptable. But then, it'd be a *big* job to get that wide body clean.

Mitch would check out the alibi, but was sure it'd hold up. Cheyenne would say she'd spent the night with Crank Ferguson if that's what he wanted her to say. That didn't mean it was true, but having met Rosie's only son, Mitch doubted he was the murderer. Somebody had physically subdued Rosie, who was a big, strong woman. This guy didn't have it in him, and why would he kill his own mother in such a gruesome way?

The murderer didn't just want Rosie Ferguson dead. He'd wanted her to suffer. Whoever had done it was one sick bastard.

Chapter Twenty-Eight

RILEIGH HAD a productive Sunday all planned out. She had all kinds of things on her personal to-do list that she could wrap up to get the jump on the week, preparing to appear at the GI's office in Gatlinburg bright and early Monday morning to see if they could use her.

She had helped Georgia clear out her mother's attic for a yard sale, and that had put a bee in Rileigh's bonnet to do the same with the attic of this old house. Mama's house was way bigger than Georgia's mother's house, and therefore had accumulated a shit ton of flotsam and jetsam that needed managing.

The first item on the to-do agenda was gather up some cardboard boxes—

Her phone rang and when she looked at the screen, she saw that it was Brandon. She didn't even try not to smile.

"To what do I owe the honor of a call from you on this lazy Sunday?"

"Iris is missing."

She kept herself from saying, "What?"

She'd heard him. Saying "what?" was just an effort to

put off for a few precious seconds the import of what he'd said. It didn't need confirmation.

"Rileigh …"

She realized she'd been silent longer than the allowed time during a phone conversation after which people thought you'd hung up on them or the call dropped.

"I'm here. Trying to absorb it. You do know that Iris is the one of Aunt Daisy's sisters who thinks she's my mother."

"I remember that. Her real name is Dora Jean Simmons."

"Tell me what happened." Though she was very afraid that she already knew what had happened and what that would mean for her aunt, and consequently, her mother.

"Same song, next verse. She was missing at breakfast this morning. And your aunt — she's hiding in the broom closet and won't come out or talk to anybody. Since she no longer had a cell phone, she's probably feeling pretty isolated."

"Got it. I'll bring Mama out and maybe we can calm her."

That's probably a good idea.

"So, how'd they inform you?"

"I got a call as soon as the seven-to-three shift came on to relieve the eleven-to-seven. They served breakfast and Iris wasn't in the room with her sisters. And this time, it's not just your aunt who's providing misinformation about what might have happened to her."

"One of the other sisters saw something."

"I don't believe any of them actually saw anything. At least not anything real. But last time the others weren't around when Rosie went missing, and Daisy's delusion was all we had to run with. This time, the others were there."

"There for what?"

"For the abduction."

"You mean they all confirmed what Aunt Daisy's been saying all this time? That an angel appeared in the room and carried Rosie away?"

"Oh, no. They can't agree on a delusion."

"Goody."

"Lucille Cramer swears that she saw Iris walk through the wall."

"Lucille Cramer… which—?"

"That's Della. She said she watched Iris walk through a wall like it wasn't there. She tried to demonstrate for the charge nurse, Betty Carrico , and she about broke her nose."

"And the others?"

"Let me see. Jasmine— that's Lillian McGranahan— she says that Iris went down the drain in the bathtub."

"Down the drain."

"Yep. Said she was taking a bath and let the water out and Iris washed right out of the tub with the bubbles."

"How about Aster?"

"Ethel Baggot. She's the only holdout. She doesn't have an explanation for what happened to Iris at all. I'm not sure, but I think she believes Iris is still there, in the room. When you talk to her, she'll turn suddenly, like maybe she saw somebody out of the corner of her eye, and then she'll look disappointed that she's not there. But Ethel isn't much of a talker anyway."

Rileigh knew that. All the other women in the room deferred to Daisy, except Aster. Aster ignored her. Not as in didn't do whatever it was Daisy wanted her to do. She ignored Daisy as if she weren't there at all, including acting like she didn't hear anything Daisy said. Which made it maddening to the others because they kept having to explain what Daisy had said to fill in the holes.

Rileigh sighed. "Aster thinks Iris is still there, Della thinks she walked into a wall, and Jasmine thinks she went down the drain."

"You've pretty much got it down. We've been searching the premises all morning — you know the drill, you helped out the last time we performed an all-hands-on-deck search."

"That was in the dark. The place creeped me out in the dark. In the middle of the day ... no, it creeps me out in the middle of the day too."

"I've notified the authorities. They should be here any minute. I called you because ..."

Brandon paused after the *because*, and she thought maybe he was considering whether or not to tell her the real reason he'd called — because he just wanted to talk to her. But that's not what he said.

"I figured you'd want to know, and that you'd be helpful in keeping your Aunt Daisy on the rails."

"I'll go tell Mama. We'll leave right away."

"Rileigh ..." Another pause. "Thanks."

Then he hung up, leaving her holding her phone, wondering what exactly it was he was thanking her for. She really didn't know. And it was possible Brandon didn't know either.

Chapter Twenty-Nine

RILEIGH and her mother went directly to her Aunt Daisy's room as soon as they got to the Carrington House. Daisy had come out of the broom closet, only to make a dash down the hall to the bigger storage closet at the end. She barricaded herself in there and refused to come out.

"Daisy?" Mama called out sweetly to the closed door. "Come out, dear. I brought you some chocolate pie."

Her mother had made a pie that morning. Rileigh had had only a taste of it and it was awful. Mama must have doubled or tripled the amount of cocoa than the recipe required. And there was something extra in there. Dark chocolate, it tasted like, little chunks of it. Rileigh could only suppose that she'd crumbled up a bar of dark chocolate and put it in the mixing bowl with the rest of the pie filling.

However, chocolate happened to be Daisy's favorite pie, and she wouldn't know until she came out of her self-imposed captivity that the juice definitely wasn't worth the squeeze.

"I ain't coming out of here. You can't make me. I seen him, them eyes. I know them eyes."

"Whose eyes, Aunt Daisy," Rileigh asked.

"The angel, that's who. Who'd you think I was talking about, the tooth fairy?"

"You recognized him? Who is the angel, Aunt Daisy?"

"I don't know. I can't imagine them eyes in a face to know the who of it. But I know I've seen them eyes before. Won't never forget them bright eyes."

"Come out and tell us about it," Mama said.

"Is everybody on the other side of this door either deaf or stupid? I done told you I ain't coming out. If I come out, he'll get me too."

"What color were the eyes?"

"I ain't gonna talk about it no more. I done said all I have to say on the subject. Now everybody, go on about your business and leave me be. I ain't going nowhere."

After another half hour of trying to talk Aunt Daisy off the ledge, one of the bigger orderlies put his shoulder to it and broke the door jamb. When they got the door open, it was a fight to drag Daisy out of the storage closet. They finally had to sedate her and strap her to a gurney.

"She'll be fine once the drug wears off," said the nurse who'd administered the shot. "And she'll be secure so she can't do any more of this dumb shit."

"How long?" Rileigh asked.

"Oh, at least half an hour, maybe longer."

Rileigh would be at her aunt's side in half an hour. She didn't like the attitude of the catty nurse. Her protective instinct was a useless gesture, given that eventually she'd go home and Daisy would still be here in the care of people who Brandon had confessed were mostly a bunch of incompetents. But she couldn't help it.

By the time she got to Brandon's office, he and Mitch were already there, discussing the case.

Discussing was a weasel word. They weren't discussing, they were on the verge of shouting at each other.

She entered to hear "… more than simple incompetence." Mitch was shaking his head. "There's more to it than that. An elderly woman just vanished out of a room with the door locked. It was locked, right?"

"Of course it—"

"And you checked it?"

"*I* didn't check it but—"

"Somebody checked to see that it was locked."

"That's correct, and not just once. They checked it at lights out. And again at 11 p.m. when they changed shifts, the three-to-eleven left and the eleven-to-seven came on. It's right here on the nurses' log. They checked all the rooms and all the hatches were battened down."

Brandon drew a breath. Mitch grabbed the ball and ran with it. "But when the seven-to-three shift came on the next morning, and they checked—"

"They checked and it was still locked. It wasn't until the breakfast cart came around, that they unlocked the door and realized Iris was missing."

"I'm having trouble picturing this in my head. So, they're in a room with a locked door and what… you just go by every so often and jiggle the knob?"

"Of course we don't jiggle the knob."

"Ah, excuse me. But could I interrupt this brawl before it starts and maybe direct all this testosterone in a more productive direction?" Rileigh said.

"You called Rileigh?"

"I did. Her aunt was in a state of extreme emotional distress. I was hoping Rileigh or Lily could calm her down."

"Did you call the next of kins of all the other women in that wing to come and——?"

"The other women in that wing didn't barricade themselves in a storage closet."

"And if anybody's interested," Rileigh glared at Mitch, "Aunt Daisy is sleeping off a sedative, strapped down to a bed."

"What about the surveillance camera. What did they show?"

"They showed nothing at all, because nothing was what there was to see. The two cameras with views of that room showed that nobody went in or came out, from the time the door was locked until it was unlocked."

"Could the staff have sabotaged the tapes?"

"No, of course not."

"I thought you said they were a bunch of incompetents."

"In most cases, I don't think they're the best person for their positions due to deficiencies in the skills we'd like for those positions. I didn't say they were criminals."

"So, you're certain the tapes—"

Brandon held up his hand. "You know what? I think we all need to take a look at those surveillance videos, to see what they do and don't show."

They went to the room where the videos could be played back on a monitor. Brandon got a technician to queue them up and run them in fast forward, starting before the room was locked for the night.

They watched in silence as perky-jerky surveillance camera footage showed shadowy figures at the door of the room, presumably locking it. As the time stamp spun slowly, they fast-forwarded through the time until the eleven-to-seven shift change occurred, and sure enough, the room was checked again. The morning footage showed a lot more activity outside in the hallway outside the room than there'd been in the late evening and night videos, but it was clear that nobody went into the room and nobody came out of it.

When the last of the video footage passed on the viewer, Brandon reached over and turned on the lights.

"Well?" he said.

"Well, what?" Mitch snapped. "That video footage could have been doctored."

Brandon sighed and Rileigh rolled her eyes.

"Do you want to take the footage with you and test it to see if it has been tampered with?"

"I will send somebody here to pick it up later this afternoon." Mitch was crisp, efficient, and behaving like a jackass.

"If you have no further need of me, Sheriff Webster, I have things to do," Brandon said. He turned to Rileigh then. "Tell your mother thanks for dropping her life and coming running down here on a moment's notice. I really appreciate it. Your aunt would have required a whole lot more medical intervention if the two of you hadn't been here."

Rileigh smiled at him, then turned and saw that the sheriff was watching the two of them.

"I'll let you know my findings on the video tapes." He turned on his heel, left the room and strode down the hallway.

"Looks like somebody pissed in the sheriff's Cheerios this morning," Brandon said, and Rileigh laughed.

Brandon smiled at her, reached out and touched her arm. "Thank you for Daisy," he glanced down the hallway where the sheriff had disappeared. "And for everything else."

Chapter Thirty

MITCH STORMED out to his cruiser, got inside, and slammed the door. Then he paused to ask himself what in the hell he is so mad about.

Well, duh, he was angry that yet another old woman had disappeared, and all that implied. Clearly, this place's standards of operation were subpar, or this kind of thing wouldn't keep happening. Mostly, he just couldn't forget the sight of Rosie Ferguson, lying on her side on that running path.

"I do know she was alive when it happened." Gus' words rang like a Chinese gong in his head.

He had thought about nothing else since.

That old lady had been tied down with something like wire. Gus said it was not rawhide rope or twine. He said from the shape and depth of the injuries she'd sustained struggling to free herself, it was probably something like those plastic zip lock ties. So Rosie had been restrained with zip ties, probably spread-eagled, and in his mind's eye he saw her on a big, four poster bed, the kind with solid oak posters.

Like the one his aunt and uncle slept on at the farm.

He shivered as the images dumped out of his subconscious and into his conscious mind. The time they had finally had enough. The time they had decided that they were going to fight back.

It had been after his brother, Hank, had almost been blinded because of a random slap from their uncle, after Hank spilled some of the milk out of the canister he was unloading from the milking machine.

"You clumsy little shit, look what you did." Their uncle grabs Hank by the collar of his shirt and throws him halfway across the milking parlor. His brother's head connects with the bottom of the shelf, where the antiseptic is held in a big bottle. The first thing the two of them have to do every morning is use that antiseptic to clean off the cow's udders. They have to scrub them clean before they can attach the ends of the milking machine to their teats, and several of the cows really disliked the cleaning process, would wiggle and try to get away. They'd kick you too, if they got the chance.

When Hank hits the wall beneath the shelf, the bottle teeters and then falls over. The lid is loose, so when the bottle hits the shelf, it begins to drain the antiseptic onto the shelf. Hank is under the shelf, looks up, and some of it drips into his eye.

Hank screams in pain, and Mitch leaps up from where he is cleaning the milking machine. He grabs his little brother, drags him to the hose he is using, and begins to squirt him in the face with water.

"It burns, it burns," his brother shrieks, wiggling and squirming in pain.

Mitch works frantically to get the antiseptic out of his brother's eye, fearing the damage it has already done. His uncle does absolutely nothing, just stands there watching as Mitch tries to get the chemical out of his brother's eye.

He washes and washes and washes. He is certain he has gotten every speck of it out, but he keeps washing anyway, until his uncle comes up behind him and switches off the water to the hose.

"It's washed out. He'll be fine. Now clean up that mess."

His uncle indicates the spot on the shelf where the container of antiseptic had turned over and the floor where it had dripped. Mitch's brother is on his knees in front of him, his head tilted back and his eyes squeezed shut. The right eye is red and swelling. Already he couldn't open it.

"Hank needs to see a doctor," Mitch says. "His eye is really injured—"

"Ain't going to be paying no doctor's bills for some runt who gets soap in his eye. If it blinds him, serves him right for being clumsy. You got two eyes. You don't need but one to work."

For the next three days, his brother is in agony, the pain in his eye keeping him from sleeping. His aunt slaps a makeshift bandage over it to cover it up, but doesn't give him so much as an aspirin for the pain.

Thankfully, the boys are working in the garden. Mitch can do the work for both of them.

After three days, Mitch eases the bandage off his brother's eye and makes him open it just a slit.

"What can you see?"

"It hurts."

"I know it hurts, but what can you see?"

"I can see… light. I can see blurry shapes."

Well, he isn't blind at least. After a week, his eye is still red and swollen, but he can see out of it, squinting. But the could-have-been-blind episode crosses some line with Mitchell. He and his brother have no say over what happens to them every summer. They've tried running away but they only get in trouble for it, are hauled back home and packed off to their aunt and uncle's anyway.

"We gotta do something," Mitch tells his brother. "If he doesn't blind one of us, he's going to kill us. I'm not going to let that happen."

"It doesn't do any good to run away."

"I'm not talking about running away. I'm talking about… I'm talking about fighting back."

His brother is appalled. His uncle is a beast of a man, and his aunt is almost as big. There's no way the two preteen boys could win a fight with them.

"I'm not talking about a fair fight," Mitch says, his jaw clenched. "I'm talking about an ambush."

Chapter Thirty-One

Sherman Plumber was ninety-one years old, and if you was to say years *young*, Sherm was like as not to punch you in the face. He hated it when folks acted like the highest value in the world was being young when any fool who'd been around the block more than a couple of times could tell you that it was the old who should be running things. The old understood what the young never could but would never admit they didn't.

Well, Sherman understood what it meant to be old, both in mind, body, and spirit. He had arthritis and as he fought the gear shift in his old pickup truck's standard transmission, as much wishing it up the incline as letting the motor pull the thing, he felt the ache in the bones of his fingers and wrists.

His thumbs didn't work right. They'd got moved somehow, and they wasn't so much on the sides of his hands as the bottoms, hanging off down off the sides of his hands so he couldn't put his palms flat on a table. Sometimes he wondered if they could even be called opposable thumbs anymore since they didn't oppose nothing.

The old truck groaned as if it was in as much pain as he was, having to climb up and down these mountains. But they was home. Sherman had been born here and he expected to die here, and in all the long years in between, he hadn't seen no work of the Almighty as beautiful as the mountains, no better place to put down roots and raise a family. When he thought about it, he realized that he'd only been truly happy in all his life when he was here. Them times he was out on the flat, fighting the great war that didn't nobody think was all that great anymore. Running that chain of grocery stores he'd built up from the first one he'd won in a poker game. All those years gone by, his body and his soul had been aching to be home, and as soon as he figured that out, he'd sold everything he had and come back here. That, and the decision to marry Mary Beth Stoner was the best two decisions he'd ever made.

He and Mary Beth had come back ten years ago Christmas. She'd died in the spring and Sherman had buried her, just like he'd been burying everybody else from the Forge for the past decade. As he pulled his truck to a stop beside the tool shed in the old cemetery, he wondered sometimes who would bury him when the time come. And it'd be coming soon. A man could tell a thing like that, when the angel of death was hovering low. He wouldn't likely live to see another summer.

He stopped and opened the truck door, had to throw his shoulder against it a time or two to get it unstuck. Then he climbed out and went to the shed, took his keyring, and found the right key for the padlock, opened it up and went inside. Today was the day he took care of the back north side of the cemetery. He'd divided it into quarters in his head when he took the job, told the boss he couldn't make one hundred percent of the huge old cemetery look good all the time, but he could make a quarter of it perfect, another quarter look real good, a third only fair and the fourth quarter was gonna look pretty shaggy and overgrown and if the boss man didn't like that, he'd have to find somebody else for the job. He'd hired Sherman, who had been tending to the dead ever since.

He'd walked among the tombstones in this cemetery so often, he knew most of the names, at least the family names. Some of them stones way up on the hillside, the words had worn completely away and wasn't no way to tell who was lying in the dirt under them.

The early morning was Sherman's favorite time here. The dew still glistened on the grass and the leaves of the flowers, making diamonds in the spiderwebs. It was like the whole place was waking up to the day, as the sun rose up over the mountaintop and shone down into the valley, the shadow of the mountain receded off the cemetery and the sun greeted them.

Sherman set out between the headstones to the north edge of the cemetery. He'd start at the narrow end, which was less than half a mile away.

First thing he'd done when he come to work was make sure wasn't no windfall in his quarter today. Wasn't no limbs that had fallen off trees or bushes laying on the graves and in the spaces in between. Wasn't like it was summertime, and he had to spend most of his time mowing and weeding, keeping the woods encroaching on the outside edges, keeping the bushes trimmed and—

Sherman stopped and looked out at the swath of headstones in front of him. There was something wrong. Out of place. He knew right off where it was. Even from here he could see that it was the Phelps family plots. Husband, wife, three children, and the baby they didn't even name 'cause it didn't live that long. Two of the children had died when they was teenagers, the last one went off to war in some jungle somewhere didn't even have a name, and they sent him home in a box.

And Herb Phelps had been a World War II veteran. He'd encouraged the boy to do his duty and then he didn't make it back alive. That was likely what put Herb in an early grave.

Because he was a WWII vet, there was a special insignia on his headstone, a mark of respect. You could see them on stones all around. Wouldn't be long before they'd be planting Sherman beside his Mary Beth and there'd be one of those insignias on his stone. He'd lied, said he was sixteen, joined up and the war ended the next day. But he'd by god served!

There was something laying on top of Charlie Phelps' grave. Sherman's eyesight wasn't what it had once been. It took him a few steps to get in focus so he could tell it wasn't just a tree limb or a shadow. There was something large laying on Charlie's grave, and even from here, Sherman could see it was dang near as long as the grave.

He approached, and as he could see more and more of what the thing was, he walked slower and slower. Didn't want to get there and see what his eyes was going to see whether he liked it or not. By the time he was thirty feet away, he was just shuffling along, hardly walking at all.

And from thirty feet he could see real clear what it was that was laying on top of Charlie Phelps's grave. It was a body. A woman's body, it appeared to be from here, and all she had on was a nightgown. He was approaching the gravesite from the bottom end and he seen that her feet was bare, then her legs, and the nightgown she was wearing. It was kinda hiked up with her leg sticking out, but she wasn't just sprawled out there. She'd been put there, arranged proper.

It was Sherman's poor eyesight that did him in. 'Cause he couldn't see it well, he didn't realize until he was right up on it, just a few feet from Charlie's grave, that the woman lying there wasn't just dead. You could tell that part from far off. But from up close you could see…

He stared at the body in horror for a moment, flashed back to the day one of his buddies had stepped on a live landmine during maneuvers and it blew him apart.

This woman had been blown apart. She was all there, except for her head. The body was stretched out longways on the grave, and it ended in the bloody stump of a neck with no head on it right under Charlie's stone, right under that insignia that showed he was a WWII veteran.

The headless corpse was laying on her back, mostly neat and tidy. Her hands were clasped on her chest and there was a single red rose in her fingers.

Then Sherman was running, didn't know when he'd started running, but he'd made it all the way back to his truck before he stopped and threw up, choked and gagged and then dry heaved for a while before he got himself in order.

Then he got into his truck, took the phone out of the pocket of his overalls, and dialed 911.

Chapter Thirty-Two

THE CRIME SCENE was all taped off with yellow police tape by the time Mitch got there. Deputies Mullins and Rawlings had responded to the frantic 911 call from the groundskeeper at Rest Haven Cemetery in the southern part of Yarmouth County. The old man had said there was a dead body in the cemetery. At first, the dispatcher thought it was a crank call — the cemetery was full of dead bodies. But when the dispatcher wanted to know what was strange about that, the old man had hollered at her that this was a recent dead body, and "all its pieces ain't there."

Mitch had been in line at McDonalds, getting some breakfast, when the call came in. He paid for it, drove forward to the trash can out front and dumped the food into it. He kept the coffee, though, because it was hot and strong and he needed all the fortification he could get.

It had occurred to him then that Gus was out of town, had left yesterday for his deep-sea fishing trip and wouldn't be back for a week. Mitch was surprised at how bereft he felt that the best friend he'd made since he got to

Yarmouth County, whose wisdom and expertise he depended on, wouldn't be there for backup. He was on the hook all by himself for this one. Then, he thought about Rileigh. In truth, she was the best friend he had made since he got here, but he'd be damned if he'd drag her into this one.

His feet crunched on the gravel road leading up to the back part of the cemetery where he could see the yellow fence of tape. He squared his shoulders as he approached, and even gritted his teeth for what he'd find. Looking at a dead body was never a pleasant experience, and seeing it first thing in the morning made it worse somehow, as if he'd needed some living in this day, some normal first, before the awful struck. It would definitely color how the rest of his day panned out. And he was definitely not looking forward to this particular corpse, given that the man on the 911 call had said it was missing some of its "pieces." As it turned out, the piece that wasn't there was a significant one.

"What do we have here?" he asked Deputy Mullins as he approached him. Mullins was shook. Mitch could tell he was holding it together with force of will. Shit, he was a deputy sheriff in a small town in rural Tennessee. He definitely had not signed up for all blood, guts and gore the shit storm of the past few months had dumped on him. None of the deputies had. He wouldn't be surprised if all six of them just quit.

Yes, he would. He'd be very surprised. The deputies had definitely risen to the occasion in the past few months. Had grown and matured both personally and professionally. He was proud of them all.

Mullins consulted a notebook he held in his hand. His voice was strained, but the hand holding the notebook was not shaking.

"The man who discovered the body is Sherman Plumber, ninety-one years old. He's the cemetery caretaker. He was coming out to do some routine maintenance in this part of the cemetery when he found it."

This was a huge, sprawling cemetery that actually stretched up the hillside into the trees. Routine maintenance on it was a big job, and he was surprised the man doing it was so old.

The "it" was a lump under a sheet on top of a grave, lying lengthwise up against the headstone. The gravestone was a big one. It stretched across the top of two graves. Herbert and Maxine Phelps. But those weren't the only two graves there from the Phelps family. Beside them were their three children. Mitch looked at the birth and death dates of the children and started to do the math in his head, how old each of them had been when they died. But he stopped. He didn't have to know how old their children had been to know that the deaths of each of them — whether as infants or adults — had ripped out a piece of their parents' hearts, their souls. And three … But maybe there were other children out there who had survived to carry on the Phelps name. He hoped so. There was also an insignia on the headstone of Herbert Phelps indicating that he had served in World War II.

Mitch made himself step forward and lift up the sheet covering the body. He flinched back, couldn't help himself, and he was extremely grateful he'd had the good judgement to dump his breakfast in the trash can before coming here, or he might be dumping it here on the ground.

The body was an old woman. She was wearing a nightgown. He glanced down to see, but knew what he'd find when he did. She was barefoot and the bottoms of her feet were clean. She hadn't been murdered here in the cemetery. She'd died somewhere else, and the body had been carried here and arranged where it was lying. But he didn't need clean feet to tell him that the woman had died somewhere besides here. If she'd been murdered here, there would be blood everywhere, buckets of it... because the piece of the body was missing was the head.

Old woman.

Another old woman. Surely this didn't have anything to do with the murder of Rosie, whose body was found on Thursday on a walking trail. Mitch let the sheet drop back down onto the body as his mind began making mental leaps he didn't like, taking the rest of him with it to places he didn't want to go. He definitely had not expected this, hadn't expected that there could be some connection to the most recent murder he was investigating. He thought he'd be asked to solve two entirely different puzzles. But maybe it was all one big puzzle. If it was ...

He couldn't process the ramifications of "if it was" right now because they were just flat out too staggering. So, he went on auto pilot for a while, "doing the do" that protocol required of him under these circumstances. Deputy Mullins had brought the old man back to the site of the grave in his cruiser when he'd responded to the 911 call.

Sherman Plumber didn't look anywhere near as old as he'd told the deputy he was. Ninety-one, wasn't it? But he was a wizened old man who looked way too frail to be the caretaker of a place the size of Rest Haven. But when Mitch approached, the old man squared his shoulders — as Mitch had done approaching the body. He was a tough old dude whom life had taught some important lessons. One of them was the old AA slogan, "Fake it until you make it." You could act like you were calm and collected and in charge even if you weren't. And if you acted like you were, you'd eventually become the role you were playing.

Mitch stuck out his hand and introduced himself. The old man's handshake was firm, his eyes clear.

"Tell me what happened, if you would please."

"Ain't my story to tell. I just come into it right here at the tail end. That woman up there on Herb Phelps' grave was kilt and then put there for somebody to find. I happened to be the somebody, but the story started long before I showed up."

"What did you do after you found the body?"

"I didn't touch nothing, just backed off and come running all the way back down to my truck. And I ain't ashamed to admit it, I tossed my cookies after I seen it. But that was down there by my truck. If they's any evidence up there, any footprints or marks or the like, I didn't mess with them."

Mitch had been thinking about tracks and knew the gravel road wouldn't likely yield any viable ones. He had also been careful where he walked when he approached the body. Perhaps there was a print somewhere near it, in damp earth or mud, but the grass surrounding the gravesite would have hidden the prints of whoever carried the body to the site. And somebody had carried it, picked it up and put it into some kind of vehicle, drove here, unloaded it, and paced it on the grave.

Just like somebody'd done with Rosie's body.

And there it was, full circle. A dead old lady and four days later, a second one. In a county this size. It couldn't be coincidental. But if not coincidence, what? Serial killer? Mitch didn't know a whole lot about the way serial killers operated, but he did know they committed their murders the same way every time. They either strangled their victims, shot them, knifed them, drowned them or whatever. Everything was the same, and — if all the television shows about it were to be believed — their signature. Their M.O. was what identified them, and often what resulted in their arrest.

The method of death of these two murder victims couldn't have been more disparate. One was tied down and somehow, the murderer had made a rat eat through her body.

Every time he thought about that, a wave of nausea washed over him. As long as he could keep that reality at arm's length, he could stay detached. But when he thought about that rat, and that she'd been awake… He couldn't entertain those thoughts for long without sinking into a place that was deep and dark and despairing.

This was a grisly murder, too. Somebody had killed this woman by chopping off her head. Or perhaps not. Perhaps she was already dead before her head was removed. God, he hoped so. But he needed Gus to tell him that, exactly how she had died and when, and Gus was out on a boat in the middle of some ocean trying to catch a prize marlin. Well, the coroner in Gatlinburg was competent. He'd met Dr. Nagasura when he'd taken the body of Tina Montgomery in to be examined last summer. He did a thorough job, but he was slow, and Mitch wanted answers to all these mysteries yesterday.

One mystery at a time now, and Mitch could still operate on autopilot for a while yet before he had to step out of automatic mode and think, really think about what the pieces added up to. He'd let that slide for a while. He wouldn't consider—

No! Oh, surely not. For the first time it occurred to Mitch that maybe this old lady in her nightgown had also been a patient at the Carrington House.

There were plenty of elderly women in Yarmouth

County to choose from to kill without going there. No, this old woman had been snatched out of her home somewhere, and when they got back the fingerprints, they'd know where. Perhaps even before they got the fingerprints. The woman's family might report her missing before they had to resort to fingerprint identification.

He prayed this old lady had nothing to do with Rosie. Rileigh was not going to get dragged into *this* murder case.

Chapter Thirty-Three

RILEIGH WOKE up early and lay in the dark thinking, which on most occasions was not a good thing. It was always best for her to keep her mind occupied, because it went places when it was bored, and Rileigh didn't want to get dragged back to those places.

But this morning, her thoughts were not about doom and gloom. They were about the blonde man who'd stood in a crowded restaurant Saturday night and belted out the national anthem. Who did things like that? And he didn't just do it, he nailed the song, had silenced the crowd and then brought them to their feet.

"My father got promoted because he'd haul me out to do this in front of admirals."

She hadn't pursued it, but it bore investigation. Brandon Hollister didn't just sing the National Anthem like he'd been paid to do it at a football game. Nobody sings only one song, no matter what they say. He'd been trained to sing, had a professional level talent. Yet he blew it off, wasn't vain about it, tried to change the subject when you mentioned it.

Was that simple humility? If it was, it was admirable. But she couldn't help wondering if he had something to hide? Oh, she didn't mean something sinister, like a sordid past. He might be hiding some experience that had convinced him not to pursue a singing career. If that was the reason, she would dearly like to know that the event was that'd so scarred him. But she wouldn't pry, absolutely wouldn't—

She smelled bacon. The aroma brought her up to a sitting position in the bed, where she inhaled a huge lungfull of it. Mama was frying bacon. Even with all her culinary disabilities, it was hard to screw up bacon, which meant Mama was fixing one of her so-called whale-of-a-breakfasts for Rileigh. And this morning, Rileigh actually was hungry enough to eat it. Well, some of it anyway.

"You up with the chickens this morning, aren't you?" Mama said when Rileigh staggered down to the kitchen with a sheet crease on her face and her hair bed-headed. Her mother was dressed, no robe and slippers for her, and she already "had her face on."

"You up for some pancakes?"

Pancakes required a recipe that you had to stick to and specific ingredients you couldn't swap out for other things. Nope, that was dicey. Best to stay with bacon and eggs.

"Thanks, but I'd just like some eggs with the bacon."

Lily turned to the refrigerator to retrieve the eggs.

"So, what glorious activities do you have on deck?"

"First thing, I'm going into Gatlinburg to the Good GI's office. I hope they have a case for me."

"And if they don't?"

"If they don't — and even if they do — I'm helping to investigate the employees at the Carrington House, doing background checks and interviews. I will work that in around whatever case the Good GI's give me."

"You're helping Mitch out, ain't ya?"

"There are too many people for anybody to check out on their own."

"You like Mitch, do ya?"

"Of course I like Mitch." What a stupid question. The man had saved her life, twice, was almost burned at the stake along with her. Yeah, she liked him a lot.

"You like him better'n Brandon Hollister?"

Rileigh was surprised by the question, but really not. Her mother had no filters these days. If she thought it, she said it, and there was something admirable about that level of honesty, even if it was a bit uncomfortable to live with.

"I like both of them, Mama."

"That don't answer my question."

"Sorry, that's all I've got. If you're thinking I'm in some kind of romantic involvement, then I hate to disappoint you, but my friendship with neither one of them is that kind."

"Riiiiiight."

Rileigh finished her breakfast and went back upstairs to dress. She stood for a long time in a hot shower, letting it turn her skin pink, then she put on her "uniform" — a button-down shirt, untucked, a pair of well-worn jeans, and a pair of New Balance running shoes.

She was thinking about what she should say if Wally told her he didn't have any work for her. She needed to have some comeback that would make him reconsider. By his own admission, she was as qualified as the other investigators on his staff, more qualified in fact. And perhaps that was the issue, she was overqualified and Wally—

She had gotten down to the bottom of the hill and there was a box sitting under the mailbox, probably because it was too big to fit inside.

But the mail didn't usually come this early.

She got out of the car and picked up the box. It was heavy. It had her name and address on it, but there was no stamp. It hadn't come in the mail. Which meant somebody'd just dropped the thing off under her mailbox — when? In the middle of the night? It certainly hadn't been there when she came home yesterday.

Turning the box over in her hands, she felt something bump inside it, but there were no markings of any kind other than her name and address. It was so wrapped tight with that plastic mailing tape, must have had half a roll on it. There was no way she could pull that off with her fingers. She'd have to cut it. So, she put the box into the car and then executed a U turn in the road to drive back up the driveway to the house. There was no backing up her driveway.

When her mother heard the screen door screech, she called out, "Rhett, is that you?"

It was another Rhett Butler day in the Bishop household. Goody.

"It's just me, Mama. There was a box under the mailbox and I brought it back to open it."

Rileigh took the box into the kitchen, then dug around in the drawers to find a knife suitable for cutting the tape away.

"Don't you use my good butcher knife," her mother said, and Rileigh froze. That's what Aunt Daisy always said. She had a special butcher knife that she kept very sharp, and she got pissed if anybody used it for anything except to cut food. And Mama had said it just like Daisy always did, with some petulance that you'd be so inconsiderate as to do such a thing.

Wordlessly, Rileigh selected a different knife from the drawer and began to cut away the mailing tape. She had a pile of it on the table before she got all the way down to the box. It was one of those boxes that are used to ship fruit or pound cakes. The pristine cardboard had a wax surface on it.

As she cut the tape away, she and Mama engaged in a game of what do you think it is? But it was a boring one as long as you stuck to reality, because she could think of nothing that'd be dropped off at her house that wouldn't be a surprise when they opened it. If you didn't stick to reality, the box could have contained the crown jewels, the Hope Diamond, a million dollars in large bills — or a football helmet — that last one only because one would have fit perfectly in the box.

Rileigh carefully drew the knife along the final taped seam and the tops of the box opened on either side. Rileigh lifted the sides away and recoiled from the smell that emanated from whatever was inside. Her mother wrinkled her nose at the smell.

"What in the world —?"

Rileigh reached into the box and began removing the wadded-up newspapers that'd been stuffed in it to hold whatever was inside in place. The third handful of newspapers were sticky. She looked down and there was something red on her fingers.

It was blood.

Whatever was in the box was …

"Mama, why don't you wait–"

"I ain't waiting on nothing," her mother said, reached into the box and began pulling out great handfuls of the paper and throwing it on the floor.

There was blood on all of it.

Whatever was in the box, Rileigh didn't want her mother to see it.

Grabbing her mother's arm, she pulled her away from the box.

"I mean it, Mama, I want you to step away from the table."

Rileigh's heart was hammering like a woodpecker in a mason jar, shoving blood though her body, up to those veins on both sides of her forehead that always throbbed when she was upset.

But Mama would not be deterred.

"If you gonna see it, so am I."

Yanking her arm free from Rileigh's grasp, Mama reached into the box and pulled out a whole handful of paper. It stuck together and a lot of it came out at one time. Then she could see what was inside the box. She couldn't see it all, but she could see enough.

Rileigh gasped and staggered back a step as if she'd been punched in the face.

Her mother began to scream.

Chapter Thirty-Four

RILEIGH BISHOP WAS anything but a hysteric, but the woman who'd called Mitch fifteen minutes ago was as close to hysteria as he'd ever heard anybody. She hadn't yet gone over the edge. But she was teetering over the abyss and she was off balance.

Mitch could hear screaming in the background, an awful keening sound that didn't stop.

"Get over here!" Rileigh demanded in a shaky voice. "Get over here right now!"

"What—?"

"Just come!"

Then she disconnected the call.

Mitch made the journey from the Cave Hill Cemetery to Rileigh Bishop's house on Bent Twig Drive with full siren wailing and lights flashing. He flew up the driveway so fast that he came very close to crashing into the fence in the front yard.

Rileigh and her mother were both in the front yard, and he heaved an immediate sigh of relief that neither of them appeared to be harmed. But Lily was totally freaking out and Rileigh appeared to be close behind her.

He leapt out of the cruiser, vaulted over the fence, and ran to them. Rileigh's face was streaked with tears. Her mother's was streaked with mascara. Lily stood with her hand over her mouth, shaking her head back and forth, as if the she could hold in her tears.

Rileigh had her arms around her mother, trying to comfort her, but her mother kept pulling free, to walk a few steps away, and Rileigh would follow her, try to hold her again.

Then he saw the red on Lily's face. It was smeared, had wiped off her hands. His gaze shot to Rileigh's hands, and they had blood on them, too.

"What—"

"In the house," Rileigh said, gasping for the air to push the words out of her throat, "on the kitchen table. The box. Look in the box."

Mitch leapt up the steps on the porch two at a time and yanked open the door. When he got to the kitchen doorway, he saw the box sitting on the table. On the table and floor all round it were pieces of wadded-up newspaper. Bloody newspaper.

He approached the box slowly, dreading what he would find inside.

Much of it was still hidden by newspaper, but enough was visible to tell what it was, and as soon as he made the connection, he felt an iron bar clamp across his ribcage, and he was unable to breathe. He turned away abruptly and saw Rileigh in the living room. She'd followed him into the house, but wouldn't come any farther.

"Where did this come from?"

"The box was sitting by the mailbox when I went down the driveway this morning." Rileigh's voice was shaking, and she had her hands clasped into fists and her arms crossed across her chest. "It was addressed to me." She stopped. "To me!"

She took a breath and continued. "It had so much tape on it, I knew I couldn't get the box open without a knife, so I brought it back to the house to open it. And when we did …"

She uttered a little peep of a cry, just a small one and Mitch was instantly at her side, folding her into his arms. She was stiff there, didn't relax into him, but neither did she pull away.

"Who would … Who is …"

"We'll find out," he whispered into her hair. "I swear to God we'll find out."

But he thought he already knew the answer to the first who, was certain he already knew.

Why had the head that belonged on the body of an old woman lying on a grave in the Cave Hill Cemetery had delivered to Rileigh? With her name on the box, there was no mistaking that the killer had been sending a message to her.

For several hours, they tried to calm Mama, to get her to a state where she wasn't hysterical and uncommunicative. When the ambulance arrived, the EMT saw the state Lily was in and gave her a shot of something. He told Rileigh what it was, but she didn't remember. He also offered to give her some pills "for her nerves," but she shook her head.

Rileigh tried to convince her mother to go into the house, to rest in Rileigh's bedroom, which was as far away from the kitchen as it was possible to get, but Mama would have none of it. Finally, Rileigh called their nearest neighbors, the Delgado family, who lived just down the road. She asked Carmen Delgado to pick up her mother and take her home to stay there for a while.

But it didn't work. Mama refused to go.

So Rileigh finally consented to have her mother sedated and taken to the hospital. Rileigh stayed behind, would follow the ambulance later.

"Okay, tell me what you know," she demanded of Mitch, after her mother had finally been packed safely away to the hospital. "I saw you talking to Jeb Rawlings. Spill it."

"I was called to the Cave Hill Cemetery early this morning. There was a body laid out on a grave there. The head was missing. She was holding a single red rose."

Rileigh made the connection. "So somebody killed a woman, chopped her head off, and then delivered it to me in a cardboard box. What in the hell for?"

Mitch didn't want to say the next part, but he had to.

"The woman was ... an elderly woman. She was barefoot, dressed in a nightgown."

Rileigh's hands flew to her mouth and she felt her eyes bugging out. "No, tell me it's not Iris."

"I have already called the Carrington House," he said. "They told me that Dora Jean Simmons was not in the room this morning when they went in to serve breakfast."

"Iris is harmless, wouldn't hurt a fly." Rileigh stopped herself. "You don't suppose ..."

"Suppose what?"

"You don't suppose the head was delivered to me because Iris thought I was her daughter? It was her particular delusion, like Mama's dating Rhett Butler. She thought so the first time she ever saw me."

"That could be the connection to you."

"If that's not the connection, what do you think is?"

"Don't have an answer for that, but it could have something to do with the fact that you've been involved in the first investigation."

"You're saying you think the two murders are connected, Rosie's and Iris. You think it's the same murderer?"

"Of course it's the same murderer."

"But he didn't kill the second the same way he killed the first. Murderers don't do that."

"Serial killers you mean."

Rileigh nodded. "They have some kind of signature method, don't they? Brandon used to work for the behavioral analysis unit at the FBI. Maybe he could—"

"I haven't officially ruled him out as a suspect."

Rileigh couldn't believe what she was hearing. She'd seen how they'd butted heads before, but was he going to let his dislike for Brandon affect his judgment when it came to the investigation?

"You don't think he did this?" she asked.

"I don't," Mitch said. "But like I said, I haven't been able to officially rule him out. And you'd best stay clear of him until we find the real killer."

We. So, Mitch wasn't going to object to her continuing to help. But he also wasn't going to take advantage of Brandon's experience, even though they might need his help if they had a real serial killer on their hands.

So she would have to be careful how she brought him in.

Because she wasn't letting the monster who'd killed Rosie and Iris go free. She'd do whatever it took to make sure he paid for what he'd done.

. . .

RILEIGH GROANED as she hauled herself out of bed. She might as well have gone to the hospital to interrogate suspects last night, instead of staying at home. She hadn't slept at all — kept waking in the middle of the night from crazy nightmares, the contents of which, thankfully, she could not recall. But she spent most of the night lying there in the dark, trying to get some rest.

Around three in the morning, she'd decided that lying there in the dark dozing off again and again amounted to a mugging victim returning to the scene of the crime again knowing she'd be attacked when she did.

The forensics team from the Tennessee State Patrol had locked down her house as soon as they got there. And they'd spent the whole rest of the day investigating. They checked for prints on the mailbox post — why? — and looked to have collected just about every rock and weed that was on the ground under the box. They took pictures of the box on the kitchen table from every angle and tested it for fingerprints, but came up with only two sets of prints, and at least from cursory analysis, it appeared the prints belonged to Rileigh and her mother. They bagged up every piece of newspaper in the box, starting with the ones on the floor and gradually unpacking the rest of the newspaper, slowly revealing the rest of the severed head.

Rileigh didn't stay in the room for any of that. She paced in the back yard, fed the chickens, then accidentally fed them again because her mind had been disconnected when she did it the first time. She also had a brief conversation with Brandon. They'd talked about the fact that Iris was missing, and she told him what Mitch would have said if he was on the phone: that the police have recovered the body — she didn't say in two different locations — but the case was still under investigation and she couldn't give out any more information than that. Brandon had told her that

Aunt Daisy was bouncing off the wall, or would have been if they hadn't sedated her and put her under restraints.

"She was yelling for Lily."

Rileigh felt a sense of relief that her mother was actually going to be spared this time. Little sister was not going to go running to the Carrington House to fix whatever was broke in big sister's life.

During many of the hours during which Rileigh had been banished from her house, she had talked to Mitch about the cases, batting one thing or another around with him, but not coming up with anything that made any sense.

"Isn't a serial killer by definition somebody who murders more than one person?" Rileigh had said.

"One person at a time."

"Okay, a killer who kills a victim, allows some time to elapse, and then kills another victim. Isn't that what a serial killer is?"

"That'd be my definition. But the fly in the buttermilk is—"

"I know, this case doesn't match what is currently known about serial killers. They don't use one method to murder the first victim and a second, different method to kill the second. But I think the key words in that statement are 'what is currently known about serial killers.' Hell, species evolve all the time. Amoebas become protozoan, tadpoles become frogs, or whatever. Can't the species of human beings labeled as serial killers, evolve, too?"

Mitch shook his head. "Meaning you want me to contact the FBI about this?"

"You didn't answer my question. Isn't it possible that serial killers could evolve?"

"As a species, no. As individuals, sure. Any given serial killer gets to make up his own rules for this game he's decided to play. An individual killer could choose, for some reason we might understand someday, to kill the victims differently. That still doesn't mean it's time to call in the FBI."

"Then when the hell is it time to call them? The way bodies are dropping around here, if you wait until the end of the month, there'll be half a dozen more of them. Brandon was an FBI profiler—"

Rileigh knew she'd stepped in it the moment his name left her lips. Mentioning that Brandon had worked for the FBI was probably not the best argument to use on Mitch to get him to call them.

He didn't exactly grind out the next words through clenched teeth, but it was close.

"I am *not* going to call in the FBI on two murders in the same jurisdiction. They're all about catching serial killers who drop one victim in Syracuse and the next in Albuquerque. We don't fit that model."

He held up his hand to forestall her protest.

"That's not to say I'm never going to go to them for assistance. But I want to understand a shit-ton more about this case than I do right now before I hand the wheel to some other law enforcement agency and let them drive the car."

Two of Aunt Daisy's friends were dead, and he was worried about jurisdiction?

"Is that it? You don't want to call in the FBI because you want to be in charge of the case? It would be a real feather in your cap when the lowly county sheriff solves the mysterious crime, catches the murder, smiles for the camera, film at eleven."

She was instantly sorry she'd said that. Mitch was anything but a glory hound. He wasn't the kind of man who sought the spotlight. Just the opposite, he'd told her often that the best police work was always done below the radar and out of the glare of media attention. And he'd practiced what he preached.

"I'm sorry, I shouldn't have said that," she apologized. "I'm just a little bit tense right now."

"I know."

Dammit, he was so understanding. That somehow made the mean things she'd said even worse.

But Mitch didn't seem upset. "I have all kinds of investigative lines in the water, and I want to see if any of those catch a fish before I throw up my hands and say 'I surrender.'"

She didn't agree with him. Vehemently disagreed with him, as a matter of fact, but conceded that these were not her chips to play. All these decisions were his to make. Just like they'd have been hers if she'd been running the show.

And she hadn't thought that thought in a long time. Running the show, as in being the lead investigator on a criminal case. That's what she'd been working so hard for in Memphis, being a good cop, the best cop, a cop's cop, doing everything by the book, while at the same time acknowledging that sometimes you just had to go with your gut instincts. All of that effort had been toward the single goal of getting her detective stripes. She'd wanted a career in law enforcement since the first time she tried on the uniform.

But then the thing had happened. The thing that shall not be named. The thing in Memphis that had shattered her career and driven her back home to the mountains of Tennessee with her tail between her legs. Suddenly she realized that she wasn't that person anymore, that broken officer. She had healed from that trauma, and she was ready to take on those kinds of challenges again.

So did that mean she wanted to be a police officer

again, put on the badge and gun and all that that implied? This time last week she would have shouted a resounding no. But something had clicked, a tumbler had fallen into place since she returned home.

All the work with Mitch had whetted her appetite for a position of her own.

Chapter Thirty-Five

RILEIGH HEADED out to check out the fourth name on the list of the Carrington House employees she and Mitch had divided between them. She'd already crossed off the first three on her list.

Mark Hannaberry was so squeaky clean, she wondered that he didn't look like the Tidy Bowl man. Husband, father, elder in his church. He probably fed the homeless on weekends, though he hadn't told her that.

Odd Pemberton had an iron-clad alibi for the time that Rosie was killed. He was in jail in a neighboring county.

And Sheila Throckmartin was five feet tall and weighed maybe a hundred pounds soaking wet, and she'd probably have to take three running jumps at the scales to get there. She couldn't have hauled Rosie's body a half-mile down the trail if she'd put it in a wheelbarrow.

Today's suspect was Horace Collier. She wasn't completely sure if he was Dr. Collier, though because his educational history was sketchy. He'd enrolled in the doctoral program in chemistry at Vanderbilt University, but she could find no listing of him on the graduation rolls of the school.

As she drove to the Grandview Condominium Complex in Pigeon Forge, she got an email that brightened her day. She'd been trying, with little success, to dig into the man's employment history. These days, it was almost impossible to check somebody's references, because there have been so many lawsuits about it. Somebody didn't get a job, so they sued the dude they'd listed as a reference who told the truth. Or a company hired an employee based on how highly you'd recommended him, and they slap you with a lawsuit, claiming it was your fault he'd turned out to be an embezzler.

A reference had come in from Casperton Memorial Hospital in Spokane, Washington, and the administrator who wrote it was definitely trying to straddle the fence on it. But he did give Rileigh a tidbit of information that might prove helpful.

He did an exemplary job, always on time, got along with other employees… yada, yada.

It did point out that Mr./Dr. Collier was "wrapped a little too tight." Then it continued. "My only issue with him was that I found him using the hospital's lab equipment for private purposes. He was doing research of some kind for a pharmaceutical company, I think, and he commandeered the use of our equipment to conduct his experiments."

So, Collier was a chemist. And he was working on some kind of research. Maybe, I don't know, something like changing the chemical nature of Fentanyl, perhaps?

It certainly bore looking into.

Collier lived on the fifth floor of the nine-story building, an inconvenient place because the windows were still below the tree line on the hillside on the east. The windows on the sixth floor, however, provided a panoramic view of the whole valley. She supposed those condos probably sold for considerably more than the ones on the lower floors.

She had called to ask for an appointment — no sense wasting time trying to track somebody down if they'd meet with her willingly —but she'd been intentionally vague in the voice mail she left, said she wanted to talk to him about some "personal matters" at the Carrington House. And that was true, either way you pronounced the word — personal or personnel.

She went up in the elevator to the sound of some rap song in which she could not pick out a single identifiable English word. When she knocked on the door, she heard movement inside, but Dr. Collier didn't come to the door. She knocked again and rang the bell. Nothing.

But somebody was in there, so she just shoved the bell button all the way in and let it *buzzzzzzzzzzzzz*.

The door opened slightly and a face appeared in the crack.

"Today's just not a good day for me. I'm sorry. You'll have to come back—"

She decided to play bad cop.

"You don't understand how this is going. All staff at the Carrington House are under investigation. Part of them, the sheriff is handling. I'm doing the rest. So if you don't talk to me, you get to talk to him, and I guarantee you, it won't be a pleasant experience."

That got him.

She didn't even need the added, "And he'll probably take you down to his office to do it."

After that, the door swung wide and before her stood a small man with a pinched face and thick glasses. And he was literally shaking. No, make that vibrating. This guy would make Don Knotts nervous.

"I don't have anything to tell you, really I don't, I don't know anything the police would want to know, and I just do my job the best I can and keep any head down, and if there's bad stuff going on around me how would I know, because I'm just—"

"Stop."

He stopped.

"You didn't invite me, but I'll just be rude and ask if I can sit down."

"Oh, of course, sit here," he indicated the settee. Then he pointed to the chair, "No, sit there, it's more comfortable." He glanced at the couch and Rileigh could tell he was about to offer that as well, so she sat down quickly on the settee. He looked visibly relieved. She wondered if he'd just have kept offering one piece of furniture after another until —

"How about you sit down too, Mr. Collier. Or is it Dr. Collier?"

Apparently *that* was a loaded question. The man was suddenly so tense he was rendered momentarily speechless. When he did speak, so many words had backed up in his head, they all ran together.

" I do have a doctoral degree, it's from Vanderbilt, that's where I filed my dissertation, but the thing is there was some kind of snafu, some kind of paperwork glitch, you know, and they didn't connect my completed dissertation—"

"I'm not interested in tracing your educational history, Dr. Collier. I want to talk to you about your job at the Carrington House. You work in the hematology lab, is that right?"

"Yes."

Just the one word. He looked like a little kid trying not

to pee in his pants, holding on as hard as he could to what-ever words he could have launched out after it.

"What is it you do there?"

Before he could answer, she held up her hand. "Don't give me doctor-speak, just tell me, do you test people's blood?"

"Oh yes, I work on blood samples that are provided to me by the doctors and the rest of the staff."

"Who's your boss?"

The man looked like he might throw up.

"Dr. Bengt Gundersen," he said.

Bengt. The man must have spent a lifetime telling people how to pronounce it. From the good chemist's response to the question, she could see there were truths to be mined there.

"Is he a good boss to work for?"

"Dr. Gundersen?"

She didn't respond.

"Why, sure he is. He's a really nice guy. He—"

"So, he's never had to reprimand you?" She just launched that out there as a hail Mary and the reward was substantial.

The chemist looked like he was about to cry.

"He told me the whole incident would be expunged from my personnel file, that nobody would ever know about it but the two of us."

"He lied." Rileigh had finally hit the jackpot. "Wonder what else he lied about?"

"It was all a big mistake. I didn't mean to ... I couldn't... it wasn't my ..."

He couldn't even complete a sentence.

"So, he told you what you'd done wouldn't be in your permanent record, right?"

"He swore."

"And what did you give him in return for his silence?"

All the color drained out of the man's face.

"I had to. I had no choice. He made me."

"Made you what?"

"Do those experiments with the drugs. He said I had to or he'd out me and—"

"What drugs?"

"Prescription drugs."

"And fentanyl," Rileigh said flatly. It wasn't a question.

He looked at her with pleading eyes.

"And fentanyl. Please don't tell—"

"What else did you have to do for him?" She thought about nosey Rosie. "Did somebody catch you experimenting, and he made you shut them up?"

He looked blank.

"What are you talking about?"

"I'm talking about the old lady who vanished out of her room on the psychiatric ward, the one who was murdered and dumped on a hiking trail. Did you kill her?"

"Dear god, no."

He leapt to his feet so violently that he overturned a coffee table next to the couch. The lamp and vase on it crashed to the floor. "I wouldn't hurt anybody. If anybody … it wasn't me, I swear to God it wasn't me."

"You'd best come clean with me right now, or you're going to be looking down the barrel of a murder charge."

Collier sat back down, perhaps involuntarily when his knees gave out under him, and in his machine-gun, staccato speech, he told her an involved story about Dr. Gundersen and a group of 'bad men, they're bad men, you can tell just by looking at them they're bad men, dangerous men.'"

Rileigh couldn't keep the whole tale straight, but she

didn't interrupt for fear he'd realize he was totally spilling the proverbial beans.

He said the doctor and those bad men were running some kind of drug operation out of the hospital, swore he didn't know a thing about it, wouldn't even have known it existed except he was working late in the lab and over-heard the men talking.

"They were making a fortune. A literal fortune. Dr. Gundersen was socking it away in offshore accounts."

She finally dared to interrupt to introduce a question.

"What did Dr. Gundersen need you for?"

"I was doing experiments on fentanyl. I had a break-through. I changed the chemical structure of it, which would necessarily change the effect it had on people."

Shit, she hoped the good doctor and his chemist friend weren't poisoning all the addicts in the county. She wanted to ask, but he rushed on.

"But Dr. Gundersen didn't want to tell the bad men about what I'd discovered, said it would just be between him and me, nobody else involved."

"So, the good doctor was double-crossing the drug dealers he was working with. That could get you killed."

"I don't know anything about that. Nothing about anybody being killed. I swear to God I don't. All I know is that he said he was going to sneak some of the altered drug I'd made out past his business partners. That's the last I heard."

He suddenly dropped to his knees before her.

"Please, you have to believe me. I didn't kill anybody. I wouldn't hurt a soul."

"I believe you Dr. Collier," she said and the happy smile that lit his face was pathetic. "But you have to do something for me."

"Anything. Anything at all. Just name it."

"Keep your mouth shut. You don't tell Dr. Gundersen that you talked to me. You don't communicate with him at all, do you understand? Not a word."

He didn't cross his heart and hope to die, but he looked like he was coming close. He got to his feet and wiped the tears that had spilled out of his eyes off his cheeks.

"I swear I won't say a word."

"If you do—"

"I won't. I swear."

Rileigh left Dr. Collier in his apartment and went down the elevator to her car. She called Mitch to tell him what she'd found out, but her call went to voice mail. So she left him a terse message, said she'd talked to Horace Collier and he'd spilled his guts, implicated Dr. Bengt Gundersen in some kind of illegal drug enterprise.

"I'm going to the hospital now to have a little chat with the good Dr. Gundersen."

Chapter Thirty-Six

RILEIGH ARRIVED at the Carrington House and parked behind the building. She didn't want to chance running into Brandon, which, of course, is exactly what she did.

He hailed her as she walked down the hallway.

"Hey, Rileigh, wait up."

She turned around and hoped her dismay didn't show on her face. She absolutely did not have the time or the bandwidth for small talk right now. She was in confrontation mode, and it was like keeping a horse that was raring to go out of the starting gate.

"Well, Hi Brandon. I didn't expect to run in to you today."

He caught up with her and walked alongside her.

"How you doing?" She could hear the concern in his voice.

"Oh, I'm fine."

He stopped dead still in the middle of the hallway and she was a couple of steps ahead of him before she realized it. Turning around she saw the look on his face, and she couldn't help it. The look melted her. He really was worried about her. Really.

"I'm not buying what you're trying to sell," he said. "You want to try again?"

She took the two steps between them and told him, honestly.

"I really am fine." she paused. "Fine right now. Give me a couple of hours and you might get an entirely different answer." She made the fish swimming in water up-and-down motion in the air with her hand.

"That's understandable. I talked to Felix, and he said what you saw was about as bad as it gets."

Felix Rodriguez was an EMT on the ambulance that had come to pick up her mother.

"Oh, it was horrific alright." She paused, then said softly. "Even compared to things I saw in the military."

He reached out and touched her arm.

"You're holding up, look good." He smiled and that, too, seemed unrehearsed and totally natural. "How's your mother?"

"She's doing ok. I'll be going to the regional hospital to check on her when I leave here. Hoping they'll let me take her home." She paused. "At least she was spared being summoned by Aunt Daisy to come see to her after Iris disappeared."

"Daisy didn't take that well."

"So I hear."

"You haven't seen her yet?"

Rileigh leapt on the opportunity. "No, not yet. As a matter of fact, that's what I'm here for. She's under restraint, yes?"

"Yes, it was the only thing we could do." He started to hail an orderly. "I'll get Vince to take you—"

"I don't need an escort. They told me where she was when I called, and I can find my way around this place pretty well." She looked at her watch. Then she hurried on before he could volunteer to accompany her himself. "Sorry, gotta run."

"Well, if you have the time, stop by my office when you get finished with Daisy. I'll be glad to get an unbiased report on her condition."

They said goodbye, and Rileigh headed down the hall toward the elevator that would take her to the ward where her aunt was under restraint. After Brandon turned the corner at the end of the hall, she changed direction and went to the board on the wall that showed the names of the staff and where their offices were located. Dr. Bengt Gundersen was on the third floor of the office wing.

As she approached his office, she rehearsed what she was going to say. She had to take him by surprise, so she had to come up with some ruse to explain her presence and get him alone.

She stepped up to the receptionist's desk and readied a response for when the receptionist wanted to know why Rileigh wanted to see the doctor. But the woman never asked.

"I'd like to speak to Dr. Gundersen," Rileigh said.

"Good luck with that."

"Excuse me?"

The woman caught herself and leapt quickly into professional mode.

"I'm sorry, but Dr. Gundersen isn't available right now."

"Would you mind telling me why not?"

The woman was surprised enough to answer.

"Because he's out doing that thing he does where he leaves and I don't know when he'll be back. He said if there was emergency, they could find him in the basement — with the construction workers."

The basement. Where the morgue was located.

The woman leaned forward and said conspiratorially, "He screws around when he's on the clock. Just because he has an MD behind his name doesn't mean he shouldn't have to follow the rules like everybody else."

"Okay, thank you."

"Would you like to leave a message for him?"

"No, I'll come back tomorrow."

Rileigh headed back to the elevator. If she remembered correctly, the elevators didn't go all the way down into the basement. You had to get off on the first floor and find one of those creepy doors in a rock wall somewhere, and behind it would be steps leading downward.

It took her a few minutes, but she found the door and opened it. The smell common to all closed up damp places wafted into her face on a little breeze from somewhere. She felt around on the other side of the steps and found no light switch. Well, there'd be light after she got out of the stairwell. She pulled out her cell phone and punched the flashlight app and started down the stone steps.

Stone. This was part of the original hospital, the one they'd constructed for tuberculosis patients out of stone and granite. The flashlight illuminated a couple of steps below where she was walking and she thought she caught movement on a distant step, out of the corner of her eye. Maybe a rat. She shuddered.

At bottom of the stairs the floor was wet. Not damp, wet.

She looked around as far as the light would reach. The door in front of her was all she could see. She pulled on the handle and it was stuck for a moment, then released with a resounding screeching sound.

The room on the other side of the door was as dark as the stairwell.

Shit. She'd gone to the north end of the first floor to go down the stairs. The basement under that older part of the building wasn't being used for anything, not even storage—not if the floor was wet. She could go back up the stairs, down the hallway and enter the basement through a different entrance. But there was basement under the whole building, every section of it. She could just as easily go across the basement here and find a door that would open onto one of the used, lighted areas. She chided herself for not asking where specifically the construction was going on in the basement.

Her shoes clunked with a hollow sound on the stone floor and she walked carefully across it, not wanting to trip over something. She shone the flashlight all around, but couldn't see any doors with light seeping out from under them.

Slowly crossing the room, she tried to head in a straight line from the door to the stairs, because if she couldn't find a lighted area where the men were working, she'd have to go back up the stairs and come down another entrance, and she did not want to lose sight of the stairs and waste valuable time trying to find them. She had already taken longer than she intended to. Getting hung up with Brandon upstairs had delayed her. She'd been glad when the receptionist said that Dr. Gundersen was down in the basement where construction was going on. That meant there'd be some other people around and those others would be men, probably strong ones.

Not that she expected any trouble from the doctor. A plastic surgeon wasn't likely to put up a fight.

Chapter Thirty-Seven

RILEIGH HAD DECIDED to come down here because she'd thought the basement offered a good place to step away and have a private conversation, while remaining within sight of humanity. Well, she wasn't having any luck finding humanity.

She stopped, stood still in the dark, listened. She couldn't hear the sounds of building that she'd hear if somebody were nearby nailing two-by-fours together to shore up a wall. But standing still did help her eyes adjust to the darkness, and when they did, she saw lighting shining through the frames around several doors on the far side of the room.

She stepped out of the dark room into one only marginally lighter. There were lights on somewhere within the space, but not nearby. And she still couldn't hear the sounds of building.

"Yoo hoo, anybody down here?" She was beginning to get a hinky feeling about finding the basement deserted, at least the part of it she was in.

She listened.

Silence.

Walking on toward where the lights were shining, she still could hear nothing. Finally, she turned a corner and saw the source of the light in the basement, the elusive light she'd been trying to find. It was shining around a doorway about thirty feet away. She went to the door and opened it, and found herself at the end of a hallway that was brightly lit. Big fluorescent lights hung from the ceiling, the old-fashioned metal kind that had long bulbs in them. The bulbs flickered, casting weird shadows on the walls.

Light. But no voices. She was reluctant to call out again and announce her presence. She didn't pull her Glock from its holster, but she was conscious of its presence there and was reassured by it.

"Hello," she finally called out.

A voice immediately replied. "You looking for somebody?"

It was a man's voice, coming from a doorway leading out of what might once have been an industrial kitchen.

"I'm looking for the construction workers. Are they down here?"

"The construction guys left, but I stayed behind, in here."

As she approached the doorway she could hear a hum of some kind, the sound of small electric engines running.

"Are you Dr. Gundersen? That's who I'm looking for."

"Sure am. Come on in and tell me what I can do for you."

His voice sounded merely conversational, not the least bit menacing. She still had an itch to pull out her weapon. Thought about it, but no. If she intended to get anything out of this doctor, she needed the element of surprise, but not the kind of surprise where somebody pulls a gun on you.

She walked into the room and saw half a dozen small machines. There was a hum coming from them. "You must've wanted a nose job bad to come all the way down here to talk about it. The receptionist should have made it clear that I don't do the scheduling. I can't work you in any sooner than the next available open date."

She approached him slowly, watching for any sudden movements. But he merely kept loading ice from a sack of it into the top of one of the machines.

As she got a good look at him, she smiled at her own stereotyping. Bengt Gunderson, with the classically Swedish name, had black hair and brown eyes and looked way more Italian than Scandinavian.

He set the sack of ice down beside the machine.

"Don't suppose you want some ice cream?"

"Excuse me."

"Homemade ice cream, from an antique ice cream maker. Not the oldest kind, those you have to crank, but the earliest model of an electric one. There's some in the freezer if you want a taste."

He gestured toward the walk-in freezer.

"Ice cream's a hobby of mine. So, who are you?" he nodded to his arms, up to the elbow in chunks of ice in a plastic tub. "Sorry, but I can't shake hands."

"My name's Rileigh Bishop." She thought he reacted to that, but maybe not. "My aunt, Daisy Gillespie, is a patient in the D ward, Room 105." He still didn't react. "I'm working with the sheriff on the cases of the two missing patients."

"Heard about those. What do you want to talk to me about?"

He didn't appear to be the least bit on guard, so maybe now was a good time to drop the bomb.

"I just had a nice chat with a friend of yours."

"Who was that?"

"Dr. Horace Collier."

He didn't exactly stop in his tracks, but his shoulders tensed and he sucked in a breath. Covered it nicely, though.

"What'd you talk to him about?"

"Drugs. The illegal kind."

He froze then, stiff as a chunk of the ice he was loading into the ice cream maker.

Rileigh continued, ready to draw her gun if he moved. "He seems to know a lot about the chemistry of fentanyl. Apparently, it's possible to make a whole new drug out of fentanyl, with entirely different characteristics."

He was as quick as a striking cobra, too fast even though Rileigh was expecting it. Whirling around suddenly, he threw the tub of ice and cold water into her face. The shock was so profound that she didn't respond quick enough. He was one beat ahead of her when she went for her gun, and he was on her before she could pull her pistol out of its holster. He was a big man, and he slammed into her and knocked her up against the wall. Her gun flew out of her hand and skidded away from her, across the floor.

Then he swung at her, a roundhouse haymaker that would have rung her bell, but she dodged out of the way and the blow just caught the edge of her cheek. Even that was enough to stagger her, and she flew in the direction of the blow and hit the floor on her side. She started to scramble to her feet, but Dr. Gundersen was now standing above her with her gun pointed at her face.

"You bitch!" he yelled. He'd gone from calm and

charming to wild-eyed fury between one heartbeat and the next. "You're not taking this away from me. I've worked too long and too hard to develop untraceable fentanyl that doesn't show up in a blood test. It's *mine*."

So that's what was so valuable about Dr. Collier's new and improved fentanyl. The drug was cheap to manufacture, if you could get your hands on the chemicals, which China was more than eager to sell to Mexican drug cartels. What would untraceable fentanyl be worth on the street?

He was panting like he'd just run a race.

"You are *not* going to tell anybody about it, or about me or that asshole Collier."

He stepped back a few steps, out of grabbing range.

"Stand up!"

She didn't move.

"I will shoot you dead if you don't do what I tell you. Now stand up!"

Rileigh got to her feet, gauging the distance between them, planning a move.

"Now step back and open that freezer door." Rileigh looked over her shoulder and saw the door to the walk-in freezer directly behind her. "Do it now or die."

Rileigh turned slowly, put out her hand, tensed —

"Don't try it. Nobody will hear the gunshot that blows your brains out."

Rileigh opened the door and started to step back, but he leapt forward suddenly and shoved her from behind. She went flying into the freezer and landed spread eagled on the floor on her back.

"You're about to become a popsicle. I set the temperature for ice cream — twenty degrees below zero. You'll experience hypothermia in five minutes, freeze to death in fifteen." He gave her a grim smile. "And frozen like that, your body will keep. I can take my time getting rid of it."

Rileigh's hands and butt were already going numb.

Then he stepped back and slammed the door shut.

Rileigh had never felt cold so intense it burned, but this did. She stood up and rubbed her hands together, could see in the pale pink light her panting breath coming out in big puffs of white. Her hair and the top of her shirt that'd gotten wet were already becoming brittle. Her lungs hurt, didn't want to draw in the frigid air. Her nose was so cold it began to freeze on the inside. The tears in her eyes were beginning to freeze.

She was going to die here.

Then she thought she heard sounds from outside, maybe scuffling sounds. Voices. She opened her mouth to cry out for help, but she couldn't make her voice work.

The door suddenly flew open and the bright light blinded her. She could only see a dark silhouette, but she recognized it.

Mitch!

Half an hour later, she sat quietly and took the tongue-lashing she'd earned, seated on an exam table in the emergency room with two blankets that'd been warmed up in an autoclave wrapped around her shoulders.

"I got your voicemail and thought — she's not stupid enough to go there *alone*. You're damned lucky I thought about it some more and decided, yeah, actually, she *is* stupid enough to go there alone."

She was still trembling, even with her hands wrapped around a cup of steaming coffee.

"You're absolutely right. I was a world class idiot to go in without backup—"

"Without backup? Hell, I didn't even know you were here."

"I'm sorry."

"If the doctor's receptionist hadn't told me about

Gundersen's ice cream, you'd be dead right now. Think about that. Dead."

She had nothing to say to that, so she didn't say anything. Brandon came into the room with another cup of coffee.

"Here, this one's hotter," he said and handed it to her.

Mitch either ran out of steam or decided there was no point in continuing to berate her, because he turned toward the door.

"I had Collier picked up, too," he said. "So he could tell me what he's already told you about Dr. Gundersen. Then the good doctor and I will have a chat."

After that he just shook his head, and as Aunt Daisy would say, he didn't say hi, bye, or kiss my foot. He just left.

"When your teeth finally stop chattering, how about you come up to my office and have a drink?" Brandon offered.

That sounded glorious.

Chapter Thirty-Eight

Mitch drove back to the sheriff's office with his hands clenched into fists on the steering wheel. Rileigh could have been killed. She almost was killed. Why in the world had she gotten it into her head to go confront that doctor on her own with no backup?

He let out a breath. He had to let this go. He had bigger fish to fry than wondering what had gotten into Rileigh. If he let himself stay in that emotional space very long, he would realize that his response was just a little over the top. And if he questioned himself, asked why it was over the top, he would get that queasy feeling in his stomach he didn't like.

He pulled into the back parking lot behind the sheriff's office and got out of his cruiser. As soon as Mitch walked in, Detective Mullins told him that the doctor they'd arrested at the Carrington House earlier was in the "interrogation room."

The interrogation room was the staff lounge. It wasn't at all like in the cop shows: a bare table with a chain coming up through it so the handcuffs can be locked down, two straight back chairs, and a one-way mirror. This interrogation room had a microwave, a small refrigerator, a big coffee maker, and lots of different coffee cups sitting on the table. All of them had slogans or cartoons or pictures on them. Mitch's favorite featured a picture of two dinosaurs standing on the shore as the ark sailed away into the distance. The caption under it read, "Damn, was that today?"

After Mitch went into his office and sat for a few minutes to gather his thoughts, he went into the interrogation room to talk to Dr. Gunderson.

The moment he walked into the room, the doctor leapt to his feet. "I want my lawyer."

"Have you called him?"

"Yes, I've called her. She's in Knoxville. She'll be here as soon as she can. And I'm not saying a word until she gets here." With that, the doctor crossed his arms over his chest and sat down in a huff.

"Suit yourself," Mitch said. He went over to the cups arranged on the edge of the sink and got his own. This one had a slogan that said, "Let's keep the dumbfuckery to a minimum today."

He went to the coffee maker and began to fill the cup with coffee.

"You want some coffee?"

"Hell no, I don't want any coffee. What I want is my lawyer. You can't do this to me. You can't go charging into the—"

Mitch whirled around so fast it was startling. He took two steps and was standing right in front of the doctor, looking down at him.

"The hell I can't. If I hadn't shown up, you'd have killed Rileigh."

"That was all a big mistake. A total misunderstanding."

"You saying you *accidentally* locked her in a freezer at 20 degrees below zero?"

The doctor stopped, regrouped. "I'm not saying anything else until my lawyer gets here."

Mitch turned around and went back to making himself a cup of coffee. "I've had a nice long talk with your chemist friend, Dr. Collier."

"He's not a doctor. He never finished his dissertation."

"*Mr.* Collier, then. He seems to be quite the chemist, and he is just chock full of information about drugs. Mostly the illegal kind."

"You can't believe a word that man says. You saw what a whack-job he is. He can't keep anything straight."

"It seemed pretty straight to me. He told me all about the illegal drug operation that you're running with some locals."

That was a total bluff. Mitch hadn't even talked to the man yet. But the bluff rattled the doctor, who began to sputter. "Well, I … I mean, it was a mistake. I didn't ever mean to…"

"Collier told me that you and he were side-jobbing with a few experiments on fentanyl."

The doctor just looked at him. Didn't speak.

"In other words, you were double-crossing your druggie friends. Not sharing your good fortune with your drug dealer friends, the ones you're in bed with now. That's never a healthy thing to do. Particularly not here in the mountains, where locals stick together."

The doctor spread his hands out on the table. He said, "Surely you don't think I would commit the crimes you're accusing me of. I'm a doctor. Do you have any idea how hard I worked—?"

"Save it for the young nurses." Mitch casually stirred a packet of creamer into his coffee. "I'm not impressed. I'll have to admit, though, you've got some stones on you—double-crossing drug dealers."

The doctor laughed nervously. "You've certainly got a vivid imagination, Sheriff Webster."

"So, tell me this? Why in the hell did you stuff that baggie full of designer fentanyl into a dead body? Surely there was an easier way to transport it."

Before the doctor could reply, Mitch added. "Witnesses, Dr. Gundersen. Credible witnesses saw you go into the morgue where Mackay's body was."

Another total bluff. That Gundersen didn't react to.

"Doesn't prove a damn thing. So I went in there. I had a reason ..." Mitch watched him frantically try to think of one. "I was looking for something."

"What?"

"None of your business what. I don't have to answer your questions. I don't even have to stay here. I'm not under arrest."

"If you try to leave, I'll arrest you. You'd best hang around and chat, unless you want all the women with big noses in the county to find out their plastic surgeon's been busted."

Mitch picked up his cup of coffee and walked to the door. He turned around and addressed the doctor.

"You should have stuck with boob jobs and liposuction. You are in deep shit here. Not just on the drug charges, I've also got you for attempted murder."

"I told you that was a misunderstanding, an accident —"

Mitch interrupted him. "And I know you're involved up to your stethoscope in the murders of the two women who went missing from the Carrington House."

The doctor was so shocked he just looked at Mitch. But then his demeanor changed. Instead of freaking out as

Mitch had expected, he calmed down, his eyes stopped darting back and forth, he relaxed in the chair. Maybe this was the state of detachment he'd heard surgeons got into right before a surgery, a place of absolute control.

Mitch had intended to shock and surprise the doctor with the accusation. Instead, it was Mitch who was surprised — by the doctor's response to it.

Chapter Thirty-Nine

WHEN RILEIGH'S teeth finally stopped chattering, she accompanied Brandon to his office for that promised drink. She'd looked at his office the other times she'd been there, but she had never before taken the time to really examine it. It was on the first floor in the oldest part of the building. The space had been renovated over the years, but somehow the general aura of the Carrington House — stately and creepy — remained. The windows were narrow and tall, with pediments over them to add charm and style. One window had a window seat she'd never noticed before, and the walls were lined with bookshelves, filled with big leather-bound volumes of classics — Shakespeare, Oliver Twist, The Old Man and the Sea. She wandered down the bookcase near the door, checking out the titles.

Brandon came in behind her. "Please have a seat."

She had plenty of choices of where to sit. There was a couch against one wall, a settee and two armchairs arranged around a coffee table, and his desk was located in the far back corner. It was huge. An old oak desk that would probably take ten men to move. The surface was at least six feet across.

Brandon gestured to the desk.

"When I get bored, I play ping-pong on the top."

"You don't really."

He said nothing, just opened a drawer and pulled out a miniature net, the kind you stretched across ping pong tables.

"I wasn't joking. When I was a kid, I used to play in my father's office. It was like being the king of the mountain. But the best place of all to play was underneath, here in the space for the chair. That's like the coolest cave ever."

Rileigh made her way to one of the armchairs around the coffee table and gestured all around her at the bookshelves. "Have you read them all?"

"Most of them . My mother fancied herself something of a writer. She was into poetry. When she read me one of her originals and it didn't rhyme, I pointed out that fact. She never read me another one. But she made sure I was well-educated in the classics."

"About that drink you promised?" Rileigh said. She still felt chilled, even though she was sure her body temperature had returned to normal.

Brandon went to a glass front cabinet on one wall and opened the door. "What would you like? I have—"

"In polite society, I think the damsel in distress is supposed to be offered a brandy. But if it's all the same to you, I'd love a shot of whisky, straight up. Makers Mark if you have it, Jim Beam if you don't."

He smiled at her and reached into the cabinets, selected a bottle that had a red wax seal. "We'll christen this one."

He pulled on the tab and wound it around the top of the bottle, breaking the seal. Then he took two glasses from the cabinet, filled them both about half full and brought them to where Rileigh was sitting.

"This should warm your bones," he said. "Bourbon whiskey neat. Good for what ails you."

Rileigh took the glass thankfully and sipped the amber liquid. The taste of it was sweet and it did indeed warm her all the way down.

Brandon sat down in the chair across from hers and set his drink on the coffee table. "You were asking about the books?"

That's when she saw the old, yellowed document framed on the far wall. It took her a moment but, were those the plans for the layout of this place?

She got up and crossed the room to stand in front of the framed plans, and that was indeed what they were, maybe even the original plans. When she tried to picture in her head the existing structure and make it fit with the construction plans in the frame, she bogged down.

"These couldn't be the original plans, could they?"

Brandon shrugged. "If they're not, I'll bet the originals are somewhere on those shelves."

He indicated high, narrow shelves where cylinders lay side by side, the kind into which rolled- up documents had been placed for storage.

Suddenly, Rileigh had an idea. She turned to Brandon. "Do you really think the original building plans might be in one of those cylinders?"

"Maybe. Probably. I've never looked."

"Do you mind if we look now?"

His gave her a quizzical look, but he went to the end of the nearest set of shelves and moved the rolling ladder over to where the cylinders were located. He climbed up a few feet, and then began handing cylinders back down to Rileigh.

The surface of Brandon's massive desk was the perfect place to unfurl them, so they took three big containers there, popped off the lids, and pulled out the first of the plans.

"Is there any particular reason you want to see the plans?"

Rileigh hesitated to tell him because it sounded so crazy. But there had to be some explanation for how two women managed to get out of a room that was locked from the outside.

"Ok, umbrella of mercy here." She touched her finger-tips together above her head, like making the roof on a house.

"What does that mean?"

"That's what we did as kids. If we were about to say something totally ridiculous, or had an idea that was way out there, we'd say, umbrella of mercy and tent our fingers. You were absolutely, positively not allowed to laugh or make fun of anything somebody under the umbrella of mercy said."

"Ok, umbrella of mercy. What do you want to see the plans for?"

"I'm wondering if maybe Aunt Daisy wasn't imagining things after all."

Chapter Forty

Mitch stood at the door of the "interrogation" room, listening for signs of movement.

Nothing.

It'd sure be handy to have one of those one-way mirrors on the wall so you could watch the reactions of the people you'd just questioned. Unfortunately, this wasn't really an interrogation room. It was the officers' break room and they'd probably not like that kind of invasion of privacy. Besides, the room on the other side of the break room where you'd have to stand to look through the mirror was a broom closet.

When Mitch walked back into the room, the doctor was totally calm.

"You think you can scare me?" There was an ugly sneer on his face. "Is that it? You're trying to intimidate me, saying I'm a suspect in murders I had nothing to do with—"

"Not a bluff, Dr. Gundersen. Fact. We have no suspects in the brutal murders of two old women who disappeared out of the psych ward at the Carrington House this past week. Nothing. Then I learn that you have been operating a drug operation out of the place."

"Pure conjecture on your part. You have no proof — well except for the testimony of horrified Horace, and that's just about the same thing as no proof at all. A first-year law student could crack him on the stand in five minutes, have him blubbering and asking for his mommy."

"Well, there's also that little thing about trying to kill Rileigh, about what you said to her before you shoved her into the freezer to die, about how the doctored, pardon my pun, fentanyl was yours, all yours, and you didn't plan to share it with your drug-dealing buddies."

"She told you I said that? She's lying." He leaned back in the chair. "You've made quite a leap here, from suspicion, and suspicion is all it is, of illegal drug violations to murder."

Gundersen's calm was unnerving. He supposed remaining calm was a skill surgeons had to cultivate. Mitch would have to figure out a way crack him.

"You keep wanting to dust that pesky little detail about trying to kill Rileigh under the rug and I guarantee that's not going to happen. You're going down for attempted murder, and as soon as I find the evidence I'm looking for, you'll go down for double murders, too. You'll never see the outside of federal prison again."

Mitch was pushing hard now. He'd looked at his watch when the doctor said his attorney was on the way. The lawyer would be here any minute. Mitch had to get the doctor to crack before his legal talent showed up and zipped the client's lips shut.

"You're crazy. You're totally crazy. What possible motive would I have to kill those old ladies? I don't even know their names."

"The first one was Rosie." He went for shock value. "You tied her down and let a rat chew though her belly."

"What!" Suddenly, Dr. Gundersen was both flushed and pale, and that was a neat trick.

"It's not common knowledge yet, but the cause of death for Lucille Ferguson was internal organ damage inflicted by a rat chewing through her body. And you kept her alive while you did it."

Again, the doctor's response was unexpected. He didn't panic, just cocked his head to the side. "You have genuinely lost your mind."

"And as for motive, you've got a powerful one. Lucille's roommates called her Nosy Rosie. She was always sticking her nose in where it didn't belong, digging around in things she had no business fooling with. I figure she caught you doing one of your drug deals and you knew you had to shut her up."

Shut her up.

Mitch hadn't put it together at the time, but the nurse, the one who'd died from drinking Drano, had gotten off work early because "a doctor told her to take the rest of the night off." What if the doctor had been Dr. Gundersen, and he'd spiked her thermos with LSD before she left, hoping she'd do something stupid? Which she did.

Her daughter had said, "Mama told me our financial problems were over." Maybe Rosie wasn't the only one who was nosy. Maybe Stella Roundtree had stumbled on something she shouldn't have seen and was planning on supplementing her income with a little blackmail.

Mitch only had a few minutes left so he ran with it.

"Just like you shut up Stella Roundtree. She was blackmailing you, wasn't she?"

The doctor's response was not fear this time. It was anger. And before his eyes, Mitch watched the doctor turn into a raving lunatic. His eyes narrowed into slits. His nostrils flared. A horrifying grimace of something like lunacy took over his face.

He leapt up and grabbed Mitch's shirt, drew back his fist to slam it into Mitch's face. Mitch parried the blow with his left hand and struck out with his right fist, landing a vicious punch in the doctor's mid-section that knocked all the wind out of him. He collapsed on his knees, holding onto his belly.

The door suddenly opened and in strode a young woman in a business suit, carrying a briefcase. She gawked at the scene — the doctor on the floor, Mitch over him — and yelled, "What's going on here? What have you done to my client?"

Mitch stood up straight. "He attacked me."

"Right. An unarmed *physician* attacked a police officer with a gun."

She dropped to her knees beside the doctor. "Bengt, are you all right?"

She looked up at Mitch, "Call an ambulance, right now. You could have ruptured his spleen. He needs medical attention."

Mitch nodded to the deputy who'd followed Bengt's lawyer in, said "Call EMS," and provided the code that meant send an ambulance, but there's no real emergency.

Gundersen held his stomach as if he was in pain, groaned plaintively — can you spell L.A.W.S.U.I.T.? — until the ambulance crew hauled him away, though it was clear he was just fine. He would be wheeled out of the E.R in an hour or so in a wheelchair, and then go play a round of tennis.

It took Mitch almost an hour to clear the pandemonium out of his office. Now, he'd be sued for punching the guy, because the proper response was to allow the man to punch him, maybe take his gun and shoot him with it, but under no circumstances should Mitch be allowed to defend himself.

His cell phone rang and when he took it out, he saw it was Gus Hazleton. He was supposed to be on vacation somewhere. Why was he calling?

"Have you caught the world's biggest marlin yet?"

"Have you caught the murderer who killed one woman with a rat and another by chopping off her head?"

"How'd you find out about that one, way out there in the South Atlantic or wherever the hell you are?"

"I got my sources. I'd tell you who they are, but then I'd have to shoot you."

"The answer is no, I have not caught the murderer yet. Not that I can prove, anyway."

"That's where I come in. The county coroner, always on the job. I get to be Gus-to-the-rescue, tell you something you don't know that'll help you solve the case."

Chapter Forty-One

"You think your aunt might have been right about what?" Brandon asked Rileigh as he spread the rolled-out plans on his vast desktop."

"Remember, we're still under the sacred oath of the umbrella of mercy."

"What happens to you if you violate the oath?" he asked. She gave him a stern look and he held both hands in front of him, palms out. "Asking for a friend."

She had to smile at that. "We never had to come up with penalties, because nobody ever broke it. So don't you start."

She took a breath. "I've been bothered from the git-go about the locked door. Maybe Rosie knew how to pick the lock, but Iris didn't. How'd they leave a locked room, unless there was another way out?"

He said nothing. Put his hand over his mouth.

"I'm not laughing, I swear." He indicated the plans on the desk. "Maybe there are all sorts of secret entrances and exits in this place. Who knows? I'm not aware of any, but that doesn't mean they don't exist."

et's take a look."

two of them poured over the plans out of all three canisters. They put weights on the four corners — big books were valuable to have around for more than their literary value — to keep the plans from rolling up like a window shade.

It took a little while to figure out what the different marks on the plans meant. There were symbols that must communicate something to architects or builders, but they just looked like little squiggly lines to Rileigh.

After she had gone over the first two sets of plans, they appeared to be the more recent of the batch. Rileigh pulled out what appeared to be the oldest paper in the containers and spread those plans out on the desktop.

Somewhat used to picturing the plans superimposed on the actual structure now, Rileigh began to trace lines from one point to another.

"What's that?" she said, indicating a dotted line that went from the north end of the basement to the rooms on the first floor. Then it vanished.

"There isn't any way to get from the basement into that part of the facility," Brandon said.

"No way that we know of." Rileigh stood up, energized. It might prove to be a wild goose chase, but it was better than sitting around doing nothing.

"You got any flashlights?"

Brandon eyed her curiously. "Surely there are some functioning flashlights on the premises somewhere."

Twenty minutes later, Rileigh and Brandon were making their way across the basement, lighting the way in front of them with twin light sabers of flashlight beams. This was the part of the basement that Rileigh had been in earlier in the day, the place where the doctor indulged his hobby of ice-cream making. If she'd shined her flashlight in that direction, she could have seen the freezer where she'd almost died.

Rileigh had taken a picture of the plans with her phone. They stopped to look at it, turned it so it ran long-ways on the screen, then zoomed in with their fingers.

"Okay, if this is that," she pointed to a large brick something that was probably an ancient, bricked-in chimney, then to another shape on the plan, "then what is that?"

There was another line near the shape, one of the dotted lines, and it didn't attach to any door in the basement.

Brandon had no idea either.

The two of them walked carefully through a floor littered with debris from wall collapses and who knew what else, moving in the direction of the dotted line, trying to figure out where it intersected the basement wall. Rileigh saw a small alcove about thirty feet away, with a low ceiling, like maybe it was under a staircase. She shined her flashlight in that direction and followed its beam. She stepped into the alcove and found that it only had three sides. Where there should have been a wall on the back side was an opening.

Rileigh's heart took up the rhythm of a timpani drum.

"It's right there on the plans. See? The dotted line starts here and goes—" Brandon gestured out into the darkness. "—that way."

He shined his flashlight all around, and they saw that what lay behind the alcove was a tunnel stretching out with a black mouth in front of them.

"Holy shit," Rileigh said reverently. "There really is a secret passageway in the wall."

Brandon held out his fist. She bumped it with hers.

Wasn't it convenient that the secret passageway was

close to where Dr. Bengt Gunderson — who'd just tried to kill her — spent so much of his time.

Pointing the flashlight up to make sure the roof was stable, the two of them made their way down the tunnel that was indicated as a dotted line on the building plans. The tunnel smelled stale, and there was the underlying odor of mildew the farther they went down it.

They passed one side tunnel that angled off to the north, but it appeared to be blocked by a rockfall about fifty feet in. They didn't investigate, just stayed on the main route underground.

Rileigh noted that what they didn't find as they went along were spiderwebs. Shouldn't they be having to fight their way through spider webs across the tunnel? Which would totally have freaked her out. Still, if there weren't any webs, didn't that mean that somebody'd been down this tunnel recently and cleared the webs away?

She looked down at the floor, stopped and pointed out with her flashlight. "Look, that looks like a footprint."

"Let's not get out ahead of our headlights here," Brandon said. "Let's just follow this thing and see where it goes. Chances are it doesn't go anywhere at all, just dead ends into some wall that got built later."

"Yeah, probably doesn't go anywhere at all."

But Rileigh didn't believe that for a New York minute. This tunnel went somewhere. It started only a few feet away from the infamous Dr. Gundersen's Ice Cream Factory. His was the footprint she'd just seen on the floor. He'd been down it. She just knew it.

Chapter Forty-Two

"WHAT INFORMATION COULD you possibly have sitting on a fishing boat somewhere trying to catch a marlin?"

"My mother always told me that wherever you go, there you are."

"And that's relevant to this conversation because?"

"Because I brought my brain with me on this fishing trip and when I heard about the second murder, that brain began juking and jiving."

"That's a scary thought. What did your juking brain tell you?"

"Tell me about the murder first, about what you found."

Mitch told him about being summoned to the cemetery where the old grounds keeper had stumbled upon the grisly scene when he started work Monday morning, how he had found a headless corpse on top of a grave, a woman in a nightgown, holding a red rose — and the woman had turned out to be another of Daisy's sisters gone missing.

"Okay, that's the way I heard it. What I know is—"

"That's not all."

"What'd you leave out?"

"That same morning that the headless body was found in the cemetery, a box was delivered to Rileigh's mother's house. It was addressed to Rileigh and—"

"No."

"Yes. It was the head that was missing from the body in the cemetery. Dora Jean Simmons, who Daisy called Iris. She was a particular favorite of Rileigh's, quiet and withdrawn, never had much to say. Rileigh said her 'delusion of choice' was that she believed Rileigh was her daughter."

"Her daughter?"

"Uh-huh."

Gus groaned. "It's worse than I thought."

"What's worse? Could you just tell me?"

"You never read about a man named Alex Cullen?"

"Doesn't ring any bells."

"Maybe it didn't make it into the whole US, but it was big news in Spokane, Washington. I was living in British Columbia at the time and Canadian news media were all over it, too. Alex Cullen was a plumber, a mild-mannered unassuming man, as neighbors described him. Of course, the neighbors are always surprised. Apparently, he spent considerable time choosing his targets, always women, but age and race didn't seem to matter to him. He picked apartment dwellers, would get into the apartment houses by telling the supervisor that one of the tenants had called a plumber. Then I think he told the women that there was a leak in the ceiling in the apartment below and he had to check their pipes. They'd let him in and that was the last thing they ever did."

"A serial killer."

It wasn't a question, so Gus didn't answer it.

"The FBI later confirmed that he had killed four women — chopped off their heads. That's significant. He didn't kill them some other way and then cut their heads off as trophies. They bled out from the neck wound. It was the only mark on them. Then he put the bodies in cemeteries, laid them out on top of the graves of World War II veterans. And the first victim, he mailed her head in a box to her mother."

Mitch only grunted, remembering the head in the cardboard box on Rileigh's kitchen table.

"He might have done the same thing to the other three victims, mailed out their heads, but he got caught before he had a chance. In an unrelated case, there had been some burglaries in Cullen's neighborhood and the local police thought the thieves were kids living nearby. So they searched the garages of neighboring houses, looking for the stolen items. They found the three missing heads of the other victims in a freezer in Cullen's mother's basement — which, technically, they didn't have a right to search, because they never got a warrant."

"Did he get off because of that legal snafu?"

"Might have, but the case never went to trial. They never found him. They looked in his computer and found where he had researched creating a new identity and living under the radar. It was a big deal for a while in Spokane, and every now and then they resurrect the mystery… whatever happened to Alex Cullen? People in his family, including his mother, said they believe he killed himself, that he was 'profoundly sorry for what he'd done' and he'd offed himself. I don't buy that angle. I think you can be profoundly sorry for maybe one murder. But after the third one, you were definitely doing the do on purpose, and remorse doesn't figure into that narrative."

There was a sound in the background on Gus' end, then excited voices.

"Well, I gotta go, appears I have a bite."

"No, wait. You tell me all this and then what? Run off to catch a fish? Do you think that Alex Cullen moved to Tennessee and decided to start killing people?"

"Well, he is a serial killer who's never been caught and that's certainly his MO."

"Rosie and the rats was a profound *departure* from that M.O. Do you think that means—?"

"Seriously, dude, I got to go. I came a long way and paid a lot of money to catch this fish, and I'm not going to let it get away. I'll call you later."

"Fine, go catch your fish."

Gus ended the call.

Mitch immediately Googled Alex Cullen and was rewarded with way more information than anybody ought to be able to call up with a search engine. There were pictures — graphic — of the heads in the freezer in the killer's basement, and shots of the bodies found on the graves, though they all were covered with blankets. He read several accounts of the crimes in a couple of different newspapers. The case had been given to the FBI for investigation, so Mitch didn't know why it hadn't become a national story. Must have been a busy news day.

Each of the stories about it had a different hook. One concentrated on the frozen heads, interviewed shrinks about what could possibly be the motivation for decapitating a victim.

Another talked about the "grave of a World War II veteran" angle, checking on the killer's military service — he'd served a hitch in the Navy, but nothing jumped out as a reason that experience would have turned him into a killer. The rose his victim was holding was never properly explained either.

A third newspaper took the angle of the head mailed to the victim's daughter. And that was grim. The daughter was pregnant at the time, and was so upset by the head in a box that she'd miscarried.

None of the newspapers ever established a link between the victims, or determined how he might have picked those particular women, if, indeed, it wasn't just random — ring a doorbell, kill whoever answers the door. The police never found out how the murderer knew the first victim's daughter, and there was speculation that he would eventually have gotten around to mailing out the other severed heads, but got apprehended before he had a chance.

Whoever killed Iris knew information even more personal than her next of kin. The killer knew that she had no children, but that she had believed Rileigh Bishop was her daughter. There were a finite number of people who knew that, so how did the killer come by the information? That suggested he must work at the Carrington House.

He considered his only suspect, who would likely be suing him, his department, the city of Black Bear Forge, and the state of Tennessee for police brutality. He was a strange man. In fact, it was almost like he wasn't one man at all but three of them. Could Gundersen be suffering from DPD, dissociative personality disorder? That was the therapeutic name for people who were once defined as split personalities.

Did he panic when Rosie caught him, causing something inside him to snap and unleash his demons? Did one personality kill Rosie and a different one Iris? And which one of them was driving the doctor's bus now? Maybe there were more of them. Were they all killers?

If Mitch had let a serial killer slip through his fingers, the guy could be on the prowl — he looked at his watch. Dr. Gundersen was out there somewhere *right now,* maybe stalking somebody else, or covering his tracks for the ones he'd already killed.

Chapter Forty-Three

BRANDON AND RILEIGH made their way down the tunnel carefully. It was dark and creepy, but it didn't appear to be dangerous, although it was hard not to think about the roof falling without warning. It had been cut through solid rock, so that was unlikely, but the roofs of coal mines sometimes fell, and they were cut through rock, so Rileigh was still careful. The tunnel twisted and turned, and several times Rileigh spotted something on the floor that looked like a footprint. She didn't mention all of them to Brandon.

Rileigh's flashlight beam fell on something white. Brandon pointed his the same way. It was lying on the floor, but not as if it had been discarded. It looked as if had been laid down there on purpose.

"It's lab coat," Brandon said.

"The kind Dr. Gundersen wears."

"Along with every other doctor in the building."

She was getting out ahead of her headlights again.

"Fine, it's the same kind of coat every doctor wears, but it's here. And it's white. It's not dirty, like it's been here a hundred years. And it's not lying in a wrinkled heap. It's laid out nice and neat. Like ... like somebody might be needing it again." Rileigh paused, swallowed before she continued. "Daisy said the angel was wearing white."

"She saw doctors in white coats every day. Why would she suddenly think this one was an angel?"

"I don't know—"

Rileigh didn't finish. When she stood her flashlight illuminated something else a few feet away from the lab coat in the shadows.

A lantern. Beside it was a rubber mask, the Halloween kind that fit over the whole head. But this one wasn't some horror creature. It was that girl from the movie, Frozen. Rileigh hadn't seen it, but she'd seen the posters. And the dolls, the tee shirts, the everything-marketable-from-a-movie. The mask had a beautiful face and long white-blonde hair.

"If you saw somebody 'in white' just suddenly appear, and they had a face like this... add dementia into the mix and a touch of Alzheimer's and stir."

"You'd think it was an angel." Brandon completed the thought.

They finally came around a bend that displayed what Rileigh had been hoping so desperately not to find. A wall. A dead end. They walked to the wall and Rileigh's heart sank.

"Like you said, a wall." She ground her teeth. "Dammit. I thought we were onto something here."

Brandon smiled a small smile. "I believe you southerners would say, 'Don't get your panties all in a wad yet.'"

"You learn Southern fast."

"I have a gift for foreign languages."

He turned back to the wall and began to examine it. It

had cracks and crevices. Then Brandon shined his light on something on the floor.

"Doesn't that look like something was dragged over that spot?"

No, actually it didn't. But then the footprints she'd seen might not have been footprints either, so she got down on knee and examined it. Yeah, something had dragged.

"Look!"

Brandon was standing near her, shining his light on one of the cracks in the wall. "This is a good-sized crack, shine your light into it."

The two of them shined their lights into the crack, but Rileigh couldn't make out anything about it. Then Brandon started feeling around the crack, above and below it.

"What are you looking for?"

"That place where something dragged. You know how a door opens across a pile of snow and makes a straight line that's circular on the top? This looks like that."

She looked at it again from his angle, and could kinda see —

"Here! Put your fingers in here."

Brandon had his fingers in a crack higher up on the wall.

"Pull."

Rileigh pulled.

Nothing.

"Pull harder."

Rileigh pulled harder — it moved!

"Did you feel that?"

"Oh, yeah."

"Keep pulling."

The two of them kept pulling, and a section of wall

began to move away from the rest of the wall, revealing a crack that ran all the way to the floor.

"You pull there," Brandon indicated the crack leading to the floor. "And I'll pull up here."

Rileigh pulled. At first nothing moved, but then it did. A whole piece of the wall became a doorway, and the door she was pulling on moved out over the floor of the tunnel, making an arc in the dirt.

As soon as the door was open a few inches, Rileigh shined her light into the space behind it. Nothing but darkness. Brandon kept pulling, opening the door wider. Rileigh leaned into the space beyond and shone her light around in it.

It was a closet. There was a bar and dresses hanging down from it.

Rileigh stepped into the closet, felt around for the knob, and opened the door.

Aunt Daisy's room. The closet was in Aunt Daisy's room.

Rileigh stepped out into the room, which was dim because the blinds had been drawn.

"Where's Aunt Daisy?"

She crossed the room and turned on the light, as if maybe her aunt would be visible if she just had better light. "Where is she?"

All the birdcages were empty.

Rileigh turned around and around in a circle. Brandon crossed the room to the door out into the hallway. He tried to turn the knob. The door was locked.

"Why would they lock the door if no one's in here? I thought you said Aunt Daisy had been returned to her room."

"She was. The other two were sent to the crafts room

so they wouldn't disturb her while she slept off the sedative."

The ramifications of that took Rileigh's breath way. And her eyes grew wide.

"Aunt Daisy was here, and now she's gone." Rileigh looked back at the closet.

"If she didn't go out through the door into the hallway, she went out through the tunnel. The angel took her away."

"No, that doesn't work. Not an angel. The angel outfit's out in the tunnel. Whoever took her away didn't bother to dress up like an angel this time. Just went in and grabbed her."

"Because we were hot on his trail. The doctor came in here and got her, took her somewhere and — *that's* why he was in the basement! He wasn't playing with his precious ice cream collection. He'd just snatched Aunt Daisy. Maybe we got him before he had a chance to do anything to her."

Even if he wasn't buying that, Brandon was encouraging. "Then she's safe now. We just have to find her."

"She's not *safe*. She's in more danger now than she was before."

"How do you figure that? Dr. Gundersen just got arrested. He's warming up a bench in a jail cell–"

"Oh, he's out by now. If he had a good lawyer, he wouldn't have been there long enough to get the seat warm. And if he's out, Aunt Daisy is a loose end. We have to find her *now.*"

"Once he got her to the basement, she could be anywhere."

"It's not like he could have dragged her kicking and screaming down one of the hospital hallways. The other tunnel, the spur–"

"That doesn't go anywhere. It was blocked."

"We don't know that, we didn't look. Maybe it ends somewhere and that's where he put her, where he's holding her until he has time to—"

Rileigh ran into the closet, out the back, and into the tunnel.

Chapter Forty-Four

MITCH SAT in front of his computer, considering his next move. If the doctor was suffering from… he paused, then typed in "Dissociative Personality Disorder" and punched enter. Nothing that matched what he'd typed in came up because he'd used the wrong word. It was Dissociative *Identity* Disorder, and there were a plethora of listings for that.

He read, "Someone with DID has multiple, distinct personalities. Each may have a unique name, personal history, and characteristics. The various identities control a person's behavior at different times. The condition can cause memory loss, delusions, or depression. DID is usually caused by past trauma."

Well, he had certainly encountered different, distinct personalities in Dr. Bengt Gundersen. He'd been Dr. Timid in the beginning. He'd been scared to death, trying and not succeeding in hiding his discomfort. His body language had been closed up, in total protection/defense mode, and Dr. Timid would have cracked, would have spilled his guts if Mitch had kept applying the pressure.

But to the rescue came Dr. Confident, who swapped

places with his mealy-mouthed self in less time than it took to spell Czechoslovakia. Dr. Confident was sure of himself, was actually Dr. Arrogant. He was condescending, blew off what he saw as Mitch's inadequate attempts to get him to open up. He was snarky and snide and absolutely in charge. Dr. Arrogant would have saved the day if he'd been left in charge, he would have buttoned his lip until the lawyer showed up, at which point he would have waltzed out the door with her a free man. Maybe he'd have flipped Mitch the bird on the way out. But when Mitch mentioned Stella Roundtree, that pushed some kind of button, tripped a trigger in his DID cadre of personalities, and Dr. Violent Rage showed up to take over and save poor Dr. Gundersen, whose real personality might have been in there somewhere, but wasn't likely any of the three people Mitch had met.

Mitch continued to scan down, stopped on an article by WebMed, which said that not everyone experiences DID the same way. "'Alters' or different identities have their own age, sex, or race. Each has its own posture, gestures, and distinct way of talking. Sometimes the alters are imaginary people. Sometimes they are animals. Each personality reveals itself and controls the individual's behavior and thought, and that is called 'switching.' Switching typically takes days to occur, but some severe cases switch back and forth in seconds."

Dr. Gundersen had his switching down to an art form, went from one to another in a nanosecond. In fact, Mitch had seen three distinct personalities over the course of less than an hour. From what he was reading, that didn't seem to be a typical scenario.

But Mitch was no shrink, had not even talked to one about the issue. He'd just hopped online and became an instant expert on a very complex mental disorder. He sighed, pushed his chair back from his desk, and started to go into the break/interrogation room for a cup of coffee. He needed the reassurance of his "Let's keep the dumb-fuckery to a minimum" cup right now.

Then he paused, sat back down, and typed some other words into the search engine. The screen filled up then too, but the results were not nearly as on point as the others had been.

He'd typed in "serial killer" and "rats."

He waded through lots of information about serial killers, and about rats. But he also found references to killers who involved rats in their murders. It was ghastly reading. A man named Richard Kuklinski had admitted to police that his favorite method of killing people was to tie them up and leave them in caves, where inevitably they would be eaten alive by rats. That was interesting. But he read on to find that the killer made all sorts of outrageous claims and the 'rat-killing' was only one of them. Police had never been able to find any evidence to substantiate the claim.

Following the entry about Richard Kuklinski were various entries about criminals who used various forms of rat torture as persuasion. A New Jersey man named David Wax was alleged to have threatened kidnap victim Israel Bryskman with rat torture unless he agreed to give his wife a divorce. Bryskman was Jewish, and in Orthodox Judaism only the husband has the power to end the marriage in divorce.

There was a reference to a "Rats Dungeon" as a feature of the Tower of London in its heyday, alleged by Catholic writers in the Elizabethan era, a cell below high-water mark and totally dark that would draw in rats from the River Thames as the tide flowed in. Prisoners in the cell would have "flesh torn from their bones" when the tide flowed back out.

Mitch stopped reading with that entry, got up and got his cup of coffee, then went back to his office, sat down at the computer, and continued to scroll.

He read that various South American dictators in Brazil, Chile, and Argentina, had used rats in creative ways either to torture victims for information or to terrorize the peasants to keep them in line. He skipped over the descriptions of these methods of torture, noticed only that they involved the inserting of rats into the bodies of living victims.

Then he came upon the case of Colby Malone, and he didn't skip any part of that one, read it straight through several times.

Colby Malone was an Indiana man who should have been apprehended as a juvenile, because he clearly demonstrated murderous tendencies even as a child. At age ten, he forced a classmate to swallow double A batteries just to see what it would do to her. What it did to her was send her into surgery to have them removed. When he was twelve years old, he caught two small children who lived in his neighborhood — little girls — and tied their braids together. Then he hung them over a clothesline, to dangle on each side of it suspended only by their braids. At age fifteen, he was caught by police on suspicion that he had tried to poison his elderly grandmother by getting her to drink antifreeze, but before her death, the old woman swore he hadn't done it and they couldn't make the charges stick.

He vanished off the radar as an adult, appearing to be an ordinary young man who went from one part time job to another, drifting all over the country. He didn't get into trouble after that, or if he did, it wasn't of the ghastly sort that would make the news.

Until Malone was twenty-six years old, when he abducted a mentally-handicapped teenage girl in Texarkana, Texas and killed her, then cut her body into small pieces and put the pieces in a barrel of lye. A few months later, he struck again. This time it was a child, who wasn't reported missing for several days because of the drug-related issues of her parents. When her body was finally found in a shallow grave, it was too decomposed to make a clear determination about the cause of death. After the death of a third child, Malone emerged as the front-running suspect in all three cases and the FBI got involved, because one had occurred in the Arkansas part of Texarkana and the other two had been in Texas. Malone had access to the first two victims, and given his sordid record as a juvenile, he was the prime lead. He was brought in for questioning in the first case. But when authorities went looking for him again after the third case, he had vanished.

Malone's next victim was a nursing home patient.

When Mitch read that part, he sat up straighter in the chair.

The victim's name was Cora Purdom, and she was taken from the nursing home in broad daylight. She'd been sitting in a wheelchair on the wide veranda port of the facility, and when the nurses came to wheel the residents back inside, she was gone, wheelchair and all. The wheelchair was found a few hours later in the woods behind the facility.

It was wintertime in Maine, and Portland was struck by a blizzard the next day that pretty much immobilized the whole town. It was several days before they dug out, and drifts of snow remained on the ground for months. But come April, the snow began to melt. That's when they found Cora Purdom's body. She had been left lying on a walking trail — would have been right out in plain sight if the snow hadn't concealed the body. But the snow also preserved the body, so the coroner was able to determine her cause of death.

She had died from internal injuries caused by some kind of small animal eating though her body.

Mitch paused, read that part again.

Malone's fingerprint was found on a hair clip he put in her hair and the FBI descended on Portland in an effort to find him. After he grabbed another old woman, the manhunt cornered him in a small cabin in the woods and literally caught him in the middle of the murder. He was arrested, but the victim was already dead.

None of the cases ever went to trial, however, because Malone somehow managed to hang himself in his jail cell, thus ending the story.

Mitch Googled Malone and was able to find a few other accounts of the crimes, but there was no big media splash about it as there would be as soon as the media got hold of the *details* of Rosie's cause of death. Mitch had kept a lid on it for over a week, which was something on the order of a parting-the-Red-Sea miracle — gave out cause of death as "internal injuries" and nothing more. He knew it would leak soon and when it did, the media would be all over it.

But that would no longer be his problem to bear alone. It was clear now he was dealing with a serial killer.

Oh, there were alternative hypotheses.

You could believe that Alex Cullen, the cut-off-their-heads killer who'd gotten away had moved to Tennessee, and had struck again — abducted two victims, but killed the first one in an entirely different way than he'd killed his four other victims before reverting to his own head-chopping M.O.

You could believe that two entirely different killers just happened to abduct women in three days from the same room in a hospital, and then killed both of them in separate, but horrible ways.

Nope.

The same person committed both murders. Or two different personalities within one person were responsible. He believed the murderer was re-creating serial killings that'd been investigated by the FBI — a copycat.

The FBI wasn't exactly on the favorites list in Mitch's phone, but he could look up the number.

Chapter Forty-Five

Rileigh ran down the tunnel as fast as she could, which wasn't very fast, until she came to the spot where the smaller tunnel stretched off to the left. She turned down it toward the rockfall that blocked…

Except it didn't block the whole tunnel. There were rocks on one side of the tunnel, but the other side was clear, at least clear enough for someone to pass through it.

Brandon grabbed her arm before she could go barreling down the spur.

"Wait. Now we stop. We call the sheriff," he said.

Rileigh's adrenaline was flowing and she was in no mood to back off.

"Fine, call him, but I'm going on." He didn't let go. "It will take time for him to get here, but maybe there's not any time. Aunt Daisy is in danger every second."

Rileigh marveled at her own feelings. She was terrified that something would happen to Aunt Daisy, the woman who'd slept with Rileigh's father behind Mama's back and killed Rileigh's sister, Jillian. Maybe. But there was no maybe to the fact that she'd tried to cut Rileigh's head off with a chain saw.

As she thought the thought, the fingers on her left hand actually began to ache, as if they were still held in place by wires beneath a cast. That was real, it'd happened. So how could she possibly be so upset now that her aunt was in danger?

Mitch had told her once that her continued loyalty to her aunt was a testimony to her own character, and maybe it was. She genuinely couldn't have come up with a reason. She just cared.

She loved her aunt Daisy.

Now *there* was a revelation, one her subconscious mind had been hiding from her for years. Rileigh loved her aunt. She loved the woman who'd wiped off her milk mustache after she ate cereal and taught her how to tie her shoes. She loved the woman who had been genuinely good to her when she was a child. Maybe that woman didn't exist anymore, had been obliterated by years of bad decisions, dementia, Alzheimer's. Maybe she had always just been a narcissistic old woman who didn't care about anybody but herself.

Rileigh didn't know.

What she did know now, a revelation from the cosmos, was that she loved her aunt. She just did. And she didn't know how to turn off that love. It was just there, a part of her, and she would have to accommodate her life around it.

Brandon didn't let go of her arm.

"We're calling the sheriff," he said firmly, pulled out his phone and looked at the screen. "Or not."

He turned the screen to face Rileigh. There were no bars showing on the signal icon. Rileigh turned and he stopped her again. "You try."

She pulled her phone from her pocket. She had one bar. She hit the favorites button, then tapped Mitch. When she put the phone to her ear, there was only silence. She hit the red disconnect button and tried again. This time the phone rang once, then the line went dead. Down here in the catacombs, she didn't have reception either.

So much for the fabulous 3G network.

"We need to go back upstairs and call the sheriff," Brandon said.

What he was saying was right. That's exactly what they ought to do.

Rileigh yanked her arm out of his grip.

"You're right, we should. You go right ahead and do that. I'm going to find Aunt Daisy." She turned and hurried down the narrow tunnel. After a few seconds, she could hear Brandon following her.

Her flashlight picked right now to blink out. Suddenly the tunnel was only half as bright, illuminated only by Brandon's flashlight beam. She shook the flashlight and the light blinked back on. Blinked back off. Blinked back on and stayed on.

This tunnel was much narrower than the main tunnel and the floor tilted. They were moving upward. The ceiling was lower, too. She felt like she might bump her head if she stood up tall, though Brandon was six inches taller than she was, and he hadn't bumped his head. He came close, though. Sometimes when an irregularity of the rock made the roof dip down it brushed his blond hair.

They wound around a turn where the tunnel grew so narrow, they could barely get between the walls, then it widened until it was just as wide as the main tunnel leading out of the basement. Around the next bend, the tunnel ended in a door.

This wasn't some disguised door, made to look like it

was rock, with the seams obscured and no knob. This was a regular door, with a door frame, hinges, and a knob. Rileigh paused, drew her Glock from its holster.

She saw that Brandon's eyes grew wide when he saw that, but he said nothing.

"You need to stay behind me."

She looked into his eyes to gauge whether or not he would follow her instructions. What she saw there was maybe so, maybe not. It was clear that he was as ramped up for a fight as she was. But he did step aside and allow her to approach the door first. She put her ear to the wood and listened, could hear nothing. She reached out and slowly turned the doorknob. It was a new knob, looked like a new door, too, and a new door jamb, like it had only been put here recently.

Rileigh pushed the door slowly inward. The room on the other side of the door was as dark as the tunnel. Rileigh shined her light around it, moving it slowly along the walls and the floor. It was completely empty, not only devoid of furniture but empty of everything else as well. Perhaps it was meant to be used as a storage room of some kind.

Except... there was another door set into the far wall. And light shone through the crack at the bottom of the door.

Chapter Forty-Six

MITCH DIALED the number for the FBI and as it rang, he fervently hoped the call wouldn't be answered by a computerized not-person.

Your call is being monitored for quality assurance purposes.

When a live person answered, he explained who he was and what he wanted, said he was a county sheriff in Tennessee and thought he was dealing with a copycat serial killer. The cases this killer was copying had been worked by the FBI, and he would sure like to talk to the agents who worked those cases.

"Which cases were those?"

"They were the cases involving Alex Cullen and Colby Malone."

He heard the clicking of a keyboard, then she said, "Okay, let me put you on hold and see what I can find out."

So, Mitch was put on hold. The music was classic Rock. He listened to Cream, Led Zeppelin, Crosby, Stills & Nash, Chicago, Beatles, the Rolling Stones—

"I think I've got something for you."

The intrusion of the voice was so startling Mitch coughed before he sputtered, "What'd you find?"

"I found the agent who worked the Alex Cullen case. He works out of the Jackson, Mississippi field office. If you don't mind holding again, I'll see if I can connect you."

"Don't mind at all. I was just getting into Smoke on the Water when you came back on the line."

She left and then the line went dead. This time there was no music, and after a minute or so Mitch understood why they played it. Made the wait time go faster.

"This is Agent Bower, what can I do for you?"

The voice was Southern.

"My name's Mitchell Webster, I'm the sheriff in Yarmuth County Tennessee. I called about … did the woman tell you what I was asking about?"

"She just said you were interested in a case I worked awhile back."

"Yes, the Alex Cullen case."

Bower made a grunting sound. "The fish that got away. You thinking maybe he's turned up in your pond?"

"Maybe. It's more likely we have a copycat."

"How can I help you?"

"Tell me about the case, anything that stood out."

"What stood out is opening that freezer and seeing three frozen heads. Had a trainee with me and he tossed his cookies when he saw it." He paused. "Let me see… well, it's all there in the reports. You've read the reports, right?"

"Afraid not. All I know is 'Google is your friend.'"

There was an audible groan.

"Friendly Google always gets at least seventy percent wrong. This is the real version."

Bower told Mitch about the case, how he had first been called in when a police captain in Pascagoula, Mississippi got a hit through NCIC on a previous beheading case very much like the one he was working. The agent was definitely local, left out the middle "is" so Mississippi became 'Miss-sipi.'

"I talked to them both," he said, "then a team of us went down there. The MOs appeared to match just about perfectly. Both cases involved a headless corpse left in a cemetery on the grave of a World War II soldier. In the first case, the victim's head was mailed to her daughter. That was ugly. We talked to the daughter, she'd been pregnant and lost the baby."

"Not surprised. I've seen a severed head in a cardboard box and it's pretty jarring when you were expecting Corning Ware from Amazon."

"Sounds like your case lines up with ours pretty closely. Was there a corpse on a grave?"

"Yup. The grave of a World War II soldier."

"Sounding better all the time. Anyway, where was I? Okay, so we've got murders in Arizona and Mississippi, and we did some digging and found a similar case in Minneapolis, so that made three of them. Then another body dropped in Bowling Green, Kentucky, which was Cullen's hometown. We went there immediately and worked it, got forensics to see what they could get off the bodies, but then we caught a break. The local police were doing a neighborhood search for some stolen goods, and they opened a freezer in this lady's garage and found the heads of the last three victims. So we started looking for Cullen. Matched his whereabouts to the other murders and were certain we had our man. But he slipped away. We literally got to the apartment where he was staying half an hour after he left. His mother called and warned him. We found on his computer where he'd researched how to make a new identity, so we figure that's what he did, but we never heard of him again, until right now, that is. What have you got on him?"

"I'm glad to tell you about the case I'm working, but I really don't think the killer is Cullen. I think the killer is a Cullen copycat."

Mitch explained what he'd found, and the similarities stood out — soldier's grave, head mailed to the daughter, right down the line. Mitch was about to describe the case that copied the murders of Colby Malone when the agent interrupted him.

"Sorry, I have to go now. I'm on a stake out and the other team may have eyes on the suspect. Leave your number and I'll call you back."

The line went instantly dead, and Mitch sat holding his silent phone. Mitch considered his next move. With Dr. Gundersen on the loose out there, he didn't have time to sit around waiting for the FBI to call back. It could be days from now, and he didn't have days.

He suddenly remembered what Rileigh had said, about Brandon Hollister working with the FBI. He'd worked with the Behavioral Analysis Unit out of Quantico. That was a pretty prestigious unit, maybe he knew somebody higher up the food chain who could grease the skids so Mitch could get the information he needed without having to wait.

And not just the information. He'd intended to ask the FBI to work with him on the two murder cases, but he'd never had a chance.

Mitch didn't have Brandon Hollister on the favorites list on his phone, like Rileigh did. He cringed a little at that. But calling the man for help proved that Brandon's interest in Rileigh didn't concern Mitch in the least. Didn't it?

His call went immediately to voicemail, which meant

the phone was turned off or didn't have cell service. He called the facility and spoke to Brandon's secretary, who said he was not in the office right now.

Mitch was spared having to decide what to do next when his phone rang in his hand. It was Agent Bower.

"False alarm. I'm still just waiting and watching. Where were we? You were telling me about a case..."

Mitch wanted to get the important part out this time before they got disconnected again.

"I was about to ask for the FBI to look into the case I'm working. It's a double murder. One of the victims was killed the way Alex Cullen killed his victims. But the M.O. on the other murder was entirely different. He killed that victim the exact same way Colby Malone killed his."

"The rat man! You definitely have my undivided attention now."

Chapter Forty-Seven

RILEIGH REACHED out with her left hand and tried the knob on the door. If it was locked …

It wasn't.

She held her breath and eased it slowly inward, aware of any creak or groan it might make. It was soundless, just swung inward. Beyond the door was a room, a kitchen — or, it had been a kitchen. There were no appliances, but there were counters and cabinets, all of them empty. There was a thin layer of dust on everything, white dust, drywall dust. Someone had hung drywall in this place recently, sanding it down, and the dust had settled out of the air on everything.

Her head on a swivel, Rileigh stepped into the room and went into search mode. With her gun in a two-hand grip, she went down the left side of the room. There was another doorway there. She peeked around the doorframe and saw other rooms beyond. Then retraced hers steps back to the door she'd come through, where Brandon still stood. She continued down the right wall of the kitchen. There was an opening there, maybe for something like a breakfast nook, not very big. She edged up to it, then spun around the corner, gun ready into the space.

It was empty.

She looked back at Brandon and motioned for him to stay where he was as she listened. There were no sounds coming from anywhere. She returned to the archway into the other rooms, this time from the right side, spun around the corner into yet another empty room. This one had likely been the dining room. The overhead light was on in the room, a dim bulb casting a bilious glow. There were two windows in the room, on opposite walls, indicating this was the corner room ... where? There was a niggling memory squirming around, trying to get her attention, but she ignored it for right now. What she could see was that the windows had something on the outside, like they were boarded up.

Boarded up windows. The niggling memory burst full blown in her mind. That night she and Brandon had searched the grounds looking for Rosie, they had come upon a little stone building out of sight behind a hedge, next to the main hospital building. The Caretaker's Cottage. She had checked that out the night of the search, but it was locked up tight with a padlock and a hasp on the outside of the front door — the only entrance that was visible from the outside.

She remembered what she'd thought when she saw it, how it looked like the fairy tale cottage where a wicked witch had kept Hansel and Gretel in a cage, fattening them up before she put them in her big oven and cooked them. It didn't look so enchanting from the inside, didn't look sinister, either. Just an unused building—

Not unused. There was drywall dust on the countertops in the kitchen. There'd been construction work of some kind in here recently. She went to the doorway opening out of the dining room and saw it opened onto a hallway with three doors, all of them closed. She hated hallways, they were too enclosed to maneuver easily and there was no room to dodge a weapon.

She went to the first doorway; it was on the right. She eased it open. As soon as she did a familiar unpleasant smell wafted toward her. It was a bathroom, but the smell wasn't the expected bathroom variety. Like wet metal.

She stepped in. It was small and she could see from ambient light that no one was inside, so she felt around on the wall for the light switch and flipped it on. She didn't breathe for a moment, looking around. The familiar smell was the metallic aroma of blood, large amounts of blood. The bathroom was awash in it. The sink, the floor, the bathtub, the toilet. All had blood splattered all over them. Dried blood stained the sink, and the bathtub was slathered with it. She used the barrel of her gun to push the shower curtain aside in the small shower so she could see into it. The shower was clean. In fact, the floor appeared to be wet, like maybe somebody had taken a shower in there recently. She remained facing the door as she looked around, prepared for the moment someone would appear there and get his ass shot.

Rileigh crept carefully out into the hallway. Two more rooms to clear. The two doors, one on each side of the hall, were bedrooms. The one on the left was the larger of the two because it stretched all the way to the kitchen, without a bathroom in between.

Eenie…meenie…minie…moe…

She walked quietly but resolutely to the door on the left, the biggest bedroom, and tried the knob. It opened and she shoved the door inward, ducking out against the wall when she did. There was a light on in the room, but she heard no sound coming from it. She put her back to the wall, gun pointed down, spun around the jamb into the doorway as she raised her gun and swept it around the room in one fluid motion, looking for human shapes, danger of any kind. There was nothing. But this room was not exactly what you'd call empty.

Rileigh stepped into the room and looked down at the floor, or down at where the floor ought to be but wasn't. The hardwood planks had been torn up in the middle of the room, revealing an area of dirt beneath the house, about six feet by ten feet. But the floorboards hadn't just been tossed aside. Somebody had used most of them to build a long wooden box, like a quilt box. The rest of the boards had been stacked so that they extended out past the closet door on the far side of the room, effective blocking it. Nobody was going to jump out at Rileigh from there.

She took a few more steps into the room. Not only were there boards strewn all around on the floor, but dirt as well, and as she approached the hole in the floor, she could see where somebody had begun to dig a hole in the dirt beneath the floor. The dirt they'd dug up was piled beside the door. The digger had made it down only a couple of feet; a couple more, and they'd hit bedrock — the bedrock that the tunnel had been cut through from the hospital to Rosie's room, and to the caretaker's cottage as well.

She'd stepped to the side as soon as she went into the room, so that the open door was never behind her. Now, she went to it, checked down the empty hallway and went to the door of the only other room in the cottage. If it was empty…

She heard noises, small ones, coming from the room. Somebody was in there. She approached the door quietly, turned the knob and it clicked open. Then she shoved the door open and leapt through the doorway, gun in a two-hand grip, sweeping the room. She was shocked at what she saw there, but concentrated on clearing the room before she did anything else.

What she saw was that this room was the only one with furniture. There was a dresser, a bedside table, and a bed.

Aunt Daisy was on the bed, tied to the headboard!

Rileigh went to the closet door in the room, flung it open, nobody there. Then she holstered her gun and hurried to her aunt's side.

Aunt Daisy looked awful. She had blood all over her nightgown, and it appeared to have come from her nose, which was still bleeding, seeping down over the piece of duct tape that had been placed on her mouth. She was tied to the headboard of the bed and the sheets were soaked with blood that had dried, making them stiff. There were also other things on the bed, that Rileigh didn't like to think about, but she knew they were pieces of … clearly this is where Rosie had been murdered. She'd been tied down to this bed and then…

Rileigh tried to pull the tape off her aunt's face, gently, but Daisy flung her head to the side and since Rileigh was holding the end of the piece of tape, it was ripped painfully off her lips.

Daisy didn't care, she was hysterical.

"Rileigh, oh dear god Rileigh, he — it was the angel and he—"

"Shhhh, shhhh now, it's okay. You're safe now."

"Not safe here, he'll come back. Oh, Rileigh, the angel is—"

Then her face froze in a rictus of terror and horror. She was looking at something behind Rileigh. Rileigh heard a sound, but she wasn't fast enough. She reached for her gun as she felt something stab into her back. She was instantly dizzy, began to collapse, tried to turn …

The world went black.

Chapter Forty-Eight

The FBI agent was, indeed, all ears when Mitch began to relate the gruesome details surrounding the murder of Rosie Ferguson.

"I really ought to stop you here, because I'm not the person you need to be talking to. Agent McCombs and Agent Petruski in Quantico worked the Rat Man case. Everybody was familiar with it, for obvious reasons, but I didn't work it and clearly you need to be talking to one of the agents who did. I'll transfer you back to Shirley and tell her where she needs to direct your call." He hesitated. "Get back to me, if you don't mind. I'm interested in the copycat angle. I'm working something else right now, but I'd liked to be involved in that if I can."

Mitch discovered that Shirley was the woman who'd sent his call to Agent Bower. She told Mitch that one of the two agents that Bower had told her to put Mitch in touch with was on vacation right now. But Agent McCombs, in the Quantico, Virginia office, was in today. She put Mitch through.

The Agent answered the phone with, "Shirley says you might have a copycat on your hands. Tell me about it."

He didn't ask who Mitch was or where he was, but Mitch identified himself anyway, and went into his spiel. He said he was working a double homicide in which the murders had been committed in vastly different ways.

"And you think the person who did them both is the same person because…?"

"Because the victims were both kidnapped from the same room in a psychiatric ward. Thelma Ferguson was killed on Wednesday and Dora Jean Simmons was killed on Saturday. The first victim was killed using the M.O. of Colby Malone, and Agent Bower— I talked to him already — said you were one of the agents looking for the killer in that case, he called him the Rat Man."

"Yeah, I worked that case. Why did you talk to Agent Bower?"

"Because I called to ask for help after the second murder. Dora Jean was killed the same way Alex Cullen killed his victims and Agent Bower worked that case."

"Heads cut off, bodies left on a grave?"

"Yes, that's it."

"But you say the first victim was offed Rat Man-style, correct?"

"The first victim was found on a walking trail, left out in plain sight."

"That squares with Malone. He left his latest victim's body in plain sight, but we didn't find it for months, until the snow melted. It'd been frozen though, so we were able to tell the cause of death, and it was gruesome."

"My coroner confirmed that Thelma died from internal injuries because a rat chewed through her body. He said she probably survived until the rat got to her heart."

"Copy that. I was the arresting officer, we caught him right after he killed his last victim, caught him in the act of killing her, in fact, but we were too late to save her."

Mitch really didn't want to know but he had to ask.

"How did he do it? How did he get a rat…"

"He tied her down, put a bucket on her belly upside down — with a rat inside it — and used an iron to heat it up. He put the iron on the bottom of the bucket, and as the bucket got hotter and hotter, the rat had to escape the heat, so—"

"I get the picture." It was an image that would haunt him the rest of his life. "I guess murders are the only cases you work, and I am here to testify that I am grateful to Mary, Joseph and the baby Jesus that I don't have your job."

The agent chuckled ruefully.

"Not just murders. Serial killers exclusively. I work with the BAU."

Mitch hadn't made the connection to Quantico.

"Maybe you know a friend of mine. His name is Brandon Hollister. He worked at the BAU years ago."

"No, the name doesn't ring a bell. Is he still an agent?"

"He never was an agent. He just worked with the BAU."

"The only people who work with the BAU are employed by the FBI. If he wasn't… wait a minute, what did you say his name was again?"

"Brandon Hollister."

"I think I remember … yeah, he's the one. We had a graduate student from some class at the University of Virginia that offered a week of observation here, just looking over our shoulders basically. I didn't like it, kept tripping over the kid, but I think I remember this Hollister dude because I caught him messing with the files when he wasn't even supposed to be in the building."

"Messing with the files."

"He lost it when I caught him, folded up and sobbed. Not a terribly well-adjusted individual. He'd only broken protocol, not the law, so we just kicked him out of the program. I did a little digging, found out UVA canned his ass, got complaints from the guys in his dorm that his room was wallpapered with bloody pictures, floor-to-ceiling. Maybe he got the pictures from our files, or maybe just downloaded them off the internet. You can get anything you want there. But they were all pictures of the victims of serial killers. He was obsessed with serial killers."

Brandon Hollister had lied to Rileigh. He'd never worked for the FBI at all, just stole pictures of serial killers' victims out of their files.

Mitch's phone beeped. He looked at the screen where he was offered the choices of holding his current call and answering the call beeping in. The caller on the other line was Agent Bower.

"I'm sorry ... would you mind ... Agent Bower is calling me on the other line—"

"You can call me back."

Mitch touched an icon and answered Agent Bower's call.

"Agent Bower. Now I get to ask what can *I* do for *you*?"

"No actually, it's still me doing something for you. I remembered that I forgot to tell you something about the Cullen murders and it's an important detail."

"I'm listening."

"All the bodies were laid out, headless, on the graves of World War II veterans and they were all holding a single red rose. I forgot to mention that."

"Nora Jean Simmons was holding a red rose, too."

The agent was silent for a moment, and when he did speak it was serious and deliberate.

"That's the most significant thing you've said today. You might really have a serious problem on your hands, Sheriff Webster."

"How so?"

"The FBI never released that information. We kept that detail a secret so we could use it to weed out the 'I'll-confess-to-anything whack-jobs.'"

"The FBI never released–"

"Nope. That was kept private. In house. So, how'd your copycat killer know about it?"

Chapter Forty-Nine

RILEIGH OPENED HER EYES. It was dark, so she closed them again. Where was she? Her mind was muddy, cloudy. She couldn't seem to focus. And she couldn't seem to move, either. It was like she was in a shoebox with the lid on it, hidden in the back of the closet.

She opened her eyes again, searching the darkness for something, anything. There was a chink of light shining through a crack in the boards in front of her. Not in front of her, *above* her. She was lying on her back somewhere on a hard surface and there were boards above her. She cast her eyes from side to side, boards around her on both sides of her. She was inside some wooden container and it had not been constructed expertly, the boards didn't fit together properly so there were small spaces between them.

She was inside a box, but it wasn't shoebox. As she became aware of that, she also became aware that her hands were bound in front of her. On top of her. She was lying on her back in some kind of box and her hands were tied.

Processing that whole thought all the way through from

beginning to end got the rest of the cobwebs out of her brain. And when the cobwebs disappeared so did her composure.

She was in a box, a wooden box... *like a coffin.*

Her heart literally skipped a beat. She felt it stutter, as she grappled with what was clearly reality. She was in a coffin.

She panicked. She wiggled and squirmed around, kicked her feet, banged on the top of the the coffin with her tied-together hands and lifted her shoulders to hit it with her forehead. She struggled to turn over, to move at all, getting more and more claustrophobic every second.

A coffin. She was in a coffin.

And hey, that wasn't even the scariest part. The really scary part was how she'd gotten there! She remembered it all now, the memories roared around and around in her mind like maniacs on supped-up Harley Davidsons. She had come through the tunnel with Brandon, found that it ended in the caretaker's cottage on the grounds of the Carrington House. She'd searched the cottage, cleared every room— correction, she must have left somewhere un-cleared, because somebody *came up behind her.* She had found Aunt Daisy, poor Aunt Daisy, tied to a four-poster bed and she'd started to untie her bonds. Then Aunt Daisy had seen somebody behind Rileigh and her reaction was too slow — dammit, she'd let her emotions cloud her judgement and she'd let her guard down.

Whoever was behind her had stabbed her with a syringe filled with who knew what. They were, after all, on the grounds of a hospital with a fully stocked pharmacy. Whatever had been in the syringe had knocked her out instantly.

Stabbed from behind... those words stood out from the others. From *behind.* The killer must have come down the tunnel himself, and when he saw her and Brandon go into the cottage, he'd followed them.

What had he done with Brandon? He would've had to subdue Brandon before he could sneak up on Rileigh. Probably gave him a sleepy time shot like he'd given her. That was the charitable conclusion, but being brutally honest it wasn't the only one, wasn't even the most likely one. You could come up behind a man and slit his throat. You had to grab his body to keep it from making noise when it thunked to the ground. The body would collapse instantly. Maybe there'd be a little gurgling sound, when the dying man tried to draw air into his lungs but drew in blood instead, drowned in it. The gurgling didn't usually last long, not very long at all. If she was brutally honest with herself, there were better than even odds that Brandon was lying out there on the floor somewhere in the cottage, dead.

She tried to let that knowledge sink in, but it flat out wouldn't. Brandon, dead. No! She banged her head on the wood beneath it and made a clunking sound of her own. She thought better of that and stopped moving, listened instead.

Where was she? Where was the coffin she'd been put in?

That had been what she'd seen in the room where the floor had been ripped up and somebody was digging a hole in the dirt.

A hole for the coffin.

Oh, dear God, a hole to bury the coffin in.

She started to hyperventilate. She started gasping, couldn't breathe, and then she totally lost it. She started screaming and yelling at the top of her lungs, kicked her feet and shoved her body from side to side. She banged her head on the bottom board and lunged upward, all in a desperate, frantic, hysterical effort to be free, to get out of this box. She kept at it, could breathe now because she was screaming.

She screamed and screamed. Screamed until her throat was so raw, she couldn't make more sound with it. She had thrown herself around as wildly as she was able and nothing had moved.

Then she began to cry. She couldn't help it. She was tied up in a coffin in a room where somebody was already digging her grave, and nobody would ever figure out what happened to her. The person who'd removed the floor would replace it, then clean up the mess and there'd be no trace of her.

She was going to die and be buried in this coffin. That thought stopped her tears, stopped her breathing, maybe even stopped her heart. Die and be buried. What if that wasn't the plan, the dying first and the being buried second?

What if the plan was to bury her alive?

That thought so terrified her, she couldn't even cry. Couldn't breathe either, and the dark world began to gray out around her. She had never fainted in her —

Suddenly the coffin moved. Somebody had shoved it. It was shoved again.

"Let me out of here. Let me go. Please, let me out."

Rileigh hated how pitiful and pathetic her pleading sounded, and she stopped in mid-plea. She was begging for her life, and she'd never have believed she could be reduced to that. If she'd been captured by the enemy during a battle, she'd have died bravely, wouldn't have begged for mercy.

She needed some of that bravery now. She tried to summon it. It was there inside somewhere, but she felt like a tube of toothpaste that had only a little remaining, so flat that squeezing it only got a little squirt to come out. And when you stopped squeezing, even that little bit was sucked back into the tube.

Then she saw the top of the coffin, the lid, begin to rise. The box flooded with light. She watched it move up and up as somebody lifted it off the box. She saw a shape briefly, before the coffin lid was tossed aside.

Now she would see the face of the killer. The man who'd killed Rosie and Iris, had probably killed Brandon and her aunt as well. The face of the man who was about to kill her.

The face appeared above her.

Brandon!

She croaked out his name.

Brandon was alive, had survived and was going to save her, get her out of the box.

She almost peed herself in relief.

"Oh, Brandon, Thank God you're alive. I was afraid you were dead, that he'd killed you, that ..."

But as she saw the look on his face, her voice trailed off. She'd never seen it on his face before, but it was a look she recognized. Oh, my yes, she'd seen that look before.

It had been on Aunt Daisy's face when she came at Rileigh with a chain saw, intent on cutting Rileigh's head off.

It had been on Sarah Park's face when she came at Rileigh with a can of gasoline, intent on burning Rileigh alive. It was a look of madness.

Pure madness.

Holy shit! It had been Brandon all along.

Chapter Fifty

IT WAS RAINING puzzle pieces out of the sky. They fell into Mitch's brain where they immediately assembled themselves into a complete picture.

The murders began when Brandon came to town. He had access — somehow— to the old women in Daisy Gillespie's room. And his motive? He was batshit crazy.

"I'll get back to you," he said to the FBI agent on his phone. He hit the red disconnect button and immediately hit Rileigh's number. The phone rang until it went to voice mail, which meant it was either turned off or had no service. The last time he'd seen her, she was wrapped in a blanket in the hospital emergency room, getting warm after she'd almost frozen to death. Where'd she go when she left there? Home, he supposed.

Then he called the Carrington House and asked to speak to Brandon again. His secretary said he was not in at the moment, did the sheriff want to leave a message?

"Do you know where he is?"

"No, I'm sorry. He must have left for the day while I

stepped out. I didn't see him leave and he's not in his office."

"Does he do that often — leave and not tell you where he's going?"

"Oh, all the time."

Mitch ended the call and called Rileigh's number again. No answer.

So, Rileigh was out there ... *somewhere*. And Brandon was out there ... *somewhere*. Neither of them were answering their phones.

He absolutely did not like the sound of that.

He called Rileigh's mother's number. Maybe she knew where Rileigh was. But her he phone rang until it went to voicemail too.

So where was Lily Bishop?

Dammit!

He ground his teeth, made himself calm down and think.

His first, primary responsibility was to find and arrest Brandon Hollister, a suspected serial killer. He had to admit that his primary personal responsibility was finding Rileigh and making sure she was all right.

On the Brandon Hollister front, the man was last seen at the hospital. He had left his office, but he could still be somewhere else in the building. It was a big building. Hollister had no idea he'd been found out, had no reason to run, unless Mitch marshaled his forces and descended on the hospital like a swarm of locusts, locked it down and searched it. But Brandon would likely hear about the search even if he'd already left, and then he'd be on the alert and in the wind. If Mitch waited and surprised him, they might get him without a struggle.

On the Rileigh front — he paused, called her again, no answer. Then he called Georgia, asked her if she knew

Rileigh's whereabouts. She didn't. Rileigh had last been seen at the hospital. But she'd likely go home after that. She'd had a harrowing day, needed a long soak in a hot bath. He called Lily Bishop's number again. Still no answer. But no answer could simply mean that Lily had left the phone in some other room and didn't hear it ring. Might be that Rileigh was home, too, but not where she could hear her phone. If she was in the garage or the chicken house, or … shoot, maybe she was in the bathtub!

Mitch made his decision. The smartest tactical thing to do to apprehend Brandon Hollister was to let the sleeping dog lie. He'd send a deputy to the hospital, just to watch it, call in if Hollister showed up. The same with Hollister's residence. Right now, his priority was finding Rileigh and warning her that Hollister was a killer. He needed to know if she was really at home and just not answering her phone. He got up from his desk, dispatched Mullins to surveil the Carrington House and Hadley to Hollister's residence, then he got into his car and raced out to Rileigh's mother's house.

Hoping he'd see Rileigh's car parked out front, he negotiated the driveway, and was disappointed. He pulled around to the back of the house and saw Lily's car. She was home. He found her in the kitchen, stirring something in a big pot on the stove.

"Well, hello, Sheriff Webster. I was just talking about you with Rhett a few minutes ago."

That was not a good sign.

"Rileigh's car's not out front. Do you know where she is?"

"Don't have no idea. You want her for something?"

"Yeah, I need to talk to her. It's very important."

"Maybe Daisy knows where she is."

"Why would Daisy know a thing like that?"

"Rileigh said she was gonna drop by to see Daisy some-time today. Maybe she told Daisy where she was going."

Mitch could go to the hospital and ask Daisy what she knew, but he knew from bitter experience that talking to Daisy Gillespie was like negotiating a minefield blind-folded. You never knew when you were going to say something that'd set her off.

"I'd call her and ask, but they took her cell phone away."

"Daisy had a cell phone?"

Lily looked chagrined. "Yeah, I know, she wasn't supposed to have the thing in the hospital, but she was all by herself out there, didn't have no family around her." Except her five imaginary sisters. "And it made her feel connected to be able to call me. That nice young man Brandon Hollister told Rileigh that as soon as the hospital inspectors finished their inspection next week, he'd let her have it back, as a favor to Rileigh."

Lily leaned close and said conspiratorially. "If you ask me, I think he's kinda sweet on Rileigh. I seen the way he looked at her."

Mitch had seen it, too, and it made his skin crawl.

Then he had an idea. He didn't dare try to get infor-mation from the explosive Daisy Gillespie, but Lily could talk to her. She'd tell Lily anything she wanted to know.

"I really need to find Rileigh. Right now. Would you go to the hospital with me and talk to Daisy, ask if Rileigh told her where she was going today."

"Don't mind a bit, Sheriff." She began taking off her apron. "Just let me get my phone. And I need to tell Rhett where I'm going. He gets worried when he can't find me. One day last week he wandered out into the woods looking for me and fell in the creek."

So, Mitch was about to take one crazy woman to talk

to another crazy woman, and that was his only link to a woman in danger of being killed by a serial killer. He had trouble picturing either of the FBI agents he'd talked to today finding themselves in a position like this. They'd seemed to have their shit together better than Mitch did. They'd been trained better and— stop it!

Self-doubt had never been one of Mitch's faults. He was letting his fear for Rileigh cloud his thinking and he couldn't afford to do. She might be in real danger right now and he could be her only hope of survival.

Chapter Fifty-One

RILEIGH GAWKED at Brandon as recognition dawned on her.

"Yes, yes, that's it!" he cried. "I've been soooo looking forward to this part. Where you figure out it's me and then your mind starts making the connections."

His voice sounded excited, Christmas-morning excited.

"I knew it would happen eventually, but in truth the snowball started rolling downhill and getting bigger and bigger, and it was all I could do to keep up with it."

"Why?"

The word popped unbidden from Rileigh's mouth, coming out in a hoarse croak because her throat was raw from screaming. She had almost no voice left.

"What on earth would you ask a question like that for? Nobody cares why. I'm telling you, the others weren't interested in motivation. At the end, all they were interested in was getting away and I certainly wasn't going to let that happen."

Rileigh just looked at him.

He sighed. "Ok, why am I about to kill you? Because it's so beautiful. I fell in love with it when I saw the first picture of a serial killer's victim at Quantico. They had all come to the extreme end of themselves, died horrible deaths, and in that grotesqueness was such beauty, I couldn't take it in. It staggered me. I put them up all over my wall and I began to ache to see something besides a picture. I've been planning this for years, and then the first one, it was such a thrill, such a high. I've never experienced anything like it in my life. There is no other act that reaches all the way out into the cosmos. When you kill someone, you have eternity in your hands. It's the most joyful and powerful I've ever felt."

The man was truly insane. Rileigh had killed people, more than she wanted to think about, and she hadn't felt joyful or powerful afterward. She'd felt sick, wanted to cry. But that was her humanity kicking in, and Brandon Hollister clearly had none of that in him anymore.

"I'm going to spend the rest of my life replicating the great masters of the art form, seeing in real life what I've only imagined from pictures before."

Rileigh said nothing. Brandon continued.

"The why-now? It's simple— opportunity. I had access to hundreds of people here. And I wanted a pure experience, no violence, I didn't want to have to subdue someone and then maybe have to fight with them. These were perfect victims — elderly women don't put up much of a fight at all." He paused and looked away, toward the next room where Daisy was tied to a bed. "I take that back. Most elderly women don't fight back. That one — I had to punch her in the face. But she'll be sorry she made me do that. She'll regret it."

He turned back to Rileigh. "My father showed me the

tunnels when I was a little boy. They were used when the place was a tuberculosis hospital. It was a way to get the dead bodies out of the building without having to wheel them down the hall where the other patients could see them. The central one at the other end was blocked years ago." He shook his head. "Such a shame, it would have been so handy to be able to take them out on the other side of the mountain and load them up. The basement was a little trickier, but I managed."

"You killed Rosie and Iris here in this cottage, didn't you?"

"I certainly did. Right in there," he nodded his head toward the other room. "On that bed. I really didn't intend to do anybody else anytime soon, so I just left the mess. But then Daisy recognized me, recognized my eyes when she was in restraints, started screaming that I was the angel of death. Nobody listened to her, of course. But I knew she'd never shut up about it and I couldn't take the chance that eventually somebody would take her seriously. It took me all day yesterday to build the coffin. Used the floor planking — multipurpose. Eventually, I'll get more plank-ing, put the floor back down and nobody'll ever know that beneath it lies … a replica."

Rileigh was beyond words, was just frozen, a mouse looking into the eyes of a cobra.

"Lloyd McNally was a schoolteacher who snatched children out of his classroom and buried them alive."

Buried *alive.*

He saw how the words affected her and grinned.

"Oh, yes. This coffin was built for your aunt, but now you're going to take her place." He paused, watched her face, and the smile on his grew wider. "Yes. Like that. Let it sink in. Let it be real. You are going to die, you really are. How does it feel to know that?"

Rileigh couldn't do much, but she did the best she could. She spit in his face. He was leaning down over the coffin talking to her, not but a couple of feet away. She nailed him. A big gob of spit hit him in the nose and splattered into his eyes, and he yanked back, horrified.

"You bitch!" he cried, hurriedly wiping his face with his hands, then untucked his shirt and wiped the rest away with the bottom of it, muttering, "… be sorry … pay for that …"

Then he collected himself. Drawing back so that he was out of range, he continued.

"I won't let your pettiness spoil this for me." His voice darkened. "Maybe I will make you pay for that. Depends on my mood. I might get the bleach out of the kitchen and pour it in your eyes."

There was as much horror in the way he said things as in what he said. He was so casual. "Pass the salt and oh, by the way, I might pour bleach in your eye."

"I'm going to have to think of a different serial killer for Daisy, now that you've stolen her exit from her. I'm thinking about Roberto Ortega. He starved his victims to death. I could do that here. Tie her to the bed and let her die there in her sisters' blood. Maybe not, though, the pictures of people who starved to death … there was no drama on their faces. Then there's Herbert Winslow. He used some kind of acid, put his victims in it and watched it eat away their skin. The pictures of that were breathtaking." He slapped his knees with his hands, the way a man will do who has things to do and needs to get busy. "I don't have to decide that now, but I do need to get you on your way."

He stood. "I need to dig the hole just a little deeper. It won't take me but a few minutes. Enjoy those minutes, because afterward you're going to stop living and start dying. And your suffering is going to be so beautiful."

He reached down and picked up the coffin lid and set it on top of the coffin, but didn't nail it down. She heard scraping and bumping sounds, then the rhythmic sounds of digging — the shovel going into the dirt, a pause, then the sound of the dirt dropping out of the shovel onto the floor of the room.

Now was her chance. As Brandon spoke, Rileigh had been slowly moving her bound hands down her body so that they were resting on the right pocket of her jeans. She was afraid he would notice her cell phone in it if she didn't do something to cover it up. She'd had no reception in the tunnel, but she was above ground now, it should work fine. As soon as Brandon was busy digging, she began to frantically dig it out of the pocket. Her wrists had been crossed, right on top of left, then bound around with some kind of nylon rope, thin but strong. She could feel the phone with her bottom hand, the left, and she tried to grab it with her fingers. But the coffin was so narrow that any movement of her arms was impeded by her elbow hitting the side of the coffin. She wiggled, squirmed, tugged, and finally it came free into her hand. The lid was only a couple of inches above her nose, so she couldn't bring the phone up to her face. She'd just have to operate it without looking at it.

Panting from the exertion, she scooted it down onto her upper thigh. She tapped it to wake it up, then tried to remember the configuration of the icons on the front. She remembered how angry she'd gotten at the Apple Store when the "genius" began to explain how you could "easily" dial 911 several different ways. She'd called bullshit on that as she listened. *Easily?* Go to Settings ... go to this app ... press this button... All the easy ways had two or three steps you likely wouldn't remember in an emergency. And right now, she couldn't think of a single one.

She had to be careful. If she accidentally did something that made a sound, bumped the side he'd hear, and he might come to investigate and take the phone away.

Then she had a horrible realization. She had facial recognition on her phone! If her face wasn't in front of the screen, she had to type in a passcode or it would remain locked! Right now, the phone was idle, waiting for the damned passcode.

Her hands were sweating.

Envisioning the front of her phone, she felt around on it with the one hand she could use, positioning it, visualizing the passcode screen. With trembling fingers, she touched the screen where she thought the correct numbers were for the eight-digit code. The numbers were all lined up in a row, one on top of the other on the far right of the screen. 936393.

Had the phone opened? She had no idea. Probably not. But if it had, and she touched the screen now in the wrong place, the Backstreet Boys could blast out I Want It That Way. Or her audio book could start playing.

Then she heard the shovel clunk on the floor. Brandon had thrown it out of the hole. He was finished digging. And she was out of time.

She began touching the face of the phone, again and again, in one place and another, trying anything. Brandon lifted the lid off.

"Hey, where'd you get that?" Brandon yanked the phone away, looked at the screen, and burst out laughing at what was there. "Google? Seriously? Were you Googling the ten best ways to get out of a coffin?"

He laughed at his own joke, dropped the phone on the

floor, picked up the shovel and stabbed it into the phone again and again. Then he turned and looked down at Rileigh in the coffin.

"Now, where were we? Oh yeah, you were about to start dying."

Chapter Fifty-Two

MITCH PULLED up and parked in front of the hospital. He and Lily went inside, and he stopped at the front desk to ask the receptionist to page Brandon Hollister. It was worth a shot.

Then the two of them wound through the facility to the desk on Daisy's ward and got the charge nurse to go with them to unlock Daisy's door.

Mitch was readying himself for bull-goose crazy and was prepared to stay completely out of it. He'd stand there as stiff as a Macys mannequin and let Lily handle Daisy.

"The others are in the craft room, to give Miss Daisy time to sleep off the sedative we had to give her. I'm not sure she's awake yet."

The nurse unlocked the door and pushed it open.

"Miss Daisy, you've got company. Your sister and the sheriff have come to see—"

She stopped and looked around.

"Miss Daisy? Where are you?"

It was clear the room was empty — not a bird in any of the cages. Now a third person had vanished out of a locked room. Perhaps the only person who could lead them to Rileigh.

The charge nurse left the room to go back to the desk to report that Daisy was missing. Mitch stood in the middle of the room, staring at nothing.

Lily's phone suddenly made a dinging sound and she jumped, then pulled it out of her purse and looked at it.

"Oh, that," she said and started to stuff the phone back into her purse.

"What? What is it?"

"I thought it was that My People app Rileigh put on my phone. But it musta been something else. This here phone got more little dots on it than a firehouse dog. Icons I mean, and I don't know how to use any of them."

"What's the My People app for?"

"Seemed to me when's she was explaining it that it didn't do diddly squat. It's a ... what did she call it ... a location app."

"Location?"

"Uh huh. That poor child is scared to death I'm going to get lost. Ever heard anything more ridiculous in your life? I've lived in this county for more than seventy years. I know every tree, rock, hollow, creek, house, and road between here and the Virginia border. Why in the world would I get lost?"

Mitch knew why, and he wasn't surprised Rileigh was concerned about it.

"What does the app tell you about location?"

"She said it was just these two phones, hooked to each other. Can't even make a call on it. There's just this little dot thingy that tells you where you are?"

"Where you are?"

"Yeah, so she can tell where I am and I can tell where she is, not that I'm worried about–"

Mitch snatched the phone out of Lily's hand and looked at the screen. The little red "dot thingy" was on a map that showed its location — the Carrington house.

"This just shows your location. Where's Rileigh?"

Lily shrugged. "Maybe her phone's turned off."

Oh, it was turned off, alright. Mitch had tried. He took his own phone out of his pocket and tried again. Same nothing, rings and then voice mail.

He gave Lily back her phone.

"I've tried to reach her a dozen times. Her phone's off."

"Well, this location thingy is supposed to show the location where the phone was turned off."

Mitch snatched the phone out of Lily's hand and looked at the screen. But there was only one dot, the one showing Lily's location. So where was the dot that would show Rileigh's ... even if her phone was turned off?

Obviously, the app didn't work.

"Did the two of you ever try it, test the app to see if it'd work."

Lily shook her head. He started to give the phone back to her, then paused.

You don't suppose...

He used his fingers to make the map where the little red dot showed bigger. He stretched it out, and stretched it out, the area around the hospital took up almost the whole screen and— there! He thought he saw. He stretched it out more. Yes. There wasn't just one red dot on the Carrington House. There were two, *one on top of the other.*

Lily was here, but so was Rileigh.

Now it was time to call out the troops. He used the mic clipped to his shoulder to call the dispatcher and began to give orders. Inside half an hour, this whole place would be locked down, nobody in or out. And then they would by god search every square inch of it.

As Mitch coordinated the search efforts on his phone, he paced back and forth in the open area of the room. Lily sat for a time on her sister's bed, then she began poking around, looking for Daisy as if she were a lost sock. She bent and looked under every bed, though you could see nothing was there. She went into the bathroom, opened the cabinet above the sink, looked on the shelves, lifting up each towel and wash cloth and looking under it. She went to the closet then and began to search it, looking through the shoes on the floor and among the hanging clothes.

"Uh, Sheriff… can you come here a minute?"

Mitch didn't have time for Lily's craziness. He stopped for a moment, looked at her, and stage whispered, "Not now, Lily," then went back to his conversation. Lily came to stand beside him, and as soon as he stopped talking, was listening to the dispatcher, Lily pulled on his sleeve.

"You really need to see this," she said.

This time he merely shook his head firmly, no.

She wouldn't give up.

She grabbed his arm and began dragging him toward the closet.

"Just a minute," he told the dispatcher, "All right, what is it, Lily?"

She opened the closet door wider so that more of the room's dim light shone. "There's a hole in the wall back there."

She wanted to show him *a hole in the wall?*

He was turning around when he saw it. One of the panels in the back of the closet was missing or had been moved. Where it had been was a hole leading out into a tunnel carved out of the solid rock.

Pieces of conversations, bits of information rose to the surface of his mind. The tuberculosis tunnels, the ones the hospital had dug so the other patients wouldn't see them carrying out the dead. This must be one of those tunnels. And that explained how two... *three* women had disappeared out of a locked room. The killer had come down the tunnel and, in the guise of an angel, had snatched them away.

Then Mitch was running down the tunnel as fast as he could using the flashlight app on his phone to light the way. Might just be the killer was at the other end of the tunnel.

But he was wrong. A few minutes later he stood panting and sweating in the basement beneath the hospital. There was no one in sight. He sagged. Well, at least he now knew how Brandon had gotten the women out of the building without being seen. That was something.

Mitch headed slowly back down the tunnel to Daisy's room, not pumped on adrenaline anymore. He spotted it then. He'd missed it before. The flashlight beam on his phone wasn't very big or bright. But walking instead running now, he saw that there was a side tunnel leading off from the main tunnel.

He turned aside and started down it.

Chapter Fifty-Three

Brandon moved out of her line of sight and was gone for a few moments, then he returned with a small box, maybe twice the size of a ring box.

"I went to a whole lot of trouble to come by my friend here, so you need to be nice to him."

Friend? In the box?

Something small.

The skin on Rileigh's arms broke out in goose bumps.

"Lloyd McNally was a nice fella and he felt bad about leaving his victims all by themselves down there in the dark. He didn't want them to get lonely. So, he gave each one of them a companion. A snake, a spider, a scorpion. Something cuddly that wouldn't breathe up what limited oxygen there will be once you're buried."

Brandon nodded to the little box in his hand. "So, I got you a roommate."

He held the box out over the coffin, lifted the lid and turned it upside down. Something fell out of onto Rileigh's leg, she felt it crawling down her leg toward her shoe.

"It's a scorpion, the biggest one I could find, though

there weren't a whole lot to choose from." Brandon tossed the scorpion's box aside, lifted the lid of the coffin and scooted it back into place. She heard and felt him driving nails in it to hold it in place.

"Brandon, don't do this, please don't do this, don't—"

"Said the woman who got all macho and spit in my face. Sorry about that now, are you?"

"Yes, I'm sorry. I'm sorry I'm not a cobra, so I could have spit poison."

She felt the scorpion skitter onto the bare skin of her hand. Somehow she managed not to scream.

"Hey, Dumbass, you picked the wrong insect to scare me."

When she was in the Middle East, scorpions were a fact of daily life, as common as a housefly. If you felt one crawling on you, and she had, many times, your best move was not to move at all. She didn't buy that, always tried to smash them. She'd been stung several times, but she'd killed a whole lot of crawly things. She slammed her hand into the coffin lid as hard as she could, crushing the bug.

When she felt the insect crushed to goo on top of her hand, she felt a momentary thrill of defiant courage. She didn't feel like a victim. But the courage was momentary, and it drained completely out of her as Brandon shoved the coffin into the hole, careful not to tip it over.

Rileigh's heart became a galloping steed. If her mouth hadn't been so dry, she'd have screamed, but she had no spit. All she had was terror, a gigantic ball of terror inside her getting bigger and bigger —

The coffin dropped down onto the hole with a bump and the terror exploded. She screamed voiceless cries, banged with her hands and her feet on the lid of the coffin, threw her body around wildly—

Clunk.

She froze.

Clunk, clunk.

It was the sound of clods of dirt hitting the lid of the coffin. Dust began to settle through the cracks in the coffin lid.

She couldn't speak. Could barely think.

"Please God," it was a tiny prayer in a small voice. "Don't let me die like this."

MITCHELL CAME to the end of the tunnel and found a door. It was closed, but not locked. He turned the knob and it opened onto an empty room, dark. There was a door on the other side of the room and light was shining under it. He pocketed his phone and pulled out his .40 caliber Sig Sauer pistol from his holster and crossed the room in three big steps. He couldn't hear any voices, but he did hear odd sounds coming from another room in the house, sounds he couldn't place.

He moved silently toward the sounds, came to a hallway with three doors. Two of them were open, on either side of the hall and from where he stood, he could see into both of them. What he saw took several seconds to register. There was a bed and furniture in the bedroom on the right. Daisy Gillespie was in the bed, tied there to one of the posts, her mouth taped shut. And the bed ... if the dark red stains he saw really were blood, it looked like a bull had been slaughtered in the room.

What he could see in the second room made no sense. The room had no furnishings and the floorboards had been torn up. Somebody had been digging there, a hole, and was now tossing the dirt back into the hole. It was Brandon Hollister.

Mitch planted his feet and aimed his pistol in a two-hand grip at the center of Hollister's back.

"Drop that shovel and turn around slow," he said, and Hollister froze. "I said drop the shovel."

Hollister didn't obey. Clutching the shovel in both hands he turned slowly around to face Mitch, a look of insane rage on his face.

"One more time. Drop the shovel or I'll shoot."

Mitch heard a sound then, coming from the hole behind and below Hollister, a thumping and bumping, something knocking against wood.

His momentary inattention was all Hollister needed. He lunged at Mitch, the shovel held high, prepared to smash it down on Mitch's head.

Mitch fired three times, so quickly it sounded like a single shot. The first caught Hollister in the center of his chest, the second hit him in the throat, and the third blew off most of his skull above his right eye.

The momentum of his lunge and the opposite force of the bullets slamming into his body must have cancelled each other out because he merely folded up and collapsed where he was, the shovel clattering to the floor.

The bumping and thumping sounds from inside the hole increased. It sounded like somebody pounding on a box, trying to get out. He stepped to the edge of the hole, saw the coffin with dirt splattered on the top. Heard a voice amid the thumping sounds coming from it.

Rileigh.

Hollister had been burying Rileigh alive.

Chapter Fifty-Four

EVERY NIGHT after Rileigh was dragged alive out of an early grave, she woke up in grip of a horrifying nightmare.

Tonight she'd managed not to scream and that was a good thing, because a scream brought Mama, all worried about her. Rileigh hated upsetting her mother.

There was no going back to sleep, so she padded barefoot out onto the swing on the front porch to watch the sunrise, wrapped up in a blanket against the autumn chill.

Oh, she was seeing a shrink. But by this time, she knew the drill. You went through life accumulating experiences. Some good. Some not. Everybody had the same fate. But some people, because of the choices they made in life, collected a boatload more bad experiences than other people, and those bad experiences were worse than the bad experiences of normal people.

Rileigh wasn't the only person that definition fit. Soldiers. Police officers. Fire fighters. Caseworkers and ministers and — the list was long.

What had happened to her in the caretaker's cottage at the Carrington house felt like the worst of all the experiences she'd collected, but maybe — she hoped, probably— that was just because it was recent. That was the only thing she'd ever found that helped. Time. Every day that passed scraped a little of the awful away, just a little. It really was the only thing that made a difference.

She'd keep going to the shrink. If she didn't, Mitch would throw her over his shoulder in a fireman's carry and take her there himself. And the shrink was helpful, gave her insight into the terror, the nature of claustrophobia, primal fears, things like that. Helped Rileigh see some parts of her life more clearly and understand better her own responses to what life threw at her.

But that spot where the rubber met the road, that place deep down in your gut, the spot that's raw because all the skin has worn away and it's nothing but tissue and nerves and bone. That's where who-you-are lives. And it hurts there, it's painful, physically, emotionally, and spiritually. You get to decide whether to stay there and face the pain, get through it, and move on, or run away from it, wall it off, pretend it doesn't exist. The decisions people make about that shape the rest of their lives.

So, Rileigh was getting through it. Doin' the do. Hangin' in there. Or whatever other inane phrase some-body had come up with to describe putting one foot in front of the other and living life.

She heard the protesting squawk of the spring on the screen door and watched her mother maneuver through it and out onto the porch balancing a tray of what appeared to be two steaming cups of hot chocolate.

So much for not waking Mama.

"You're gonna freeze to death out here, child," Mama said, setting the tray down on the table. She picked up a cup and handed it to Rileigh. This was a gamble. It could be glorious hot chocolate or some other of Mama's concoctions that just happened to be brown … what could that be?

She took a sip. It was hot chocolate.

"Thanks Mama. Sit with me?"

"Oh, I got to get Rhett's breakfast. He likes them three-minute eggs that take half an hour to make. Is Mitch coming to supper again tonight?"

Mitch had been in helicopter-mode for the first week after, and had just downgraded into surveillance mode a couple of days ago. They'd spent a lot of time together.

A lot.

"He's sweet on you, you know," Mama said.

Rileigh didn't bother to protest, because it wouldn't stop Mama from thinking it and because sometimes Rileigh thought it might be true.

"Jillian likes him a lot, you know. She told me so last week."

No matter how Rileigh prepared herself, the mention of her dead/not-dead older sister always hit her in the chest like a wrecking ball.

"Mama, please … *don't.*"

"She said he was a fine man and the two of you would make a great couple. And she give me money to buy the two of you a bottle of wine, but they wouldn't take the money at the Sav-A-Lot."

"What money?"

Her mother dug around in her pocket and brought out a coin encircled by what looked like a ring of bronze around the perimeter, with a stylized number one and lines and swirls and stars, the word "REAL" and the year 2021.

Where did Mama get a coin from Brazil?

The End

What To Read Next:

A lavish riverboat casino should be the perfect place to unwind after nearly being buried alive, but ex-police officer Rileigh Bishop knows better.

The killer wants to turn the casino into a floating graveyard.

And Rileigh is his big prize.

Get your copy of A Gamble Either Way today.

About The Author

Lauren Street has always loved a mystery. As a kid growing up in bible belt country she devoured every whodunit book she could get her sticky little hands on and secretly investigated all of her (seemingly) normal boring neighbors. Sometimes their pets and farm animals too. All grown up now and living in the UK with her thoroughly unsuspicious (and often unsuspecting) husband, she writes domestic psychological thrillers about families torn apart by secrets and lies. And she sometimes still peers over garden walls to check up on the neighbors.